TEAROOM
mysteries

Dear Reader,

This series is close to my heart. It is set in the area where I was born and lived for most of my life—beautiful Central Maine. The town in the story, Lancaster, is a fictional place. We decided to use a traditional English name for our setting, as many of the Maine towns are named for places in the British Isles. Chickadee Lake is also fictional, though it's a lot like lakes I've been on in Central Maine.

My grandmother started a tearoom during the Great Depression. She was a young farm wife and trying to make ends meet, I'm sure. She didn't keep up this business later. By the time I knew her, she had closed it. But we kids knew there would always be cookies in her cookie jar—soft molasses more likely than not—and, if we were lucky, some homemade fudge on the sideboard.

Elaine and Jan also sprang out of my imagination, but they have borrowed some characteristics from people I love. I hope these cousins will be your new friends.

If you live in northern New England, where you spend March and April waiting for spring and the "ice out," you have my empathy. If you're where it's warmer and the rivers and lakes don't freeze, we say you're "from away." We welcome you as "summer people."

Come explore a new world. Fix yourself a nice cup of tea, sit back, and enjoy *Tearoom for Two.*

Blessings,
Susan Page Davis

Tearoom Mysteries

Tearoom for Two

Tearoom for Two

SUSAN PAGE DAVIS

Guideposts
New York

Tearoom Mysteries is a trademark of Guideposts

Published by Guideposts Books & Inspirational Media
110 William Street
New York, New York 10038
Guideposts.org

Acknowledgments

Cover and interior design by Müllerhaus
Cover illustration by Ross Jones, represented by Deborah Wolfe, Ltd.
Typeset by Aptara, Inc.

Printed and bound in the United States of America
10 9 8 7 6 5 4 3 2 1

Tearoom for Two

CHAPTER ONE

Elaine Cook found a parking space in the crowded lot of the Mainely Bargains Flea Market. Her cousin Jan Blake, in the passenger seat, looked at her watch.

"Good! We have an hour and a half before we need to be at the lawyer's office."

Elaine smiled. "Plenty of time. And the best part is, this is the first week the flea market's been open this spring. It hasn't been picked over yet."

The two women got out of the car, and Elaine locked the doors. As they walked toward the large, barnlike structure that housed the flea market, she placed a hand on Jan's shoulder.

"Do you realize that in two hours, we'll be owners of that gorgeous house on the lake?"

Jan looked up at Elaine with the same giddy smile she used to wear in junior high when they learned school was canceled for a snow day. "I know! I'm so excited. We're actually going to do it!"

Inside, four long rows of tables awaited their exploration. Elaine liked to look at everything when she went to a sale, and she realized she'd have to pace herself if she wanted a glimpse of every booth.

She leaned toward Jan and lowered her voice. "Now, remember, we need some small, decorative items for the tearoom, not just dishes."

"Got it," Jan whispered back.

They meandered along the first row, lingering briefly to check prices on a lamp here and a serving tray there. Elaine caught a glimpse of the two of them in an oak-framed mirror—two women in their midfifties, neatly dressed in pants and tailored jackets. Jan was more petite, an occasional gray strand showing in her dark brown hair, wearing glasses through which her blue eyes peered at the merchandise. Beside her, Elaine also had the intense blue eyes that ran in the family. Her hair had once been blonde, but was now a soft brown with just a hint of gray.

Seeing the reflection of them together gave Elaine a feeling of belonging. Her husband, Ben, had died only six months ago, and she had lost their dream of retiring together. But reconnecting with her cousin had given her new purpose. That both Jan's and Elaine's husbands had died before reaching sixty was shocking and devastating, but Elaine had to believe that the Lord works all things for the good for those who love Him, and perhaps the tearoom they were opening was part of that good plan.

Though she had been away from Maine for many years, Elaine knew she had made the right decision to come back, and to enter into this new venture with the cousin who had been like a sister to her.

"Elaine, look." Jan tugged at her sleeve, pulling her toward the next booth, where she pointed to some tall, square tins.

"Fantastic," Elaine whispered, not wanting the vendor to see her eagerness so that she would have more leverage in negotiating. She picked up one of the colorful old tea tins. "These would be perfect," she said quietly. She and Jan quickly settled on two that had especially pretty labels. Jan handed the tins to Elaine so she could get out her wallet.

As Jan opened her purse, Elaine scanned the remaining contents of the table and caught her breath. "Oh!" She stepped closer and reached to lift a square blue-and-white teapot reverently.

"It's just like Nana's," Jan said at her elbow.

Elaine held the cover on firmly and turned the teapot over so that she could see the markings on the bottom. "I think it's identical to the ones we have."

"That's genuine Nanking china," the woman sitting behind the table said, rising from her chair.

Elaine smiled. "Yes, I know. I have one just like it."

"We both do," Jan said with a hint of pride. "Our grandmother had a tearoom during the 1930s. We each have one of the teapots she used."

"What a wonderful legacy," the vendor said.

"And we're opening a tearoom ourselves," Elaine told her. "It's called Tea for Two. We hoped to buy more teapots to use for serving our customers." As she spoke, she turned the tag tied to the handle so that she could read the price.

Jan leaned in to look too and sucked in a breath. "Oh my, that may be outside our budget."

Regretfully, Elaine nodded and replaced the teapot on the table. "I'm afraid you're right. It's lovely, but we wouldn't be able to afford one for every table at that price."

The vendor reached out and turned the tag for a glimpse. "Four-fifty. I could take off twenty-five dollars."

"Thank you, but that's still beyond our budget. But it's good to know what ours are worth." Elaine smiled at Jan. "We'll go with our original plan—mix-and-match china."

"Well, I have this one." The woman held up a plump white teapot with a spray of dainty violets on the side.

Elaine nodded. "I like that one."

"It's only five dollars," the woman said. "Not old, of course."

"We'll take it," Jan said, "and those two tins." She nodded toward the tea containers. The cousins hoped to find older pieces they could use in their new business instead of ordering new china. Collecting their tearoom service would be a labor of love.

"Where is your tearoom?" the vendor asked.

"In Lancaster," Elaine said. "On Chickadee Lake."

Jan held out a twenty-dollar bill. "It's in the most beautiful old house, right on the water."

"We hope to open by Memorial Day, but we have a lot of work to do," Elaine added.

The woman wrapped the teapot in newspaper and bagged it with the tins. "There you go. Thank you, ladies. And good luck with your tearoom."

They moved on toward the next booth.

"I had no idea Nana's china was so valuable," Jan whispered. "I was thinking maybe fifty or a hundred dollars for our teapots, but four hundred and fifty? Maybe we should sell them and use the money to buy less expensive ones. We'll need at least a dozen."

Elaine shook her head. "You know we don't want to sell Nana's teapots. And we talked about this. We'll just have to pick up more at yard sales. The money we budgeted will cover it, and no one will care if they don't match."

"True. We can mix up the cup and saucer patterns too, but I think we'd better lock up our Nanking pots," Jan said.

Elaine stopped walking and faced her. "That's a good idea. We can use your hutch, if you don't mind, in the tearoom. It's such a beautiful piece, and it locks. We can have an antique display in it, with Nana's teapots as the centerpiece." Jan had more large pieces of furniture than Elaine did, since she'd lived in one house for the last thirty-five years, while Elaine had circled the globe with her army officer husband.

"I love that idea. It will be a good conversation starter. Would you want to display some of the teapots you've collected in your travels?"

"That would be a nice touch," Elaine said.

Jan went on eagerly, "And I was thinking that if we find enough tins, we could put a narrow shelf up high on the parlor wall, like a plate rail, and display them there."

"Good thinking." Elaine was as pleased by the glint in Jan's eyes as she was with her cousin's decorating ideas.

They ambled along the length of the row and started up the other side of the aisle, watching for teapots and anything else they could use in the Queen Anne house. Elaine scooped up three little white ceramic cream pitchers. They would need a lot of those.

Jan stooped to look at a box of books that sat on the floor at the end of one booth. “Cookbooks!” She began rooting through them. The balding, bearded man who ran the booth threw her an amiable glance, then his face sharpened as he looked at a boy of about seven who was playing with some of his sale items, lining up glass insulators and egg cups in a row on the floor.

“Cut that out, Mikey. I told you not to take things out of the boxes.” He caught Elaine’s eye and shrugged. “My grandson.”

Elaine smiled. The boy was cute, but he paid little attention to his grandfather’s instructions.

The man leaned toward him without leaving his chair, and Elaine got a good view of his bald spot. “Put ‘em back.”

Mikey heard the sternness in his voice this time and began shoving the items into the nearest box.

“How much for the cookbooks?” Jan asked.

“Oh, let me see…” The dealer rose and shuffled toward her. “I haven’t really gone through those. How about ten bucks for the box?” He stooped and hefted it onto the table. “Oh, there’s something else in there.”

“It’s a teapot!” Elaine reached into the carton and picked up a small round pot with sides that went nearly straight up, like a can, and a rounded spout. “Isn’t it odd?”

“I don’t think I’ve ever seen one like that,” Jan said. The pot was painted a buttery yellow, and on the side was a bunch of amateurish pansies. “It’s hand-painted, isn’t it?”

"I think you're right." Elaine peered closely at the clumsy design. "They say that in Victorian times, ladies of leisure did a lot of china painting. I wonder if it's that old."

"I couldn't say."

"Well, the kid probably put that in there," the dealer said. "I don't think it was in there before."

Elaine turned it over. "Well, it doesn't look new," she conceded, viewing the rough, unglazed surface of the underside.

"Twenty bucks, including the teapot," the dealer said quickly.

Elaine kicked herself mentally. If she hadn't sounded so interested, he probably wouldn't have raised the price of the box lot so much.

The vendor turned toward another customer who had picked up a vase farther down his table.

"Don't feel we have to buy it," Jan whispered. "I think I do want the cookbooks though."

Elaine considered that for a moment. The teapot had something about it that made her think it might be Asian. "Well, the painting is kind of sloppy, and it's small, but I love the shape, and it seems like it might have a story. Let's get it."

"Sure," Jan said. "If you like it, that's all that matters."

With a smile, Elaine opened her purse. "Let me write a check on the business account."

The vendor had been bargaining with the other customer, but he now accepted some cash and turned his attention to the cousins. "All set, ladies?"

"Yes," Jan said firmly. "We'd like the box."

"You got it," the burly man said. His close-trimmed beard and heavy eyebrows gave him a menacing air, until he smiled broadly at them. He reminded Elaine of the jovial Paul Bunyan statue in Bangor. "Something unusual, eh?"

"That's right," Elaine said. She tore off her check and handed it to him.

"Enjoy."

"Uh...do you have any newspapers? To wrap the teapot in?"

"Oh, sure." The man stooped and fished a section of the Waterville paper from beneath his table and rolled the little teapot in it. "There you go."

"Do you have any more teapots?" Jan asked, scanning his wares.

"I don't think so—not today. Check back next week though. You never know."

Elaine smiled. That was what she loved about tag sales and flea markets. They gave her the feeling that she might discover something that had lain hidden in the attic of a New England farmhouse for the last two hundred years. She checked her watch.

"I'm afraid we'd better get going," she told Jan. "We have only twenty minutes left to get to the closing."

"Oh, then let's skedaddle," Jan said, picking up the box. They hurried to the exit and out into the parking lot.

A thin man of about forty with short, sandy hair was striding toward the entrance of the flea market. He scowled as he spoke into the phone held to his ear. "*What*? You sold it already? But I..."

He pushed through the door, and Elaine heard no more of his conversation.

"Someone's not happy," Jan observed.

They walked to Elaine's car, where they nestled their packages in the trunk.

"It will only take us ten minutes to get there," Jan assured her as they buckled their seat belts. "I think it's a good sign that we found two teapots, don't you?"

Elaine smiled. "I do. And there may be more in there. We only saw about half the booths."

"We'll have to come back again soon." Jan settled contentedly beside her as Elaine headed the car toward the lawyer's downtown office.

TWO HOURS LATER, Jan's heartbeat quickened as they drove along the narrow main street of Lancaster's village. The old houses, the quaint businesses, and the glimpses of the sparkling blue water between buildings lifted her heart. This town had been her childhood home, and now she was back. They rolled up before the house they had purchased, and Elaine shut off the engine.

"Here we are."

They sat in silence for a moment, looking at their new home. The three-story Queen Anne sported a pristine coat of white paint, and the patterned shingle siding and corner tower satisfied something in Jan's soul. Already she could picture rocking chairs with colorful cushions on the deep front porch, and hanging baskets of fuchsias.

"I'm just glad it came on the market when we were looking for a place." Jan reached for her tote bag, in which rested her copy of the deed and her new keys. "Shall we?"

"I am so ready." Elaine grinned and opened her door.

A cool breeze blew in off the lake as they walked up to the front steps, and Jan pulled her jacket a little closer. The last of the ice had melted from the lake only a couple of weeks ago, but the large maple in the front yard was starting to leaf out. In the flower beds, daffodils and Johnny-jump-ups were blooming.

She and Elaine had toured the house twice before their final decision to buy it, but she still noticed new things—the carved brackets under the eaves and the cast-iron knocker. One thing that had drawn them both to the house was the wraparound porch that offered views on two sides. They could put a few tables out there in summer. Another feature that had appealed to Jan from the start was the flight of wooden steps off the back screened porch, leading down to a lower level deck that had been added in recent years. From there a few more steps would take them down to the dock, where they could tie up a rowboat or just soak up sun.

Jan could hardly believe they had found such a perfect house, or that the two of them together had been able to buy it outright once Jan's house had sold. Of course, it would take time to add all the little touches she envisioned—curtains with a Victorian look at every window, for instance, or a hand-painted sign, and a welcome wreath on the door. But with hard work over the next few weeks, she thought they could meet their goal and open for Memorial Day weekend—the unofficial start of the tourist season in Maine.

They reached the porch, and Jan stepped forward eagerly, her key in her hand.

"I wish we could sleep here tonight, but Brian promised to help move my furniture tomorrow if the closing went off without a hitch."

"And I can call the moving company and have my things shipped now," Elaine said. She didn't have as much as Jan, nor did she have a son living nearby to help her. She had learned over all the years she spent traveling with Ben how to pare down her belongings. But now Ben was gone, and so was Jan's husband, Peter, and they had a twelve-room house to fill. The prospect excited Elaine.

A noise from inside the house jerked her to earth.

"Wait, Jan," Elaine said. "Did you hear that?"

Jan froze with her key not quite touching the escutcheon below the doorknob. "What was it?"

The sound came again, and Elaine eyed her sharply. "Someone's inside."

CHAPTER TWO

Elaine and Jan stood on the porch of their dream house, staring at each other for a moment.

"What on earth?" Elaine said.

"Should I unlock the door, or call the police?" Jan asked.

After a moment's hesitation while perusing her cousin's pale face, Elaine reached out and grasped the doorknob. To her surprise, the heavy door swung inward, revealing the central entry hall and the curving staircase that wound up to the second floor. Light filtered into the entry through the sidelights by the front door and the windows of the rooms to each side. Everything looked just as it had when they had last toured the house.

Hearing another sound, Elaine stepped forward. "Hello? Anyone home?"

A form stepped out from beneath the stair landing, where the opening to a short hallway was camouflaged by the shadows. Elaine's heart tripped.

"Well, hi! I meant to disappear before you got here, but it's good to see you again."

Elaine relaxed and her pent-up breath whooshed out. "Sharon! We just came from the closing." She turned to Jan, who stood in the doorway, blinking. "Come on in, Jan. It's only Sharon Reddick."

"Oh, hello." Jan came inside and extended her free hand to the real estate agent. In her gray pants, white blouse, and menswear jacket, Sharon looked very professional. She wore an understated gold chain at her neck, complimenting her short blonde hair.

"Welcome, Jan," Sharon said. She shook Jan's hand briefly and stood back, spreading her hands to encompass the entire house. "Your new home awaits you. I came to take down the Sold sign, and I wanted to be sure you had water when you arrived today. Remember, I told you that pump was temperamental?"

"Yes," Elaine said. "The first time you showed us the house, there was no water in the taps."

Sharon nodded, her coral lips pressed together. "I still had a key. I know the seller agreed to put in a new pump, and he assured me it was done, but I wanted to make sure. I didn't want you to have any unpleasant surprises. Everything seems to be working fine."

"Wonderful," Elaine said. "We didn't want to have to worry about that once we're in business, or in the middle of the winter."

"Are you moving in today?"

"Tomorrow," Jan said. "Elaine is staying with me tonight, and our things are supposed to be delivered in the morning."

"It will be a big day for us," Elaine said.

Sharon smiled and checked her watch. "It surely will be. Well, ladies, I'll get going. I'm meeting a client for a showing in fifteen minutes. I wish you the best, and I'll stop in to see you when the tearoom is open."

"Be sure you do." Elaine walked with her to the door.

"Oh, I almost forgot." Sharon held out the extra key. "I'm really glad this transaction went well for you."

"Thanks for all your help, Sharon." Elaine watched her walk down the driveway to where her car was parked at the curb. She hadn't even noticed it when she drove in.

With a contented sigh, she closed the door and turned to face Jan. "We did it."

"We sure did." Jan laughed and dropped a little curtsy. "Tea for one, madam?"

Elaine joined her mirth. "For two please. But let me get the kettle from the car first."

They had come prepared for this moment and went back out to the driveway, where Elaine unlocked the trunk of her car. Jan managed two folding deck chairs, while Elaine took in a box holding her own Nanking teapot, a small copper teakettle of Jan's, a pair of bone china cups and saucers, two spoons, linen napkins, loose Lady Grey tea in a tin, a tea ball, honey, and creamer. They had no table, so they set up on the kitchen counter with the deck chairs nearby. Jan filled the kettle and put it on a burner to heat.

Elaine couldn't resist a peek into the other rooms downstairs. The double parlors at the front of their house would become their tearoom. Jan had done endless calculations and decided they could put six small tables for four in each of the two rooms. They could be pushed together for larger parties.

Elaine walked over to one of the tall windows in the east parlor, which was on the left side of the entrance hall when people walked in. She looked out over its deep windowsill and across the side porch outside, catching a glimpse of calm water. "This is going to be wonderful." She turned and gazed at the massive fieldstone fireplace on the inside wall toward the back of the house and the intricately carved woodwork around the built-in window seat in the front bay window nook.

"May I show you your bedchamber while the kettle heats?" Jan asked in her formal voice.

"I'd love it." Elaine loved Jan's dry sense of humor. She could almost picture her cousin with a little mobcap and nineteenth-century maid's white apron. "Lead the way." They went out to the entrance hall, linked arms, and walked up the curving staircase together.

"Thirteen, fourteen, fifteen," Jan said as they reached the upper landing.

"That's a lot of steps." Elaine chuckled. "I guess we have to stay in shape in this house."

"Or maybe the stairs will *keep* us in shape," Jan said.

"Oh, that would be nice, wouldn't it?"

They peered first into the large front room that had probably been the master bedroom.

"Are you sure you don't want this room?" Jan asked.

"No, I still think I'd prefer one at the back. Less traffic noise. And this will make us a great sitting room."

"True."

Elaine backtracked in the upper hall and walked into the room she had mentally chosen as her own. Three large windows gave plenty of light, and two faced the lake. She could see a spruce-dotted island in the distance, and several small boats plying the peaceful water.

"Yeah. This one for me." The room would be her sanctuary. She and Ben had moved frequently, and Elaine had enjoyed her travels, but lately she had wanted to leave the constant uprooting behind. Over the years of her marriage, her letters from Jan—and later, e-mails—had been an anchor to home.

The idea of the two of them settling down together had formed in Elaine's mind soon after Ben's death. Jan had seemed surprised at first that she would want to tie herself to the tiny lakeside town. The more they discussed it, the more Jan had admitted that she longed for something new as well, and that she was tired of living alone. There was no one she would enjoy sharing a home with more than Elaine, she had confessed. Both had prayed about the sprouting idea and discussed it by phone until it grew and became a real possibility and then a plan. Elaine had returned to Maine, and they had begun their search for the perfect house.

It was amazing that God had provided this one, which was only a few miles from the farmhouses the two women had lived in as children.

She turned around slowly. The floral wallpaper must be at least fifty years old, but she loved this space. It would be cozy with her bedroom set, one of the few large items she had kept from the last house she had shared with Ben. "I love the wide baseboards and the plaster decorations in the ceiling."

"So do I," Jan said. "And you've got that gorgeous lake view and your own bath."

Elaine smiled at her, remembering how Jan's eyes had glowed the first time they saw these lovely rooms. Yes, the high ceilings and large windows in the house would mean extra money for heating, but the look of the place was worth it, both for the authentic feel they wanted in their business and for their own satisfaction. Elaine had lived in base housing, cramped city apartments, and flimsy prefabs. She could hardly wait to move into this solid, spacious, gracious old house and surround herself with beautiful things.

"Remember when we first looked at it?" she asked.

"How could I forget?" Jan asked. "I still couldn't believe you wanted to do this with me."

"Why wouldn't I?" Elaine gave her a squeeze. "When I saw this place, I knew it was right, for both of us. Plenty of private nooks when you want to study, and I can satisfy my social cravings in the tearoom and the village."

Jan nodded with an air of contentment. "We'd already rejected at least a dozen houses. But this one—I mean, it has a *tower*, Elaine."

Elaine laughed in delight. "I know. And a dock and a fireplace. A few days from now, it will have your dream kitchen too." Jan was probably thinking she didn't deserve those things, but Elaine would disagree. This house would bring them both a great deal of contentment.

Elaine took Jan's arm and walked with her to the front room Jan had chosen, opposite their new sitting room. "When we first saw this room, we talked about how you could have a cozy nook over by the windows. Your love seat will fit if you want it in here, and Grandma's rocking chair. You can look down and see what's going on and who drives in."

"I do like to be able to see people arriving," Jan admitted. "I can have a bookcase too."

"Of course! You can put your craft books in here if you want. Though we've got enough bedrooms up here to turn one into a sewing and craft room. That smaller back room across from mine would be perfect for it. We can put extra bookshelves in there."

"Great. But my science books"—a wistful look came into Jan's eyes—"they can go in here."

"Sure. I think I'll put my tea references in the sitting room, and maybe some of my fiction collection. There's lots of space in there."

Jan nodded. "We can put my TV in there if you want. I don't really like to watch in bed, and we could both use it that way. And the braided rug I had in my living room." She arched her eyebrows as if seeking approval.

"That will be lovely." Elaine caught the sharp whistling of the teakettle from downstairs. "Sounds like our tea water's ready. Come on. We should make a list of what we want where before the truck arrives tomorrow with your furniture."

Jan walked over to her. "Thank you. For everything."

Elaine's eyes misted as she squeezed her cousin's hand. "When we were both alone, God brought us together. This is going to be great."

Jan returned the gesture. "Yeah. Now, let's get our tea and take it out on *our* back porch."

They had been settled in their chairs on the screened veranda overlooking the lake for only a few minutes when Elaine's cell phone played the catchy ring tone she had chosen. She dug it out of her jacket pocket, wondering who would interrupt the quiet morning.

"Hi," said a tentative male voice. "Mrs. ...uh...Cook?"

"Yes," Elaine said.

"This is Carl Joiner. I have a booth at Mainely Bargains, the flea market."

"Oh, right." Elaine frowned at Jan, and her cousin raised her eyebrows in question. "How may I help you?"

"Uh, you bought a teapot from me today. It was in a box of stuff."

"Yes, I remember," Elaine said.

"Well, I wondered if you'd be willing to sell it back."

Elaine's mind spun. "Is there a problem?"

"No, no. No problem. I just...uh, I had a customer who had looked at it before. He came in right after you left, and he said he wanted it."

"Well, I'm sorry, but I don't want to sell it," Elaine said. "I like it."

"Oh, sure, but uh..." Joiner hesitated. "He was kind of upset. Had his heart set on it. What would you say to giving it back for fifty bucks?"

"What?" Elaine almost choked. "Just a minute please." She pushed the mute button on her phone and looked at Jan. "You are not going to believe this."

"Who is it?"

"It's the flea market dealer we bought the box lot from."

"My cookbooks?" Jan squeaked.

"Yes, but he doesn't care about those, apparently. He wants the little teapot that was in the box. Someone else wants it, and he'll give us fifty dollars for it."

Jan snorted. "If he's offering that, it must be worth more."

"Yeah." Elaine tried to puzzle that out. "What do you think? We'd make a nice profit, but…"

"I say let's find out what it's worth before we agree," Jan said. "We bought it fair and square, and we have the receipt."

"True. And I do like it."

"If you give it back now, you'll never forgive yourself," Jan said. "I know you. You wouldn't be able to stand not knowing the story behind it. I say keep it."

Buoyed by Jan's words, Elaine returned to her phone conversation. "Mr. Joiner? I've decided to keep the teapot, but thank you for your offer."

"Wait! How about a hundred?"

Elaine froze. Something was very odd about this conversation, and about that teapot.

"I don't think so. Have a nice day, Mr. Joiner. Good-bye."

She ended the call and looked at Jan, shaking her head. "That was strange."

"What did he say?" Jan asked.

"He offered me a hundred."

"No. Where is it now?"

"In the trunk of my car."

"Did he give you a reason?" Jan asked. "Did he sell it by mistake?"

"I don't know. He just said he has another customer who is really eager to get it."

"So he underpriced it, and now he has seller's remorse."

"I think you're right," Elaine said. "He wants to get it back and sell it to this other person for a big profit. I mean, if I thought it was a true mistake, I'd probably return it to him. But he just sounded greedy." She smiled at Jan. "Let's not worry about that. Once we get settled, I know someone I can ask about it. If it's anything special, he'll tell us."

"All right," Jan said.

Elaine picked up her teacup and took a sip. She wondered if she had done the right thing. She shivered.

"Are you okay?" Jan asked.

"Yes. It's a little chilly, that's all."

CHAPTER THREE

The cousins returned to the house early the next day, and the workmen they had hired to renovate the kitchen were in the house working by eight o'clock. The truck with Jan's things arrived on schedule a couple of hours later. Elaine and Jan scurried about, directing the movers about where to place each box and piece of furniture. Jan began to realize that she really had spent her last night in the old house in Augusta, and her new life with Elaine was beginning in earnest.

They had planned to dedicate the next few days to cleaning the house and arranging their possessions. Because of the work in the kitchen, they held back on unpacking most of the cookware and utensils. Their bedrooms were a priority, as they both wanted to move in as soon as possible. Barely twenty-four hours after the closing at the lawyer's office, they made up Jan's queen bed and fixed Elaine a temporary place to sleep on a twin bed in the guest room.

"It's official," Jan said, surveying the suitcases and cartons littering her room and covering the quilt on her bed. "We're sleeping here tonight."

"We sure are," Elaine said. "No turning back now."

Jan's house—the one she and Peter had bought more than thirty years ago as a young married couple—would be turned over to the new owner for occupancy at the end of the week. She had lived there so long that she expected some separation anxiety. She thought she would toss and turn on her first night in the new location, but instead she slept deeply, hardly turning over in the night. She woke early on Wednesday to the sound of robins and phoebes calling to each other in the trees outside. She sat up and smiled. "Thank You, Lord."

She had a million things to do, but she reached first for her Bible. She had placed it, her glasses, and her phone within easy reach on her maple nightstand, the same one she had used for more than thirty years. It seemed odd to see her old things in this dignified new setting.

She turned to Psalm 52 and focused on the words of praise. The last verse especially seemed fitting: *I will praise thee for ever, because thou hast done it: and I will wait on thy name; for it is good before thy saints.*

"You've done it all right, Lord," she prayed silently. "You've brought us here. Let us use this house for Your glory."

She had just finished her devotion time when she heard the sound of a power drill in the distance. A discreet knock came at her door.

"Hi." Elaine poked her head around the jamb. "Bill and his crew want to get an early start and knock off at three."

"That's fine," Jan said. "The sooner they're done, the happier I'll be." She could hardly wait to take charge in that big, gorgeous kitchen. But first, the workmen had to install a new commercial oven, dishwasher, and refrigerator, as well as new countertops.

Elaine chuckled. “Let’s go out for breakfast.”

“Do you think so?” Jan swung her legs over the side of the bed and reached for her robe. “I hate to spend more money. I mean, we’re putting so much into the remodeling.”

Elaine stepped over near her and squeezed her hand. “It’s on me. We won’t eat out a lot once we’re settled, but we can’t do much in that kitchen while they’re working on it. And we need a good breakfast, considering all the work we have to do today.”

Jan held up her hands, palms out. “Okay, you talked me into it.”

“That was easy. I’ll meet you downstairs.”

When Jan came down the stairs after getting ready for the day, Elaine was sitting on a carved bench in the entrance hall, with her purse over her shoulder and her car keys in her hand. She looked charming in green capri pants and a striped blouse, with a jade necklace at her throat.

“Ready?” When Jan nodded, Elaine hustled her around to the door between her office and the dining room that opened into the garage. “Where do you want to eat?”

“Do we need to drive?” Jan asked. “There’s a diner just down the street.”

“You’re right—Kate’s, isn’t it?” Elaine smiled. “Let’s walk.”

During the short stroll, they could see the village coming to life. Between the buildings, they caught glimpses of sunlight sparkling on the water. A woman with a low black ponytail was unlocking the door of the shop next door, Sylvia’s Closet, and she smiled and waved at them. A black-and-white sheltie trotted down the driveway of a gray Cape Cod house on the other side and wagged his tail, obviously expecting attention. While Elaine stopped to pat him, Jan spotted a flicker winging toward the woods behind the library and a swallow industriously working on a nest under the eaves of the gift shop called A Little Something. Across the street, a delivery truck was backed up to the side door of Murphy's General Store.

"I expect by the end of the month, the population will explode," she said.

"You're probably right. Summer people are this town's lifeblood." Elaine straightened but didn't break eye contact with the sheltie. "Go home now. Good boy."

Jan took her arm. "Just walk away, Elaine."

A few minutes later, they entered Kate's Diner. The long, narrow room had a counter with stools on one side and a row of small tables on the other. Elaine chose a spot near the windows, and a woman in her late twenties came over to their table. She had short, dark hair and vibrant brown eyes, and she wore a white apron over jeans and a lavender camp shirt.

"Hi. I'm Lydia. Would you ladies like a menu?"

Jan hesitated. She would have liked a chance to study the offerings but Elaine had already scanned the board above the counter.

"I'd like two eggs scrambled, with bacon and a bran muffin please. Orange juice, and hot tea."

"The muffins are great today." Lydia smiled as she wrote Elaine's order on her pad. She looked expectantly at Jan.

"I'll have the same. And lemon with the tea, if you have it."

"Sure do."

Lydia swung around and headed for the gap at the end of the counter, stopping for a moment to greet a white-haired man who sat at another table.

"She seems nice," Elaine said.

Jan nodded.

The waitress returned almost immediately with their teacups on a tray and two small metal pots of hot water, with the tea bags and a dish of lemon slices on the side.

"My mom says to ask if you're the folks who bought the Queen Anne house." She deftly transferred the items from the tray to their table.

"Well, yes, we are," Elaine said. "I'm Elaine Cook, and this is my cousin, Janet Blake. Jan and I are planning to open a tearoom."

Lydia's eyes widened. "Fantastic. That will be a great addition to the village businesses. Do you plan to open right away?"

"By Memorial Day, we hope," Jan said. "We've got a lot to do first though."

"Well, that's great. I'll help spread the word if you like."

"Thank you," Elaine said.

A woman's voice called from the grill area behind the counter, "Pick up, Lyd."

Lydia grinned. "That's me. Back in a bit."

"Well, she's certainly friendly." Jan unwrapped her tea bag and poured hot water over it, into her cup.

"I wonder if her mother is Kate," Elaine said.

"I think so, but I've been away from town so long, I don't feel as though I know anyone."

"Me too. It feels as though I should know everybody, but it's been more than thirty years since I spent much time here."

"Even though we grew up here, it's almost like moving to a new town," Jan said. "It looks the same, but a lot of the shops have changed hands. There used to be a tractor store and a hair salon on Main Street, but they're gone now. We lived several miles out of town anyway, so I didn't know the people in the village very well, other than the kids at school."

"I feel that way too," Elaine said. "A lot of the older folks who knew our parents are gone, and I get the feeling there's been a significant turnover in the population since we moved away."

Jan knew she would love living in Lancaster again, even though she would now be one of the Main Street entrepreneurs, not a farmer's daughter. She nodded firmly. "Well, we can have a lot of fun getting reacquainted with Lancaster."

SINCE THE BULK of Elaine's things were still in transit, she was free to help Jan unpack. When they got home from the diner, they opened more boxes marked "BR" for Jan's bedroom, "LR" for the upstairs living room, or "GR" for the upstairs room they had settled on for guests. That still left a bedroom on the second floor, and Elaine's idea of a sewing room seemed to make a lot of sense. Boxes marked "yarn" and "patterns," along with Jan's portable sewing machine, found their way into the empty bedroom. The swarm of kitchen boxes were temporarily left in the parlors, but they began to put dishes into Jan's hutch in the dining room.

A small chamber off the kitchen was to be their office. The dining room, behind the west parlor, would remain their private place for meals, unless it was needed for private parties. Elaine envisioned bridal showers and special high teas being served in there, away from the public space in the two parlors.

While Jan put her clothes in her dresser and closet that afternoon, Elaine unpacked another carton for her. One of the first items she encountered was a cross-stitched sampler with the words "Peter and Janet Blake" surrounded by twining flowers.

"You made this, didn't you?" she asked.

Jan glanced over at what she held.

"Yes, ages ago. When I was pregnant with Brian, if you can believe that. And then I made a little nursery sampler for him."

Elaine smiled and set it aside. The next item in the box was a framed photograph, swathed in bubble wrap and then shrouded in a bath sheet.

"Oh, your wedding picture." Smiling, Elaine laid back the protective layers and gazed down at Jan and Peter, young and beautiful in their wedding finery, with the sheen of hope in their eyes.

"Your wedding was so lovely," Elaine said.

Jan emerged from the closet and came to stand beside her. "Thirty-three years ago." Her smile drooped a little.

"You hardly look any older now," Elaine said.

"Oh, stop. You know that's not true."

"It is." Elaine squinted at Jan's dark hair. "You barely have any gray, and your skin is so smooth."

Jan made a face and waved a hand in protest.

"And I absolutely loved your gown." Elaine smiled at the tiered lace on the gown's bodice and Jan's floral headpiece topped with a fingertip veil. "What happened to it?"

"Amy wore it when she married Van."

"Aw! I wish I could have been there for that wedding."

"I think you and Ben were in Japan, or someplace ridiculous like that." Jan nodded, a wistful look on her face. "I remember you sent her the most gorgeous tea set. She takes great pride in it."

"Japan was one of Ben's more interesting assignments." Elaine placed the photograph carefully on Jan's nightstand. "Is this where you want the picture?"

Jan sighed. "It was hanging in our room in the old house. Leave it there for now, and I'll decide if that's where it belongs. Hey, what happened to *your* wedding dress?"

"It got lost when we moved the second time. I had an entire trunk of clothes lost in transit."

"Too bad."

Elaine shrugged. "Yeah. It was when we were on our way home for Ben's leave, between Italy and Hawaii. I lost my favorite Italian shoes and my wool coat too. But we all got home safely, and the kids' toys and Ben's uniforms came through all right. There are things it would have been harder to lose than a few of my clothes."

"You always have such an upbeat attitude," Jan said.

Elaine chuckled. "Part of it's from my mom, and I think part of it is just from realizing there are some things you can't do anything about."

"So true. Do you think I should put my desk up here?" Jan asked doubtfully, looking around. Her bedroom was roomy but not huge.

"There's probably room for it, but if you'd rather have it down in the office...Or we could put it in the sitting room up here."

"You should have *your* desk in the office," Jan said firmly. "You'll be doing most of the bookwork while I'm cooking, and I don't think there's enough room for two desks in that room. Not with a file cabinet and a printer and some shelving for you."

"Maybe yours should be in the sitting room, then."

The chiming doorbell claimed their attention.

"I'll get it." Elaine rose and hurried down the magnificent staircase. She opened the front door and blinked. Jan's son stood on the front porch. "Hi, Brian!"

"Hi, Elaine. How's it going?"

"Good. Your mom's upstairs. Come on in."

Brian was about four inches taller than Elaine, and solidly built. He looked more like Peter than his mom, with medium brown hair and brown eyes. *If only he'd smile more,* Elaine thought. He stepped in and looked around the entrance hall with grudging approval.

"I thought I'd take off from work early and see if you could use some muscle."

"Oh, thank you. We were just discussing whether or not to put Jan's desk upstairs."

The sound of men's voices and hammering came from the kitchen.

"What's all this?" Brian asked.

"Oh, just some changes we needed before we open the tearoom," Elaine said quickly. "You know, state regs for places that serve food."

Brian's forehead creased. "Not too expensive, I hope. I'd hate to see Mom go through her savings first thing."

"Nothing we hadn't planned on when we made our offer on the house," Elaine assured him. Jan had told her about Brian's misgivings toward their venture. She didn't mention that an electrician was also coming to revamp some wiring tomorrow, or that the tables and chairs Jan had collected over the last couple of months for the tearoom would be delivered soon.

"Maybe I'll just step through and have a word with the contractor," Brian said.

Elaine opened her mouth, but Brian was already striding through the entry toward the kitchen. She hurried after him.

CHAPTER FOUR

The contractor's two employees were still hard at work when Elaine entered the kitchen, but Brian had cornered the boss.

"That and the countertops," Bill was saying. "The old ones were out of date, and Mrs. Blake said she needed more space for all her baking, so we're giving her an island as well, with cupboards beneath."

"And what's the bottom line on that?" Brian asked sharply.

The contractor flicked a glance toward Elaine. "The owners have my estimate sheet."

"That's right," Elaine said. "We do, and we're pleased with it, Bill. Brian, I'm sure Jan will want to see you. Won't you come upstairs?"

Brian turned to follow her, sweeping a gaze around the chaotic kitchen as he did so.

Elaine started a cheery monologue as they went up the stairs.

"We're going to be very happy here, I know. We already love the house, and it's perfect for the business. Now, this will be Jan's room. Come on in. She'll have room for a small sitting area where she can read or knit." Elaine stepped well into the room and called out, "Jan, look who's come to visit."

Jan swung around. She'd been unpacking a large suitcase and placing sweater bags and folded clothing in a dresser drawer. On seeing her son, she straightened.

"Hi, Brian." Her initial smiled faded, and her lips quivered. She ran a hand over her short, dark hair and pushed up her glasses. "I'm probably covered with dust."

"It's okay, Mom." Brian stepped forward and leaned down to kiss her cheek. "So it's final, then?"

"What? Oh!" Jan glanced at Elaine, scrunching her eyes a little, and Elaine took it as a plea for support. "You mean the house? Of course. I told you we closed on Monday. All the paperwork is done. Signed, sealed, and delivered." Her laugh sounded a little nervous.

"Yes, everything is in order," Elaine said.

Brian shook his head. "I guess you've got to try it. I just hope you don't lose your investment and have regrets."

"We won't," Elaine said.

"It's an old house," Brian countered.

"Yes, but we had several inspections done, and we were assured the roof and the foundation were in good condition." Elaine tried to put a note of authority into her voice.

"Yes," Jan said. "The remodel downstairs isn't a big deal, Brian. It's just a few things we need for the tearoom."

"So I'm told, but it looks like an extensive operation to me. Granite countertops."

"That was my suggestion," Elaine said quickly. "It's great for baking, you know. Kneading bread, rolling out dough. And so durable." Elaine hoped her soothing tone would outweigh the uneasiness in Jan's eyes.

"Well, I don't know how you're fixed, Elaine, but I do know Mom's circumstances. She made a little on selling the old house, but she's got to live too. She can't afford to sink a lot of money into an old house that needs work and a business that might not make it in this economy."

Elaine stared at him and stepped closer to Jan. "But the house is sound, and our venture will succeed. We've been to the Small Business Administration and worked out a viable business plan. We've gone over everything we'll need for initial expenditures and operating costs. I assure you, Tea for Two is going to be a healthy business. Your mother and I are going to have an income from it soon."

Brian huffed out a big, concerned breath. Elaine could see that this was coming from a place of love for his mother. He looked around the room. After a moment, he turned to Jan. "Sorry, Mom. I don't mean to discourage you. I just want to know you're all right."

"I know," Jan said.

He nodded. "This is a nice house. I mean, what I can see of it. Nice room for you too." His gaze drifted over the familiar bedroom set, the door that stood open on a roomy closet, the cedar chest, and the antique rocking chair, then lingered on the doorway to Jan's private bathroom. "How many bathrooms are there?"

"Four," Elaine said.

Brian's eyes bulged. "Four bathrooms?"

"Yes, the previous owners had a couple of new ones put in up here. Your mom and I will each have a private bath."

Jan smiled. "Isn't it ridiculous? I feel sort of presumptuous moving in here."

Brian seemed at a loss for words, but after a moment he said, "Well, I expect you'll be comfortable here. And I'm glad you've got room for all your stuff."

"Thank you," Jan said.

Elaine smiled at her. "You'll have to come back in a few days, Brian, after we've got everything in place. And bring Paula and the girls with you."

"Paula's curious," Brian admitted.

"Let me show you the front room we'll be using as our sitting room," Jan said.

Elaine followed a few steps behind as they crossed the landing. Brian walked in, looked around the spacious room, and stepped closer to the large front bay window. "There's another truck out front."

"A truck? We weren't expecting anything else today." Elaine stepped closer and looked down toward Main Street. The contractor's pickup was in the driveway with Brian's car, but out at the curb was a large box van with a shipping company's logo on the side. "Oh my! It's my things. How could they have gotten here so soon? I was resigned to waiting a couple more days for them."

She dashed out to the landing and down the staircase, arriving at the front door just as the bell rang. Panting, she swung it open and faced a man in a work uniform with a clipboard in his hand.

"Elaine Cook?"

"That's me," she said. "You got here so fast!"

"That's one of our trademarks, ma'am. Quick delivery, great service. Sign here please."

Elaine signed a form, and he tore off one copy and gave it to her.

"Now, where would you like your boxes and things?"

"Well, the bed and dresser upstairs, and the desk down here. I'll have to look at the boxes as they come in."

Brian and Jan came down the stairs as the deliveryman went toward the truck.

"Do you have a lot of furniture?" Brian asked.

"Not really. A bedroom set and a desk, and several boxes of books and clothing. A few dishes. Ben and I moved so often, I culled things over the years to a small amount that I really wanted to keep. We always bought a used dining table and things like that wherever we moved."

"You know, Elaine," Brian said almost gently, "you shouldn't have signed for the delivery until you made sure it's all here."

Elaine gulped. "Yeah, you've got a point. Ben always handled things like that when we moved. I'll try to be more cautious. I was so excited to see they'd arrived."

"I'm sure it's okay. Well, there seem to be two men. Maybe they can use a little help." Brian went out on to the porch.

"Brian's a good boy," Jan said, almost in apology.

"He is. And he ought to be," Elaine replied. "Look who raised him."

"He's just worried about me."

"I know. He really loves you and wants everything to go well."

"He feels like I've kicked over the traces though, I'm afraid."

Elaine smiled. "He probably had a sedate and safe future all planned out for you. Then I stirred things up. I'm afraid he's not too pleased with my part in this."

"Well, he'll get over it. And when he sees how beautiful our new home is—after all the workers are gone and we have a chance to decorate—and how popular our tearoom is, why, he'll just have to accept that I'm not going to spend the rest of my life knitting."

Elaine slipped an arm around her cousin's shoulders. Outside, Brian was hefting a box marked "Ben."

"You have some of Ben's things?" Jan asked.

"Yes. I gave away a lot, but there were a few things I wanted to keep, and some I wanted to go through later."

"Of course." Jan patted her back. Her eyes widened as the mover stacked several cartons that appeared to be heavy on a dolly. "How many boxes of books did you bring, Elaine?"

"Uh...eight, I think."

"Eight?" Jan stared up at her, aghast.

"Well, I couldn't give up any of my favorites."

"I think all books are your favorites," Jan said.

"Pretty nearly, I suppose."

Jan laughed. "Remember how we used to trade Nancy Drews when we were kids?"

"I sure do. And I still love mysteries. But it's no mystery where I want those books."

WHEN ELAINE'S BELONGINGS were inside and parked in the rooms where she wanted them, Brian and the deliverymen left. The two women worked at unpacking and arranging things for another hour, while Bill and his men continued their work in the kitchen. Jan was happy to help Elaine. Late in the afternoon, she was in the upstairs sitting room, where they were shelving some of Elaine's books.

"I am starved," Elaine said. "I suppose it's too early for supper."

"Yes, but I admit I usually take a tea break about now myself." Jan took three books from a box and handed them to Elaine.

"I'd hate to interrupt the workmen, even to make tea."

Jan sighed. "I'll be so glad when I can get in there and whip up a batch of macaroons."

Elaine smiled at her. "I can hardly wait. I love your macaroons. I hope you'll make them often for the tearoom."

"I've made a long list of breads and sweets to offer." Contentment settled over Jan. "Bill says all the appliances are operational except the new oven, and the electrician is working on that. They're supposed to be done with the counters by tonight."

"So we can use the new refrigerator now. We'll have to shop tomorrow and stock up on groceries." Elaine slid a novel into place and straightened. "I'm getting a little tired of fast food and sandwiches myself."

"I started a subscription to the *Penzance Courier*, and it came here this morning," Jan said.

"Yes, I saw it. I'll have to read it later, if you're finished."

"I am. There's an ad for an estate sale tomorrow in the classified section." Jan watched her cousin's eyes for a sense of Elaine's feelings on that. "Do you think...?"

Elaine nodded. "Maybe we ought to reward ourselves. We've done an awful lot of work the last couple of days. Where's the sale?"

"Waterville."

The small city, about ten miles away, was the same one where they had gone for the flea market and the closing on the house Monday. A college town of about sixteen thousand people, Waterville would provide most of their shopping needs, as well as some special attractions like the art museum at Colby College and plays at the community opera house.

"That sounds like a plan," Elaine said. "We can go to the sale first, and then get groceries before we come home."

"Mrs. Cook? Ma'am? Mrs. Blake?" The male voice echoed up the stairway and along the upper hall.

"Sounds like the electrician," Jan said. She walked quickly to the door and out to the landing. Elaine followed.

"Hi," Jan called down to the bearded man in the entry below. "How can we help you?"

"Looks like we'll have to make a small hole in the wall, like we discussed, for the new outlet for that heavy-duty range. It'll be easier if I go in from behind, but that would mean a hole in the wall in that other room."

"How big a hole?" Jan asked.

"Not more'n a foot square." He pronounced it "squay-uh," and Jan caught Elaine's suppressed smile. She would have to remind Elaine that, not so many years ago, her own Maine accent had been as thick as his.

"Let me put a sheet over the computer and the desk," Elaine said.

"Good idea. Keep the plaster dust off." The electrician glanced at his watch. "It's kinda late. If it's okay with you, we'll open 'er up so we can see what we're up against. I'll have to finish it tomorrow though."

So much for having the kitchen to themselves tomorrow. Elaine hurried to her room for a sheet. Jan walked down the stairs until she was almost on the electrician's level. The embroidery on the pocket of the middle-aged man's coveralls said "Roland."

"I think I can open it up without too big a mess," he said. "I'll try to fix it after so it doesn't look bad."

"*Hmm.* Maybe Bill Bridges should do that."

"Do what?" Elaine asked from the landing above.

"Patch up the hole they make," Jan replied.

"That wall is likely old lath and plaster," Roland said, "not Sheetrock. Might be best to have Bill do it. He's got a lot of experience with that sort of thing."

"Is Bill still here?" Jan asked.

The electrician nodded. "Want him to take a look?"

All four of them—Jan, Elaine, the electrician, and the contractor—ended up in Elaine's new office. It was a little crowded, and Jan wished they hadn't moved all the furniture in before the workmen were done. Elaine threw her an apologetic look as the men moved her shredder and printer stand away from the wall in question.

"It's all right," Jan assured her. "We didn't know they'd have to cut into the wall. And we won't say a word about this to Brian."

Elaine exhaled heavily. "Right. Help me with this sheet, will you?"

Together they managed to cover the computer and the printer with the sheet and anchor it with books and paperweights. When they had finished, Bill turned away from the wall, his pocketknife in his hand.

"Roland's right, it's old plaster with horsehair in it."

"Really?" Elaine and Jan gazed at each other.

"I can fix it after and smooth it up," Bill said. "I guess you're keeping this wallpaper?"

Elaine nodded. "For now. We'll probably change it someday, but it seemed in pretty good shape, and we wanted to move things forward quickly."

"Do you have any extra?"

"Did the former owners leave any wallpaper scraps?" Elaine asked Jan.

"I don't think so. At least, I haven't seen any for this room. There's some for one of the upstairs bathrooms in the hall closet up there."

Bill cocked his head toward his right shoulder, frowning at the spot on the wall where Roland wanted to breach it. "How about if I make a little wooden door and frame it in when he's done? I think we could make it look decent. And it would give access for any future electrical work."

"Well, yes, I think that would be nice," Jan said. "If it won't take you too long."

"Nah. And I could paint it white to match the baseboards."

They talked about it a few moments longer and decided this was the best solution.

THE NEXT MORNING, Elaine and Jan let the workmen in and headed off for the estate sale. This one was not an auction but was more like a big tag sale. They went through the large brick house, looking at all the items offered.

Elaine spotted several things she liked, but she had already settled in her mind that she wouldn't make any large purchases unless they would help in the business. She did pick up a framed Wallace Nutting print to hang in the restroom that would be open to their customers.

"Elaine, come look!"

Jan's quiet summons held a note of excitement, so Elaine left the shelf of knickknacks she'd been examining and went to her cousin's side.

"Look at this corner cupboard," Jan said. "Remember we talked about displaying Nana's teapots in my hutch? This is smaller, but it could go right in the corner of the west parlor, and it wouldn't take up too much floor space."

"You're right. And it would let us keep your hutch in the dining room, where it belongs." The cherrywood and original finish on the old cabinet would blend in beautifully with their Victorian decor, and the locking door would keep their treasured items secure. "I could put some of my international teapots in it too, if you like the idea."

"I do," Jan said with a big smile.

Elaine flipped the price tag. "Hey, that's not a bad price."

"Do we have enough left in the business account?" Jan asked. "I know we still need more chairs and things..."

Elaine wondered if she was thinking about what Brian would say. Would he question every purchase his mother made? She and Jan had started a business account together, putting in equal amounts of cash for their expenses, but they hadn't reckoned on buying more furniture other than the tables and chairs for the tearoom, and they did have a lot of smaller commitments.

"I can just buy it, if it's okay with you," she said.

"Are you sure?" Jan asked.

"I'm sure. I can afford it, and I like it. Unless you really think it should officially belong to the business."

"No, that's fine with me."

Elaine smiled. "All right then."

She made her purchases, and a young man helping with the sale loaded the cupboard into the trunk of her car. The lid wouldn't quite close, but he tied it down, making the trunk lid low enough so that she could see out the rearview mirror with no trouble.

"Jan Blake!" They both turned toward the excited greeting. A woman about their age was hurrying across the parking lot toward them.

Jan's jaw dropped. "Julie Yeaton!" She embraced the newcomer.

"I thought that was you," Julie said.

Jan turned eagerly to Elaine. "You remember Julie? She was a year behind us in school."

"Oh, of course," Elaine said as the woman's identity clicked in her mind. Julie had been a cheerleader, she recalled, and had taken the same French class as Elaine during her junior year. "It's great to see you again. But Yeaton's not your maiden name."

"Dennison," Julie supplied.

"She married Chuck Yeaton," Jan said.

"Oh, I remember Chuck." Elaine could picture the tall, sandy-haired boy who had been the high school basketball team's center.

"Elaine, are you just visiting Jan, or are you back in Maine to stay?" Julie asked.

"To stay."

Jan tapped Julie's wrist. "You won't believe this. We've bought a house together in Lancaster."

"No! Wait a minute." Julie eyed them speculatively. "Not the old Victorian on Main Street?"

"Yes," Jan said with a delighted smile. "We're going to have a tearoom."

"Oh, that sounds like so much fun!"

"Stop in," Elaine said. "We hope to open by Memorial Day. Maybe sooner."

"I will. We live about a mile out the Spruce Hill Road."

"So what are you and Chuck doing now?" Jan asked.

"I'm teaching at the university in Augusta. Social Sciences. And Chuck works in Augusta too, so we can carpool. He's at the state office building. Desk job in the retirement department. And guess what *else* I'm doing."

"What?" Jan asked.

"I'm now on the board of selectmen in town."

Jan's jaw dropped.

"Wow," Elaine said. "I'm impressed."

Julie chuckled. "The qualifications aren't too rigid. You just have to be a resident of Lancaster and care what happens to the town."

"You'll be great at it," Elaine said.

"Yeah," Jan added. "Congratulations."

With promises to be in touch soon, they parted. Elaine drove home listening to Jan's enthusiastic plans for the corner cupboard display, which involved the two Nanking teapots and others Elaine had acquired while living overseas with Ben, vintage doilies, and several bone china cups and saucers Jan had inherited from her mother-in-law. They agreed to put off their grocery shopping until they had unloaded the cupboard at home.

When they reached the house, they went inside, accompanied by the sound of a power tool coming from the office.

"Go ahead upstairs if you want," Elaine said to Jan. "I'll see if a couple of the men can bring the cupboard in for us."

She went to the door of the office, and Bill looked up from where he was measuring a short length of board.

"Bill, there's a cupboard in the trunk of my car. It's in the garage. Do you think...?"

Bill nodded. "I'll have the boys bring it in. Where do you want it?"

"In the west parlor. Thanks!" She watched him for a moment. "How's it going?"

"I'm almost done, and then I'll paint it. I've got a latch set for it too."

"Great." Elaine looked over at the rectangular hole in the wall. Bill had framed it in neatly with pine molding boards and had only to hang the door and paint it. She nodded in satisfaction and then looked around. "Is Roland all done?"

"*Ayuh,*" Bill said, using the Maine version of "yeah." "He left about an hour ago." His eyes sharpened, and he stood straighter. "Oh, he said to be sure and show you what he found in the wall."

"In the wall?" Elaine wrinkled her nose, thinking maybe they had found a dead mouse.

"Yeah. Maybe you ought to sit down."

CHAPTER FIVE

Bill laid aside his tape measure and the board and moved over to Elaine's sheet-draped desk. He picked up a small box that had been resting on top of the shroud.

"When he was working on the new connection for your oven, he found this on the floor between the walls, just to one side of the hole." He held out the box, and Elaine took it.

The small box was of carved wood, perhaps rosewood, she thought. It was only about two inches square.

"It looks like a jewelry box."

"Open it." Bill's blue eyes fairly sparkled.

"All right." A small hook on one side kept the box shut, and Elaine turned it carefully. She pulled the lid up and caught her breath.

Twinkling at her out of a creamy plush nest was a ring with a burnished gold setting and a brilliant blue sapphire.

Elaine stared down at the beautiful ring. "Oh my!"

"I'm betting that's been in there a long time," Bill said, smiling broadly.

She looked at the wall and back at the carved ring box. "How did it even get in there?"

Bill shrugged. "My best guess?"

"Yes, please."

"When Roland first found it, that box had a string tied around it."

"String?" Elaine looked at him sharply.

"It's right here." Bill walked to the other side of the desk and stooped to retrieve something from Elaine's wastebasket. He laid a small wad of white cotton string on top of sheet-covered desk.

"You see there's a round cover plate up there, high on the wall?"

He pointed, and Elaine followed his indication. She had never noticed it before, but sure enough, about a foot below the top of the wall was something flat and round, about five or six inches in diameter, sticking out from the wall about an inch. The outer surface was covered with wallpaper that matched the rest of the room.

"What is that?" she asked.

"It's a flue cover. There used to be a stovepipe there. They probably had a small heater stove in this room. The pipe connected it to the old chimney that the cookstove in the kitchen used."

"There's a chimney in there?"

He laughed. "Sure. You can see it if you take a flashlight and shine it in the hole Roland made. You don't have a wood range in the kitchen now, so you don't need it. But if you look outside, you'll see there are two chimneys. There's one for the big parlor fireplace, and there's this one. And no doubt some of the bedrooms upstairs had fireplaces that connected to them too."

"There's a mantelpiece in my bedroom, and one in the big front room upstairs," Elaine admitted. "But the fireplaces must have been covered over."

"I can take a look if you want. Some houses had false mantels in them, but this one's old enough and posh enough, I'm thinking the original owners had full fireplaces up there. Probably a lot smaller than the parlor one though."

"How interesting! But where does the string come in?"

Bill shrugged. "We're not sure, but Roland and I both think someone wanted to hide the ring, so he—or she—tied one end of the string around it and lowered it down through the flue hole. It's possible they planned to get it out later and caught the other end of the string between the wall and the flue cover when they put it back on. That way, they could carefully remove the cover later and grab the end of the string and pull the box up. But somehow, the end of the string got loose and fell down inside the wall. Maybe someone who didn't know about it took the cover off, or the person who put it there accidentally lost hold of the string. Roland found it in a heap on top of the box."

"So whoever hid it couldn't get the ring out without tearing into the wall." Elaine frowned, gazing at the old-fashioned wallpaper. "But why would they want a stove in here in the first place? It's so close to the kitchen. Wouldn't the heat from there warm this room?"

"Oh, you'd be surprised how cold these old houses would get in the days before insulation and thermal windows," Bill said. "Bedrooms close to the kitchen like this were sometimes called 'birth and death rooms.' They were handy for nursing, and so the elderly, the sick, the women with new babies—they'd sleep in here, and the woman running the household could tend to them easier while she went about her kitchen work."

"Fascinating." Elaine looked up at the flue cover again. "Why did they wallpaper over the stovepipe hole?"

"It wasn't needed anymore, once they put in the central heating, was it? You burn fuel oil now," Bill said.

Elaine nodded, thinking about this information. "So you think this ring got into the wall... how?"

"Couldn't have been an accident. You don't just drop a valuable ring down a hole in the wall without meaning to."

"I agree. It would be very hard to do that. So someone did it on purpose, that's what you're saying?"

"Your guess is as good as mine." Bill picked up the tape measure and pulled out a couple of feet of the thin metal strip. "It was directly under that flue cover though."

"Maybe someone wanted to hide it," Elaine said.

He chuckled and shook his head as he checked the length of his board. "I've found a lot of odd things in walls over the years, but nothing like that. Pretty nice doodad."

"Yes. Thank you very much. I'm going to show this to Jan right now."

JAN STOOD WITH the little carved box in her hands, gaping at the ring.

"Wow. Imagine that!" Nothing like this had ever happened to her before, and she couldn't think what else to say.

"I'm going to give Roland a super-good rating on Angie's List," Elaine said. "An unscrupulous person could have pocketed that, and we'd never have known about it."

"It was good of him to turn it right over," Jan said. "And Bill too. I think we struck gold when we hired those two." She eased the ring out of the box and slid it on to her right ring finger. The beautiful gemstone was larger than any she would normally wear. It would certainly draw attention to the wearer. "It fits. Do you think the sapphire is real?"

"It sure looks like it, but I'm not an expert."

Jan took the ring off and held it up toward the light coming through her bedroom window. "Eighteen k. I don't see any initials or anything like that."

"It would have been nice to have some kind of a clue, wouldn't it?"

"So what do we do with it?" Jan asked.

"Take it to a jeweler for an opinion, I guess."

"Probably best." Jan stuck the ring band into the slot in the box and closed the lid. "Here, you take it. Put it somewhere safe until we have a chance to do that."

Elaine chuckled. "It's a bit ironic, isn't it? It's been 'somewhere safe' for who knows how many years—and now we have to worry about it."

The doorbell chimes echoed from the bell on the landing.

"Company," Elaine said.

Jan rolled her eyes. "I hope it's not Brian, or if it is him, I hope he's in a better mood today. I love him, you understand, but…"

"Yes, I do understand. Let's both go."

When Elaine opened the front door, a woman of about thirty, wearing plaid pants and a turquoise tunic, faced them. Her short blonde hair was showing its dark roots, but her eyes held a hopeful, expectant look.

"Hi. I'm Carlene Eastman."

"Can we help you?" Elaine asked.

Carlene smiled. "I used to live here. I wondered if I could take a look inside the house, for old times' sake." She peered past the cousins, and apparently noticed some cardboard cartons in the hall. "Oh, you're moving in. I heard the house had been sold."

"Uh, yes," Elaine said with a glance at Jan.

Jan shrugged. Personally, she would call first if she wanted to go back to visit the house she grew up in, but it was the era of unlisted cell phones, and after all, manners weren't always what they used to be.

"I guess it's all right," Elaine said hesitantly. She stepped back, and Carlene moved into the large entrance hall, her gaze darting about.

"I'm Jan Blake," Jan said.

"And I'm Elaine Cook. We're cousins."

"Oh, how nice. Will you both be living here?" Carlene asked.

"Yes," Elaine said, "and we'll be opening a tearoom here soon."

"A tearoom? Fabulous!" Without being invited to do so, Carlene walked to the doorway of the east parlor and looked in. "Will you have it in here?"

"Yes," Elaine said, following her into the room. "Both parlors. Was this your living room when you lived here?"

Jan hung back, content to let her more outgoing cousin do the honors.

"Oh yes." Carlene's quick gaze seemed to take in every detail of the carved woodwork around the window seat and the ornamented plaster ceiling. "I always loved that fireplace. It was so cozy in winter."

She walked past Elaine into the entrance hall again and crossed to the opposite room. Jan looked helplessly at Elaine. Her cousin hurried after Carlene, and Jan trailed them, wondering if she and Elaine would ever get to the grocery store.

Carlene barely paused in the west parlor, which had only two tables and a few chairs in it, with boxes of dishes and cookware scattered about. She walked through the connecting door to the dining room, where Jan's walnut table, chairs, and matching hutch were in place.

"Oh, how nice." She started toward the other door of the dining room.

"The kitchen is under construction," Elaine said quickly. "Probably best to stay out of there."

"Oh." Carlene's face fell. "Too bad. My mom used to make the best chocolate chip cookies out there."

Elaine's noncommittal *Mmm* seemed to sink in, and Carlene stopped and faced them.

"Well, could I...uh...see my old bedroom? I won't keep you long, but I'd love to take a quick look, if you don't mind."

"Sure," Elaine said with a note of resignation.

Carlene went out the nearest door and stood uncertainly for a moment, looking to left and right.

"This way," Elaine said.

"Oh, sorry." Carlene hesitated, peering into Elaine's office. "Are you sure I can't get a look at the kitchen? I'd like to be able to tell my mom about it."

Jan stepped forward. "The stairs are this way, Ms. Eastman."

"Of course. How silly of me."

Elaine led the way, and Jan followed Carlene around to the stairs and up them, feeling as though she was riding drag on a wagon train to make sure nobody fell out of line without being noticed.

"Which room was yours?" Elaine asked.

Carlene paused on the landing and looked around. "This one." She walked briskly to the doorway of the large front room that was slowly transforming into the cousins' sitting room.

"Really?" Elaine asked in a cheerful voice. "I thought this was probably the master bedroom. It's the biggest by far."

"Oh, well... my folks let my sister and me sleep in here, because we had to share."

"How many children were in your family?" Jan asked from the threshold.

"Just my sister and me."

Jan said no more but caught Elaine's eye and threw her a skeptical look.

Elaine walked closer to their guest. "You must have a lot of memories of this house."

"Oh yes." Carlene smiled at her. "When I lived in this room, it had yellow-striped wallpaper. So sunny and colorful."

"I can imagine," Elaine said.

Jan couldn't. The flowered wallpaper on the walls looked older than Carlene Eastman, if she was any judge.

"So the window seat was here back then," Elaine prompted.

Carlene looked at it. "Oh, yeah. We used to curl up on it and read. I don't think that shelf was there though." She nodded at a shelf on the wall above the television.

"You and your sister had lots of room to play," Jan said.

"Yeah." Carlene turned to Elaine with a smile that was almost a wince. "I don't suppose I could..."

"We really need to get on with our work," Elaine said firmly.

"Of course. Well, thank you."

Both cousins walked down the stairs with Carlene and saw her out. Elaine closed the door with a big sigh.

"You're too softhearted," Jan said.

"I kept trying to imagine if the shoe were on the other foot." Elaine shrugged. "Besides, we don't want to give anyone reason to say bad things about us."

"True, but don't you think it's odd that two girls had to share a room when there are five bedrooms up there, not to mention the third story?"

"Well... Okay, I do. I admit it."

"I felt like..."

"Like what?" Elaine asked.

"Like she was looking for something."

"The ring, maybe?"

Jan met her gaze. Elaine's blue eyes were clouded with uncertainty.

"I don't know what she wanted," Jan said. "But I don't think she ever lived here. And I think we should be careful."

CHAPTER SIX

Bill Bridges made the welcome announcement at four o'clock that he and his crew were done in the kitchen. His helpers packed up their tools while he walked about the room with Jan and Elaine, who had just finished unloading their groceries. He pointed out the special features he had added.

"You've got your island here, with cupboards below. Two outlets, one on each end. And you've got this pull-out cutting board." He slid a butcher-block board about two feet square from beneath the edge of one of the granite counters.

"This will be your baking center," Elaine said to Jan, who nodded happily.

They both exclaimed over the new oven and dishwasher.

"It's my dream kitchen." Jan clasped her hands together.

Elaine gave her a hug. "I'm so glad you've finally got it." She remembered all too well the tiny, dark kitchen in Jan's old house, not to mention the aging refrigerator that hummed too loudly and occasionally took a notion to stop working and leak water all over the floor. Jan had never owned a dishwasher.

Unloading the clean dishes might be their evening entertainment until the novelty wore off.

"So you think you can squeeze us in next week and build us a checkout counter in the entry hall?" Elaine asked. She had given Bill a rough sketch of what she envisioned—a five-foot surface for the cash register they had ordered, and a set of display shelves on the front, facing the customers. In it she would place retail items they would sell to tea aficionados: packaged teas, infusers, perhaps a few copper teakettles, porcelain teapots, and bone china cup and saucer sets.

"*Ayuh.* That shouldn't take long," Bill said.

"Great. Give us a call and let us know when to expect you, Bill." Elaine felt that the plans she and Jan had made so carefully were coming together nicely. Jan would reign in the kitchen, and Elaine would take care of ordering, keeping the financial records, and scheduling events. She thought she would be good at it, and she was eager to put her social skills to work.

After Bill's crew left, they spent an hour unpacking "K" boxes. Elaine let Jan arrange her pans, utensils, baking supplies, and spices the way she wanted them, while she unpacked dishes, kitchen linens, and cookbooks.

Elaine had brought only a few items for the kitchen. She hadn't invested in china and high-quality pots and pans during Ben's military years. She had preferred to buy inexpensive ones when they reached each new destination. Only two boxes of her belongings could remotely be called kitchen wares.

One held her small collection of teapots from around the world. The other carton was largely occupied by a smaller box. Eagerly, she lifted it out. "Oh, my Shona crane!"

"What's that?" Jan swiveled around to look at her, with a jar of paprika in one hand and a pepper grinder in the other.

"It's a sculpture Ben brought me from one of his trips when I couldn't go along with him." She lifted the lid of the box and took out the statuette. The graceful crane's body and partly folded wing formed the bulk of the piece, and also were shaped so that it could stand. Less than a foot high, the bird could sit on a table or shelf. Its long neck looped around, and its head and long beak dipped down along its body, resulting in a graceful, fluid form.

"That's nice," Jan said. "Is it from Japan?"

"No, actually, it's from Botswana. The people there carve animals from soapstone. It's not very valuable, but it's sentimental."

"I like it."

"Thanks." Elaine glanced about. "It doesn't belong in here though."

"In the dining room, maybe?" Jan suggested. "Or the sitting room upstairs?"

Elaine thought for a moment. "Would you mind if it went on one of those little side shelves on your hutch?"

"I think that would lovely. It would balance the salt glazed vase I put on one of them."

"Thank you. I'll take it in there now."

Elaine carried the crane sculpture into the dining room and set it on the empty knickknack shelf on one side of the hutch. With Jan's dishes inside, sheer curtains and pleated green-and-white drapes, and a pair of pewter candlesticks Elaine had contributed, this was beginning to look like a fine dining room, and the perfect setting for the private parties she envisioned as a special offering at Tea for Two.

Smiling, she went back to the kitchen.

"How's the spicery coming?"

"Almost done," Jan said. "Now I want to cook us some supper."

Elaine smiled at Jan's typical mood. The kitchen was ready for action. She looked at her watch. "Can I help?"

"Not unless you really want to."

"Okay, then, I might pop over to Murphy's and see what they've got for office supplies. I need some file folders, and I thought they might have sales pads. And when I come back, I'll start working on those ads we talked about for the opening."

The general store across the street and down a few doors had gas pumps outside and all wonder of delights within, from stovepipe to beach towels, bubble gum to baby bonnets. Elaine was sure Des and Jo Murphy, whom she and Jan were just getting to know, would have the file folders at the very least.

"Oh, and if you don't mind, see if they have any onions," Jan said. "I forgot them in town."

"Sure," Elaine said with a laugh. "But don't forget I have to go back to Waterville tomorrow to see the dentist. Start a list for me to take along then."

"Oh yes, I remember you set up that appointment."

"I also thought I'd take the little teapot. I have a friend who's an auctioneer, and I want him to take a look at it. Do you know Nathan Culver?"

Jan shook her head.

"Well, his dad and mine were friends," Elaine said, "and we used to go to Mr. Culver's auctions a lot. I got to know Nathan when I was a kid. His dad's gone now too, and Nathan has the business."

"Interesting."

"Yeah. He specializes in antiques. I haven't seen him in years, but I subscribe to his auction catalogs online. I'd really like to get his opinion on the teapot."

"It's cute," Jan admitted, "but those pansies on the side are dreadful."

Elaine chuckled. "That's part of what I want to ask him—if there's a way to get rid of them without ruining the pot. But with the odd things that have happened, like the dealer wanting it back, I'm thinking the sooner we get some information on it the better."

"I can't argue with that," Jan said. "It was sort of weird."

Elaine crossed the street and strolled down to the general store. Murphy's had been a fixture in Lancaster for more than fifty years, having been built by Des Murphy's grandfather. For Elaine, entering the squatty, one-story building was like stepping back into childhood. Her father had always filled his gas tank here, and her parents found it convenient when they needed a pound of butter or a gift card. Elaine and Jan had bought penny candy and popsicles here in the old days. Des ran the shop now with his wife, Jo.

Elaine took one of the small carts and wheeled slowly through the aisles, stopping to gaze at Des and Jo's displays of seasonal merchandise. She found the file folders and Jan's onion and took them to the checkout, along with a pot of pink dianthus in full bloom.

"Hi, Elaine." Jo Murphy smiled as she rang up the items. "Aren't those plants pretty? I'm going to plant some as soon as I'm sure we're past our frosts." Elaine smiled. "These are a surprise for Jan."

On arriving home, Elaine dropped her purse and the folders in the office and took the dianthus and onion to Jan in the kitchen.

"Oh, how pretty," Jan cried on sight of the flowers. "Let's use it as a centerpiece." She had brought her own houseplants, which had found new habitats in various parts of the house, but none of them were blooming at the moment.

"I just thought we should celebrate a little," Elaine said. They set the dining table with Jan's best china, Elaine's silverware, and a lacy tablecloth that had belonged to Jan's mother. Jan expressed her delight through her culinary skills, making their first dinner in their new home a memorable occasion.

The highlight of the evening for Elaine was not the delicious chicken casserole, rolls, and salad Jan prepared, but a Skype session with her son, Jared, who lived in Ohio. He had called to wish her a happy housewarming. Elaine's two grandchildren, Lucy and Micah, also talked to her for a few minutes. Elaine's heart warmed at the look of love on their faces, but the distance between them gave her a pang of regret. She had spent a week with Jared's family before coming to Maine, and four days before that with her daughter, Sasha, in Colorado.

"I hope you'll be able to come and visit this summer," she told her daughter-in-law, Corinne.

"We're going to try to make it happen," Corrie said. "The kids want to see the lake and the new house and—well, everything, but especially you."

That message buoyed Elaine as she puttered about the office that evening, setting up her files and working online to arrange advertising for the tearoom. Jo Murphy had advised her to ask Lydia Pierce about the possibility of a "new business" feature in the *Weekly Wave.* The small-format newspaper was Lydia's summer project when she wasn't working at her mother's diner, Jo had explained. The first edition of the season would come out the last week in May, and tourists could pick it up for free locally. Elaine felt advertising in it would be worthwhile, even if Lydia didn't give them a free article. She put inquiring about that on her to-do list.

She set out the next morning, leaving Jan happily creating in the kitchen. Elaine had great faith in her cousin's ability to turn the staples they had stocked into something wonderful, and Jan was already bubbling over with plans for the pastries she wanted to offer their customers.

Elaine's dental appointment went quickly, and she was glad she hadn't needed any Novocain. She wouldn't have wanted to see her friend Nathan for the first time in five years with one side of her face numb.

She decided to go to the auctioneer's place of business before tackling the grocery list, so that the food didn't have to sit in the car while she talked to him.

The auction hall resembled a one-story, sprawling barn. The white clapboard siding looked freshly painted, and the building had a large parking lot to accommodate the hundreds who attended the famous Culver auctions.

Elaine entered through the front door. The cavernous room where merchandise was displayed and bidders could find folding chairs for the sales loomed before her. To her left was a small, enclosed room with a window like a bank teller's. This was where one registered for a bidding card on auction day. To her right was the refreshment stand, empty and dark now, but one could always get a hot dog or a whoopie pie when a sale was in full swing, along with a cup of coffee or a can of Moxie.

She walked farther into the big sales room. A young man was unloading crates of merchandise from a dolly. He looked up at Elaine and paused in his work.

"Is Nathan in?" she asked.

He pointed toward the office door, which was to the left, beyond the registration booth. She walked to the open door and knocked.

Nathan looked up from his computer screen, and his smile burst out at the sight of her. In her eyes, he still looked boyish, though the sprinkling of gray in his light-brown hair showed that he had aged since their last meeting. He stood and hurried to her side.

"Elaine! Just the break I needed. How are you doing?" He took both her hands in his, his blue eyes radiating concern.

"I'm well," she said.

He nodded and drew her into the room. "Have a seat. I've been thinking about you a lot lately. Well, since Ben died. What a blow!"

"Yes. Thank you." She sat down opposite his desk, and Nathan resumed his seat in his swivel chair.

"That must have been a shock."

"Not entirely," she said. "He'd had some heart trouble, and that's why he retired last year. His last couple of physicals concerned us."

"I'm so sorry you didn't get to enjoy your retirement together," Nathan said.

"Thank you."

"Are you in the area for long?" he asked.

"Yes, actually. I'm staying. My cousin and I have bought a house in Lancaster."

His eyes widened. "Wonderful!"

"We're opening a tearoom." Elaine watched for his reaction.

Nathan's grin returned full-blown. "That's perfect for you. I should have known you'd have something in the works. You never could sit still when you were a kid."

Elaine tucked that away to think about later. She had always admired Nathan when she was a girl, and often tried to impress him, seemingly without success. Three years her senior, he had indeed treated her like "a kid." But he always got her a bottle of pop when her father took her to the auctions his dad was running and pointed out any oddities among the wares.

"I brought something for you to look at." She picked up the tote bag she had placed on the floor and took out her flea market find, swathed in bubble wrap.

At once intrigued, Nathan sat forward and watched every movement as she carefully unwound the padding and set the squatty little porcelain pot on his desk.

He frowned at it for a moment. "What can you tell me about it?"

"Not much. I got it at Mainely Bargains a few days ago. Jan and I paid twenty dollars for a box of cookbooks that had this in it. I thought the shape was unique. Well, not unique, but different from usual."

He nodded. "It's small, and the sides are straight." He took the lid off and set it on the desktop, then lifted the teapot and looked inside. "*Hmm.*" He turned it over and squinted at the bottom, his eyebrows drawing together. After a moment, he pulled a pair of reading glasses from his shirt pocket, put them on, and examined the bottom more closely.

"I couldn't find any markings on it," Elaine said.

"I don't see any either. But that could be good. Almost everything modern is marked, and this is obviously old."

"How old?"

The distasteful look with which he studied the teapot made Elaine think he must hate it. But when he spoke again, she took heart.

"It could be *very* old. I'd like to know what's under the globs of paint."

"Pretty sloppy," Elaine agreed.

"That's an understatement." Nathan took off his glasses. "I've got one for the next auction that is from the Qing dynasty. It's stoneware, made from Yixing clay."

"What's that?"

"Yixing is a city in China. They've used the clay there for making dishes for centuries. They still use it today. But I don't think this pot you've brought is too modern. And it might not be from there at all. But what I can see of this one on the bottom makes me think of the one we took in for auction. Would you like to see it?"

"I'd love to." They rose, and Nathan led her out into the auction hall and farther along the wall to a locked room nearer the auctioneer's platform. "I'm very particular who is allowed in here," he said with a smile as he unlocked the door.

Feeling privileged, Elaine followed him inside. The room was a virtual vault of antique treasures—jewelry, lamps, glassware, pottery, bronzes, and paintings were stored on shelves and special racks. She stared around at the bounty.

"It's...overwhelming, seeing so many beautiful things at once."

"Yes, I overload on it myself frequently. How much nicer to have one good piece, showcased by itself, to be studied and pondered."

He lifted a brown teapot from a shelf and set it on a small, square table with a fabric covering in the center of the room.

"It's square," Elaine said immediately.

"Yes, and yours is round. But notice how simple it is. This one has a raised vine-and-leaf design, but otherwise, it's plain. Functional." He turned it over and showed her the unglazed bottom. "Something in the color of the clay made me think yours might be Yixing."

"Yes, I see it." He was right—the color of the fired clay on the bottom of her little flea market teapot, where it had not been glazed or painted over, was very similar to that of his Qing teapot.

He put the square pot carefully back on the shelf and led her out, where he stopped to lock the door. As they walked back to his office, he said, "Tell you what—there's a restorer in town. She does a lot of glassware and china. She has a studio on College Avenue. She might be able to get that outer layer of paint off without damaging the piece. I'm afraid you might need to have that done before we can tell more about it."

"That sounds like a good idea to me," Elaine said.

Nathan opened his flat desk drawer, rooted about for a moment, and pulled out a business card. "There. Heather Wells. She's good. I've had her grind down some glassware with chips before it went to auction, things like that, and I know she's restored the finish on porcelain vases for people. She does a beautiful job."

"I'll go see her. Thanks."

"Before you do, let's take some photos, if you don't mind. When I have time, I can look for something similar in my reference books. It reminds me vaguely of another one I had in an Asian lot last year."

"Sure," Elaine said.

He looked up at her and smiled. "So. Teapot. Tearoom. I sense a theme here."

She laughed. "I've always loved tea, and I've done some reading on its history. My cousin and I decided to go into the business. We're buying up mismatched teapots and cups for the tearoom. This one caught my eye. The surface is ugly, but..." She gave a little shrug. "I imagined some woman in the 1890s painting over it because it was so plain."

"Could be. I've seen cases like that before. And you never know what's underneath."

Nathan took the teapot to a cabinet at one side of his desk, where he set it on a small display stand. A velvet-covered board was propped up behind it. "I take a lot of photos for our catalog here."

He took out his cell phone and snapped a few pictures, then reached for a digital camera. Elaine was surprised at the amount of attention he was giving her flea market treasure.

Was it because the teapot was really special, or just because she was the person who brought it in?

"Thank you very much," she told him when he began to wrap up the teapot. "I'll stop in at Heather's studio before I do my grocery shopping."

"Are you busy all the time?" Nathan asked with a quick glance up from what he was doing. "I'd love to see you again."

Elaine wasn't sure what to say. Was Nathan just being friendly, or was he making an overture to something more? Only six months had passed since Ben's death. She certainly wasn't ready to start thinking about dating or romance. Not at all. She swallowed hard.

"We're pretty busy. We hope to open Memorial Day weekend, or even before. We still have a lot to do. But maybe Jan and I could come to one of your auctions."

"We've got a big one a week from tomorrow," he said. "Lots of antiques."

"What sort of antiques?" Elaine lifted her tote bag and held the top open so he could slide the wrapped teapot inside.

"That teapot you just saw, for one thing, and some of the other items in my lockup. Some furniture. A few lamps. Some dishes and pottery. Several paintings, and a collection of old pistols. The detailed listings are going up this afternoon—if I get them done."

"Then I should leave you alone and let you finish your work," Elaine said. "I'll take a look online after you post it."

"That's all I can ask."

She smiled and accepted the hand he extended. "It's good to see you again, Nathan. I'm sure we'll meet again."

He nodded. "Soon, I hope."

Elaine's mind was in a haze as she drove to College Avenue. Seeing an old friend like Nathan made her feel welcome here in Central Maine. She hoped she *would* see him again soon, and that she could look up some of her other friends from the past.

With her thoughts elsewhere, she went right past Heather Wells's shop with its discreet sign for We Restore, and had to turn around and go back. She pulled in at the small, modest building. When she entered the shop, a woman was hard at work at a table in the center of the room. All around were shelves and file cabinets. A desk in one corner held a laptop computer and printer.

"Hi," the woman said. "May I help you?"

Her dark hair framed her face, and she removed a pair of tortoiseshell-framed glasses, revealing striking brown eyes.

"Ms. Wells? Nathan Culver recommended your work to me." Elaine stepped forward so that she stood across the workbench from her.

"Yes, I'm Heather. That was kind of Nathan. I've done some work for him in the past."

"I'm Elaine Cook. Nathan and I are old acquaintances, but I've just moved back into the area." She took out the teapot and unwrapped it on Heather's workbench. "I recently bought this at a flea market, and he thought it might be worth removing the outer layer of paint and finding out what's underneath."

Heather gazed at the small teapot for a long moment and then leaned across the table and lifted it gently. Holding the cover on, she looked at the bottom and then turned it upright, holding it out at arm's length and studying it thoughtfully.

"Can you tell me anything?" Elaine asked.

"It's got the shape of a very old pot."

"Older than Nanking?" Elaine asked, thinking of the square blue-and-white ones she and Jan owned.

"Oh, much. The Nanking period was really only a decade," Heather said.

"Really? I didn't know that."

Heather nodded. "It was when the Chinese government was located at Nanking, in the 1920s and thirties. 'Twenty-eight to 'thirty-seven, if my memory serves me right."

"My cousin and I each have one of our grandmother's teapots, and we were told they were Nanking. She had a tearoom during the Great Depression."

"They would have been fairly inexpensive then." Heather lifted the little pot. "But this one...it's a good deal older, unless I'm mistaken."

"Is that what they call the drum shape?" Elaine asked.

"Almost. It's a tiny bit rounder. Softer. I can remove the paint layer, if you want to leave it here."

"Yes, I think that would be the best thing."

Heather quoted her price, and Elaine was agreeable.

"Let me give you a receipt for the item and put a work tag on it," Heather said.

Elaine left a few minutes later, excited about the prospect of having found a special teapot even older than Nana's.

CHAPTER SEVEN

I'm so glad you're home," Jan said when Elaine entered the kitchen with several plastic grocery sacks. "Is there more in the car?"

"A few more things."

"Let me help you." Jan wiped her hands on a dish towel. "I've been baking ever since you left. I hope you brought me more eggs."

"I did. I got everything on the list and a couple of other things that took my eye. Oh, and I was able to get sales pads and an ink cartridge for the printer at the stationery store."

"That's good," Jan said.

"What did you make while I was gone?" Elaine gazed around the room. Every flat surface was covered with baking pans, cooling racks, and plastic food containers.

"Miniature cream puffs and cinnamon snaps and macaroons," Jan said as they went out to the garage. "You did bring the dark chocolate, didn't you?"

"It's in here somewhere." Elaine took several more bags from the trunk of her car.

"What did you find out about the teapot? Did you see your friend?" Jan asked. She gathered the remaining bags and shut the trunk.

"Yes, I did. Nathan was optimistic about the teapot. He gave me the name of a restorer who may be able to get the paint off, and I took it straight to her and left it at her shop. I like her. Heather Wells is her name."

"Sounds good so far." Jan followed Elaine into the kitchen and puffed a little as she lifted all her bags to the counter.

"They both think it's old," Elaine confided. "Older than Nana's."

"Wow."

"Yeah. We'll see."

"I hope you don't mind," Jan said, with a glance at the clock. "I invited a few people in to sample the pastries at two o'clock."

"Oh. I'd better grab some lunch." Elaine eyed her cautiously. "What people? And how many?"

"Just a few neighbors. Kate Pierce from the diner. She closes at two, and I told her that she and her daughters can drop around after if they want. And Sylvia Flood, from the vintage shop next door, and the woman who runs the gift shop between her and the diner. Oh, what was her name? Anyway, I asked her and a customer who was in her shop when I was there."

"Goodness. I'd better get changed too." Elaine had not only missed lunch, but she felt crumpled after her morning in town. She helped Jan put away the food she had bought and fixed herself a sandwich, which she carried upstairs with a glass of milk. As she buttoned a fresh blouse fifteen minutes later, she heard the doorbell ring. Her hair got only a quick brushing.

She went downstairs to find Jan in the big east parlor, pouring out tea for three other women.

"Hi, Elaine," Lydia Pierce said with a contagious smile. "This is such a great idea. My mom and sister will be over in a few minutes."

Jan set down the teapot near a glass plate of her macaroons and cinnamon snaps. "Do have a seat, ladies. Elaine, I think you know Jo Murphy, from the store..."

"Yes. Hi, Jo. Thanks for coming."

"Thanks for having us in," Jo said with a grin. "I left the boys in charge, so I can't stay long, but this is such fun!" She took a seat at one of the small tables.

"And this is Sylvia Flood, from Sylvia's Closet," Jan said, nodding toward the ponytailed woman Elaine had seen entering the vintage shop once before.

"Hi. Glad to meet you." Elaine extended her hand to Sylvia.

"Thanks. You too." Sylvia glanced around the big room. "This place is gorgeous. I've always wanted to see inside."

The doorbell rang, and Jan said, "I'll get it." She went into the hall and returned a moment later with a blonde woman of about forty, who wore a yellow T-shirt and a knee-length jean skirt.

"Elaine, this is Faith Lanier, from A Little Something."

"Welcome, Faith," Elaine said. "Do you know everyone else here?"

Faith looked around at the other. "Think so. This is great! I don't usually get to see any of you ladies during business hours."

"You won't either, once the summer people start arriving," Sylvia said.

"Well, I didn't think customers would beat the door down today, so I took a break from getting my inventory out and turned the sign to Closed." Faith smiled apologetically at Jan and Elaine. "Ten minutes—that's all I can stay for, but thanks for inviting me."

"You've got to try one of these cream puffs before you dash off," Lydia said from her seat beside Sylvia. "They're to die for."

"Did you make these, Jan?" Jo asked.

"She sure did," Elaine said. "Jan made all of this. She's going to do most of the baking for the tearoom. If you haven't had one of her macaroons, make sure you do. They're one of my personal favorites."

"Oh, I agree," Sylvia said. "They're my *new* favorite."

Faith accepted a cup of tea from Jan and selected one each of the macaroons, cream puffs, and cinnamon snaps. She was still with them, chattering eagerly about the upcoming tourist season, when two more women joined them. Lydia Pierce jumped up to introduce her mother, Kate, and her sister, Patti Garland, to Jan and Elaine. All of the women sat down, and Elaine soon found herself getting to know the businesswomen better. She was especially intrigued by Kate Pierce's relationship with her daughters and felt they were a good example to her and Jan of how families could succeed in business together.

"So, ladies," Lydia said, sipping her second cup of tea, "my first *Weekly Wave* of the summer comes out the Friday before Memorial Day. I'd love to do a feature on your tearoom."

"Thank you," Jan said, nodding at Elaine.

"We'd love it," Elaine assured Lydia. "In fact, I was going to ask you about it."

"Great. I'll call you and set up a time when we can talk. I'd love to get a picture of this room set up for business."

"That should happen by next week," Elaine said.

They all continued talking about plans for the summer and new ideas they were going to try to draw in customers.

After about ten minutes, Faith jumped up. "I've really got to get back to my shop, but thank you so much. Jan, Elaine, I'll be over here any chance I get, and I'll recommend you to my customers."

"Oh, me too," Sylvia said. "Your tearoom will be a great addition to Main Street. And your goodies are indescribable, Jan."

Jan's face went pink as she graciously accepted the compliments. The ladies took their leave in ones and twos, and soon the cousins were left alone in the big entrance hall.

"I hope you don't mind," Jan said immediately.

"No, that was wonderful."

"Next time, I'll try to give you more warning. I didn't expect Jo Murphy. I think Lydia invited her. But Faith's customer didn't come, so I guess it all evens out."

"That's fine. I was glad to get to know Jo a little better," Elaine said. "Sometimes it's nice to see someone outside their own workplace." She gave Jan a hug. "Thank you for doing that. I loved it, and I think they did too. Now, come on. I'll help you clear up."

"There are so many cookies left," Jan said mournfully as she surveyed the leftovers.

"Can you freeze them?"

"The cinnamon snaps, but not the cream puffs, and macaroons don't freeze too well either."

"Then we'll make plates in plastic bags and give them to the mailman and anyone else who comes by," Elaine said.

The doorbell rang, and they looked at each other.

"I didn't invite anyone else," Jan said.

Elaine laughed and went to open the door.

"Brian."

"Hi." Fatigue lines creased the skin at the corners of his eyes. "I just came by to see if you and Mom are doing okay."

"We're fine." Elaine stepped aside so he could enter.

"You're just in time, Brian," Jan said. "We have a gazillion cookies and cream puffs, and I'll send some home with you."

He followed her into the parlor and stood staring incredulously at the empty teacups and platters of sweets on the tables.

"You're not open already?"

"No," Jan assured him. "We just had a few neighbors in."

"You threw a party?" His brow wrinkled.

"Networking," Elaine said hastily. "We wanted to tell the other business owners on the street about the tearoom. They'll give us some great word-of-mouth advertising."

While she talked, Jan hurried out and returned with a plastic box, which she proceeded to fill with cookies and cream puffs.

"One of the ladies is giving us a free article in her weekly newspaper," Elaine went on.

"Free publicity is good," Brian said a bit grudgingly.

"You make sure everyone gets one of these cream puffs," Jan said to Brian as she sealed the container. "Especially Kelly. They're her favorite."

Brian sighed. "Okay, Mom. I just don't see how you think you can make a profit if you're making more food than you need and giving it all away."

"It's all good advertising," Jan said. "Are you going back to work?" Brian was the manager of a busy auto parts outlet in Augusta and often worked long hours.

"Yeah, I decided to take a late lunch hour and run out here."

"Well, put the cookie box in the shade," Jan admonished, walking with him to the door. "And tell Paula to bring the kids over."

"They're still in school."

"Well, yes, but this weekend, maybe."

"Okay. How'd the kitchen turn out?"

"It's fantastic," Jan said.

"Good."

Brian went out. Jan stood in the doorway and waved, then shut the door. "Why do I always feel exhausted after he leaves?"

Elaine smiled. "It's not just Brian. You've been on your feet all day. Let's just sit for a minute."

"But the dishes..."

"Later." Elaine took her arm and walked her through the kitchen and out on to the screened porch. "Let's go down to the deck."

"Well, okay."

They went down the stairs to the platform between the house and the lake. They could see across the water to the docks at the marina. Though the lake had been covered with ice a month ago, the owners already had a dozen small boats, several cabin cruisers, and two pontoon party boats moored at the docks. On the lake, a sailboat silently glided along, and a couple of motorboats carved the water, leaving frothy wakes behind them.

Jan sank into a deck chair. "I do love it here."

"Me too." They sat companionably for a few minutes. The sound of the outboard motors faded. "Let's come down here at dusk," Elaine said. "Faith told me there are still loons on the lake, and sundown is a good time to see them."

"Okay." Jan shifted in her chair and looked over at her cousin. "Sometimes I worry that Brian's right—that the house will need a lot of repairs."

"You know we've covered that. Bill says we're in good shape."

"Yes. That was such a relief when he said the roof would last another ten years or more. I suspect Brian may be thinking I'm spending what should be his inheritance. Is that terrible of me?"

"No," Elaine said. "But the truth is, you're growing his inheritance. Your share in this house and this business will be worth more than your old house was, and you'll be able to build up a retirement fund. Brian and Paula won't have to take care of you in your dotage."

"Brian liked thinking I couldn't get along without him," Jan mused. "The truth is, I've been independent since Pete died, but he doesn't see it that way. Oh, don't get me wrong. He does a lot for me, and I appreciate it."

"Of course. Brian has done well for himself. You should be proud of him."

"I am. I think he's starting to get used to the idea of the tearoom. I felt so stressed at first—he was so negative about it."

Elaine couldn't hold back a smile. "Worse than he is now?"

"Yes, if you can believe that. He sat me down last month and tried to convince me it was the worst idea since the Edsel." She looked over at Elaine, and her eyes brightened. "But now that you're here, and we're really doing it, he seems a little more open to it. And I know it's going to be great."

By prior agreement, the cousins got ready for church on Sunday morning and set out for Lancaster Community Church, the one place of worship in the little village. The white clapboard building was set on a rise on Pine Ridge Road, about a quarter mile off Main Street. Its location enabled residents to see the steeple pointing skyward from nearly anywhere in the village. Jan had fond memories of attending Sunday school at the building when she was a child, but she had never met the current pastor, the Reverend Michael Ryder.

She parked in the gravel lot beside a black pickup truck. As Jan and Elaine got out of their car, a couple was just climbing out of their red Toyota across the row.

"Hi," the woman called, walking toward them. She had dark blonde hair that caught the sun, and her blue dress brought out the hue of her eyes. "I think you're my new neighbors. I'm Bristol Payson, at the Bookworm."

"Oh, we're so glad to meet you," Elaine said. She introduced herself and Jan. Meanwhile, the man had sauntered over to them.

"This is my husband, Mark," Bristol said. "You may have met him already."

"I don't think so," Jan said, trying to place the tall, fortyish man with dark hair and thick eyebrows.

"He's the town clerk," Bristol said. "I thought maybe you'd been in the office."

"Hi." Mark shook their hands, and the four of them turned toward the church as other vehicles drove in.

Jan let Elaine give the Paysons a quick rundown on the tearoom, and she learned that the couple had a twenty-year-old son who was away at college.

"I've been wanting to get over and see your shop," Jan said as they entered the sanctuary. She had walked over to the Bookworm when she invited the neighbors to tea on Friday, but the shop had been closed, so she hadn't met the owner.

"Come anytime," Bristol said with a smile.

Jan and Elaine found seats in the sanctuary, and a younger couple soon filed in the other end of the pew with a little girl between them. The woman slid over toward Jan.

"Hi. I'm Kit Edmonds."

"Jan Blake." The two were soon exchanging information, and Jan turned excitedly to Elaine. "Did you hear that? Kit is Will Trexler's granddaughter. You remember him, don't you?"

"Isn't he the one who invented the bug repellant?" Elaine asked.

Kit laughed. "Yup, that's Granddad. Everyone remembers Trapper Will's Fly Dope."

"Does he still make it?" Elaine asked.

"Oh no, he sold the formula long ago. He's eighty now, but he's still sharp as a tack. In fact, he and Grammy should be here this morning."

"Didn't they have a boy named Billy?" Jan asked, racking her brain. "He was younger than I was, I think."

"He's my dad. He lives in New York now. He's a commercial pilot, but he'll be up to see the family this summer."

In the short time left before the service started, Jan also learned that Kit taught school at Lancaster Elementary, where her daughter Marcella was in the first grade.

"And my husband, Russell, is the marine postman in summer," Kit added. "He takes the mail around to all the lakeside cottages by boat." She pulled her little girl over. "Marcella, this is Mrs. Blake and Mrs. Cook. They're cousins."

"I don't have a cousin," Marcella said.

"Sure you do. Remember Lisa and Timmy?" Kit smiled apologetically. "She just doesn't see them very often." She turned back to the little girl. "These ladies are starting a tearoom at that big old house beside the Bookworm."

Marcella studied Jan thoughtfully for a moment. "What's a T-room? Is it where you make T-shirts?"

Jan smiled. "No, it's the kind of tea you drink, like coffee. A tearoom is like a restaurant, but we'll only serve tea and pastries."

Marcella grinned. "I think I'd like that. Mom, can we go there for lunch sometime?"

"Not lunch, but maybe for a snack," Kit said. The minister stood up behind the pulpit, and she pushed Marcella gently down on to the pew. *"Shh."*

"She's adorable," Elaine whispered in Jan's ear, and Jan nodded.

The congregation sang several hymns she was familiar with and a new worship song that Jan had never heard—though it seemed to be a favorite of Marcella, who sang it loudly while bouncing a little on her toes. Jan exchanged a smile with Elaine and tried not to stare at the little girl, whose long braid bobbed on the back of her yellow dress every time she bounced.

Pastor Ryder had a warm speaking voice and a delivery that made Jan feel he was addressing her individually. He was finishing a series of sermons on the book of Philippians, and Jan was encouraged by his words.

After the service, Kit introduced her and Elaine to several other church members, including her grandparents. Will and Pearl Trexler were delighted to hear they had returned to Lancaster to live and open a new business.

"I knew your father well," Pearl said to Jan.

"How nice. Elaine's mom, Virginia, is his sister."

"Oh, sure, I know Virginia. Doesn't she live in Augusta now?"

"Yes," Elaine said. "My dad passed away, and she's at the Millpond Senior Community now."

Pearl nodded. "That's a nice place. I have a friend who lives there. Now, were you two in Billy's class?"

After some figuring, Pearl and Jan determined that Billy had been two classes behind Jan and Elaine in school.

"Well, I'll have to stop in once you open the tearoom," Pearl said.

Maureen Oakley, whose leg brace was a reminder that she had survived polio as a child, also took an interest in the tearoom. When Jan mentioned a few of the sweets she would be baking for the menu, Maureen licked her lips.

"I've definitely got to come. When do you open?"

"Well, the original plan was Memorial Day weekend," Jan said, "but things are coming together so well that we're starting to think we'll open the week before, just for practice."

"Sure," Maureen said. "It would be good to work the kinks out before the big rush hits."

After Maureen had drifted off to talk to someone else, Elaine whispered to Jan, "Did you know her husband is one of the selectmen?"

"No." Jan followed Maureen's path with her gaze and saw her join a white-haired man near the door. "I'll never remember all the names."

"You don't have to," Elaine said. "If they come into the tearoom and you don't remember, just laugh and ask them to help you out and tell you who they are."

When they reached the entry, Pastor Ryder was shaking hands with people as they went out. Jan looked up into the tall man's gray eyes.

"We're so glad to have you ladies join us." He smiled at the woman by his side. "This is my wife, Sarah. She works over at the clinic. She's a nurse."

"Welcome." Sarah clasped Jan's hand. Her dark auburn hair was swept back into French braids, and she wore a pale-green linen dress.

"Thank you," Jan said. "I came here some when I was a child, but it's been a long time."

Elaine and Jan assured the Ryders they would be back another time. In the parking lot, the Paysons were headed for their car.

"Oh, Mr. Payson," Elaine called, hastening her steps.

He turned toward her. "It's Mark."

"Oh yes. I'll get it after a while." Elaine smiled sheepishly. "I wanted to ask you—you must know everyone in town, since you work at the town office."

"Pretty much," Mark said. "How can I help you?"

"I wondered about the people who used to own our house," Elaine said.

"The Binnses?"

Elaine nodded. "Yes, the man we bought it from was Jonathan Binns."

"His father had the house, if I remember right," Mark said. "I'd have to look up the details. Come by the office when you can, and I'll see what I can find."

"Thanks very much."

"No problem."

Jan and Elaine said good-bye to Bristol and Mark, promising to visit the Bookworm soon, and headed for Jan's car. The morning was well spent, Jan felt. The church service had encouraged her spiritually, and she had met a lot of new people who might become friends. She had been able to put aside her reticence with many of them, especially the Trexlers.

"What are you going to do this afternoon?" she asked as she pulled into their driveway and Elaine hit the button on the garage door opener.

"I thought I'd get the menus ready for printing, if you've finalized what you want on them."

Jan nodded. "We agreed on six sweets that we'll offer every day, and also the cookie of the day, and muffins."

"And I'll put prices for boxed treats by the dozen on the back," Elaine added. "What will you be doing?"

Jan smiled. "I expect it will sound dull, but I thought I'd look into that horsehair plaster in our walls. I'd like to know more about how it was made, and when they stopped doing it that way. It might help us learn more about that sapphire ring."

CHAPTER EIGHT

By Thursday, Elaine was convinced they had things well enough in hand that they could even open for business before Memorial Day.

"Do you think the Monday before, then?" Janet asked.

"We could. That would be the twenty-third. Or how about Saturday, the twenty-first? That would give us the weekend to recover."

Jan laughed. "Do you really think we can be ready? I mean, that's only nine days from now."

"We got the rest of the chairs and two more tables," Elaine said, ticking essentials off on her fingers. "Bill finished the checkout, and I'll stock the retail shelves today. We have enough china cups and saucers to serve twenty-four at once, and backup mugs for coffee drinkers and emergencies."

"We are going to hire someone to help serve and load the dishwasher, aren't we?"

Jan seemed a little anxious, and Elaine patted her shoulder. "Of course we are. I've placed the ad in the *Penzance Courier* and the Waterville paper. We may eventually need a second server, but I think if we hire one for now, it will be plenty."

Jan nodded, still frowning. "Until we see how it goes."

"Right." They had agreed on tearoom hours of 10:00 a.m. to 4:00 p.m., six days a week. They would stay closed on Sunday. Of course, they would put in many hours outside those, but the schedule ought to work for an establishment that didn't serve meals.

"So are we going to take that ring to the jeweler?" Jan asked. "I'd like to know what it's worth."

"So would I. Let's go this afternoon."

Jan untied her apron. "Fine with me. I'd like to stop by the shoe store too."

That settled the matter, and they headed into Waterville with the ring, in its rosewood box, tucked into Elaine's purse. She also took along the mockups she had made for their menus as well as small posters they could place around Lancaster to announce their early opening.

The jewelry store Kate Pierce had recommended to them was on the main street, and both cousins walked in and made a beeline for the counter. As often happened, Jan seemed happy to hang back and let Elaine do the talking.

"Hi," said the woman behind the counter with a bright smile.

"Hello," Elaine replied. "I'm told Mr. Martel gives appraisals for old jewelry."

"Let me tell him you're here." The woman went through an open doorway at the back of the showroom and returned a moment later. A balding man of about Elaine's height followed her. He wore a pale-blue dress shirt, open at the collar, and black-framed glasses.

"Hi. I'm Kenneth Martel. May I help you?" he asked.

"Yes," Elaine said. "We wondered if you could tell us anything about this ring—how old it is, and if it has much value."

He took the box and peered at the ring. "Would you like to step into my workshop?"

"Thank you."

Elaine had never seen a jeweler's workroom. She and Jan followed him into a small room crowded with cabinets, shelves, and a large safe built into an interior wall. Mr. Martel sat down on a stool at a workbench strewn with tools. A row of bins at the back of the surface, against the wall, held various items with paper labels tied to them. They looked like the work order tag Heather Wells had placed on Elaine's teapot, only larger. Elaine supposed these were all items customers had brought in for Mr. Martel to fix for them.

He turned on a high-intensity lamp and placed the ring under a magnifier. Elaine glanced at Jan while they waited in silence, and Jan gave her a little smile.

"I believe this is a natural sapphire," Mr. Martel said at last. "It has a small occlusion, but that's not unusual."

"What's that?" Elaine asked.

"A flaw. But most natural sapphires have them. That's one way to know it's not man-made. Of course, there are flawless natural stones, but one this size would be very rare, and extremely valuable."

Elaine swallowed hard. Their ring was a real sapphire.

"What else can you tell us?" she asked.

"See this?" He held the ring under the lamp and tipped it back and forth. "It doesn't sparkle like a diamond does. That's normal too. If it were made of glass, it would reflect colors."

Jan cleared her throat. "Isn't it paler than most sapphires?"

"No, actually." Mr. Martel turned around on his stool to face them. "Most natural blue sapphires are paler than lab-made ones. People like the deep colors, so if you're making one to sell, why not make it dark blue?"

"Interesting," Elaine said.

"Yes, well, sapphires come in a variety of colors."

"They do?" Jan asked. "I thought they were all blue. Or do you mean shades of blue?"

"No, some look red, orange, pink—even purple."

Elaine let out a slow breath. "I had no idea."

"How long have you had this ring?" Mr. Martel asked.

"Not long." Elaine glanced at Jan, and she nodded. "It was in an old house."

"Ah." Mr. Martel slid the ring back into its box. "Well, the setting is old. From the design, I'm guessing it's from the 1930s or before."

"The Depression?" Jan asked. "Who would buy a ring like this back then?"

Mr. Martel smiled. "You might be surprised. On the other hand, even if it was made then, that doesn't mean it was sold right away. But the setting is quite plain. It could be older. And if you want to learn more about the stone, you could take it to a gemologist. He or she might be able to give you more precise information. A gemologist could also give you a certificate of authenticity, in case you want to sell the ring."

"That might be a good idea," Jan said, turning wide eyes on Elaine.

"Yes, I think so too," Elaine said.

Mr. Martel handed her the ring box and stood. He walked to a cabinet, opened a drawer, and came back with a small brochure. "This man is reputable."

"Thank you," Elaine said.

Mr. Martel walked them out into the showroom. They thanked him again and left.

"Maybe we should put it in the bank for now," Elaine said. "I mean, neither of us is going to wear it."

"I certainly wouldn't dare," Jan said.

Elaine chuckled. "What do you think about his suggestion that we take it to the gemologist?"

"Let's read that pamphlet he gave you and decide later. But I do think the bank is a good idea. I can put it in my safe deposit box if you want."

Elaine gave her the ring. "Thanks. And maybe when I get a few minutes, I can do some more digging on the Binns family. If it's worth that much, I feel as though we ought to make an effort to find out who left it in the wall."

"Yes," Jan said. "We ought to do everything we can to find the owner. Maybe we can return it to the family."

Elaine pulled the strap of her purse up on her shoulder. "I'll head over to the office supply store while you're in the bank. I'd like to get the menus and posters printed up."

"I can walk over when I'm done," Jan said. "I'll meet you there."

Successful in her errands, Elaine had dropped off her materials with the printing clerk and was ready to leave the store before Jan arrived. She walked toward the door, looking out through the plate glass in hopes of seeing her cousin approaching.

Instead, a man who looked very familiar entered, and Elaine caught herself staring. His dark hair was streaked with silver at the temples, but the resemblance was too uncanny to be ignored.

"Bobby?" she asked. "Bobby Claybrook?"

He whipped his face toward her and hesitated.

"I'm sorry—Robert. It is you, isn't it?"

"Yes." He still looked puzzled.

"Elaine Cook," she said, stepping forward. "Well, Elaine Willard."

She could tell the exact moment when the light dawned. "Of course! Elaine! How are you?"

"Great. And you?"

"Good." He drew her aside so they wouldn't block the door for customers coming in. "I don't think I've seen you since graduation."

"I know! You were going to law school, right?"

He nodded. "I'm practicing here in Waterville now. Have been for thirty years."

"How time flies." Elaine wished she had come up with something more original, but Robert smiled in agreement.

"It sure has."

"You used to wear glasses," she said.

He shrugged. “Contacts. So do you live in the area? I was thinking you married a military man or something.”

“I did. But my husband passed away about six months ago.”

“I’m sorry.”

“Thank you,” Elaine said. “It was our dream to move here when Ben retired and start a B and B in Lancaster. I decided to move back anyway, and I’m starting a new venture.”

“Oh? A bed-and-breakfast?”

“No. Do you remember my cousin, Jan?”

“Sure,” Robert said.

“She’s also widowed, so the two of us are joining forces. We’ve bought a house on the lake shore in Lancaster, and we’re opening a tearoom. We’re calling it Tea for Two.”

“Charming!”

“You’ll have to stop in,” Elaine said.

“Uh...what if I’m not a tea drinker?”

“Oh, we’ll provide coffee and lemonade for those who refuse to be civilized.”

He grinned. “Sounds like fun. I still live in Lancaster, you know.”

“You do?”

Robert shrugged. “Well, I’m nearly in Penzance, but my taxes and my loyalty go to Lancaster. My wife’s gone too. She passed away about four years ago.”

“I’m sorry.”

“Thanks. We had a good life together. And I have a daughter, Susie, living in Portland.”

“That’s nice. Say, could I ask you something?” Elaine paused, wondering if she was committing a faux pas. “It’s sort of a legal question, so if I need to make an appointment, please don't hesitate to say so."

Robert shrugged. "Is it complicated?"

"I don't think so. What would happen if someone bought a house and then found something valuable inside it?"

He raised one eyebrow, and she saw the gangly high school boy in his expression. "Unless there's more to it than that, the 'find' is yours—that is, it belongs to whoever bought the house. Usually anything left in the house goes with it, unless that's spelled out in exclusions prior to the sale."

"Thanks," Elaine said. "I thought that was the case, but I wanted to make sure. As you've probably guessed, Jan and I found an unexpected bonus in the house we just bought."

"I don't think you need to worry, but if the item is extremely valuable, you might want to look up the previous owner. It's up to you, really."

The door opened, and Jan strode in, looking utterly charming if a little flustered, her cheeks a becoming natural pink and her hair a bit tousled.

"There you are," she said to Elaine, with a cautious glance at Robert. She stopped in her tracks. "Oh my goodness! Bobby Claybrook!"

He grinned. "It's me, all right. How are you, Jan?"

"I'm great."

"Elaine was just telling me about your business partnership," Robert said.

Jan smiled. "We're convinced it will be a thundering success."

Elaine studied her cousin's face. Jan looked more animated than usual, and Robert's eyes had taken on a sparkle as well.

"I'm surprised you remember me," Jan said.

"What? How could I forget the fraternal cousins?" Robert asked with a laugh.

"That's right, you boys used to tease us in junior high and call us the fraternal cousins, as opposed to the identical cousins…"

"Patty Duke and Patty Duke," Robert finished.

Memories of the 1960s television show and the ribbing she and Jan had taken at school rushed back to Elaine. It was out of production before she and Jan reached middle school, but all their classmates had seen it in reruns. Those were good days, so carefree and uncomplicated.

Jan laughed. "Yeah, I always said that I was Patty and Elaine was Cathy. And it turned out that way too. She's the one who's lived all over the world and got sophisticated."

"Oh, stop it," Elaine said, trying to control her laughter. "I never cooked a crêpe suzette in my life. You're the one who's a gourmet cook."

Robert reined in his chortling. "It's great to see you gals again. I might just have to stop by the tea shop."

"Do. You won't regret it."

He nodded. "I've got to pick up something and get back to the office, but I hope to see you again soon."

"Good to see you, Bob," Jan said as he headed for the printer cartridge display.

Elaine took her arm and scooted out on to the sidewalk with her.

"That was a surprise," Jan said.

"Doesn't he look great?"

"He sure does." Jan looked over her shoulder toward the store, and Elaine thought there was a wistful look in her eye.

"Have you seen him since graduation?" Elaine asked.

"Maybe once or twice, but it's been years."

Elaine wanted to ask if she knew whether Robert was married, but she decided to hold back on that. She didn't want Jan to think she was pushing any particular train of thought—or that she was interested in Robert herself. Elaine wasn't ready to think about romance, but her cousin might be a different story, and she was sure she'd seen a spark between Robert and Jan.

THAT EVENING, CONTENT with their day's work, Jan brewed chai tea, knowing it was one of Elaine's favorites, and prepared a tray with two cups.

"It's warm tonight," she said to Elaine, who had loaded the dishwasher. "Want to take this down to the deck?"

"Lovely, but I think I'll get my sweater anyway. Warm in Maine at the middle of May is not the same as warm in a lot of the places I've lived."

They both fetched sweaters, and Elaine picked up the tea tray. Down on the deck, they had placed a small white wrought iron table and two old-fashioned garden chairs that could be left there most of the time. Jan was sure only the wildest gale would sweep them into the water, while modern deck chairs were so light they couldn't be left outside for fear of losing them.

"This is nice." Elaine settled in on the striped cushions they had purchased to soften the seats and backs of the metal chairs. Jan took the other seat and reached for her teacup. A light breeze fluttered over the lake, making tiny waves that gently slapped the dock pilings and rocks on the shore. The sun was already low behind the dark pine and spruce trees on the west side of the lake. Only a few lights shone from houses and cottages on the perimeter of Chickadee Lake, but a couple of docks over, the marina's main pier was lit with powerful floodlights. Small boats bobbed in their slips, and the back of the marina store was clearly visible from the tearoom's lakeside deck.

"Do they leave those lights on all night?" Jan asked.

"Yes, but it doesn't bother me, since my bedroom windows are on the back and east," Elaine replied. "I think it's for security."

"I suppose so, with valuable assets sitting out there twenty-four–seven." Jan sipped her tea. "Is it tomorrow that we're interviewing applicants for the server job?"

"Yeah. We got five replies, and I've asked the three that sounded best to come in for interviews."

"I'll let you do most of the talking," Jan said, "but I'd like to see them. Not that looks are everything, but we want someone with a neat appearance. After all, we're serving food."

"Right," Elaine said. "And age isn't a factor. We've got one coming who told me she's in her twenties, and one who sounded a little older. The third one is a high school girl, but she lives in town. We might want to give her a chance."

"Well, we'll see. All females?"

"We didn't get any male applicants. If none of these three seems right, we can take another look at the other two, or we can run the ads again." Elaine sat forward. "So about the ring."

"What about it?" Jan asked.

"I asked Robert Claybrook about it—well, I didn't tell him it was a ring, but I told him we'd found something unexpected in the house and asked if it belongs to us."

"What did he say?"

"He says it does. But I still feel as though we ought to try to find out more about it. We've been so busy that I haven't gone to the town office yet, but I want to. I'm not sure how much Mark can tell us, but Bill Bridges seemed to think that ring had to have been in the wall a good long time. And with what you found out about the plaster..."

Jan set down her cup and saucer. "Yes, the research I've done so far indicates that plaster and lath was used sometimes up until the 1950s in this country, although wallboard was introduced in the thirties. I'm not sure when they stopped putting horsehair in the mortar though. I think I'll check at the library and see if they have a book on the construction of old houses. If nothing else, it's been interesting to learn about it. For me, anyway."

Elaine chuckled. "Even so," she said, "we know that wall has been there at least sixty-five years because of the plaster. Probably more. The papers we got from the real estate agent said the house was built in the 1880s. And Bill said the plaster hadn't been broken through or repaired. So that was untouched for at least sixty or seventy years, probably twice that."

Jan nodded. "But that doesn't mean the ring was there that long. I mean, someone could have dropped it down that hole a month ago. Not that I think that, but you understand what I'm saying."

"Yes. In fact, it probably wasn't put there as soon as the wall was finished. It's been there awhile, but there doesn't seem to be a way to pinpoint how long. But nobody would have put it in through the hole when it had a stovepipe in it." Elaine spread her hands helplessly. "Of course, no one knows how long they used a stove in that room."

"Maybe your approach is better," Jan said, mulling it over in her mind. The plaster was interesting, but it didn't really help in their search. "Mr. Martel thought the ring was made in the 1930s."

"Yes, or earlier. But that doesn't really help. It could have been put in the wall right up until we bought the house." Elaine lifted her teacup to her lips. "We'd never know if that flue cover was removed and replaced a hundred times."

"The box didn't have a jeweler's name in it, and Mr. Martel didn't find anything that told him who made the ring." The breeze tugged at Jan's hair, and she shoved a hand through it. "We might have more luck learning about the people who lived here."

"Let's hope so. I wonder why they put it there," Elaine mused. "If they just wanted to get rid of it, you'd think they would have sold it."

"Maybe it was stolen."

Elaine smiled, and her eyes took on a gleam. "That would be a good place to ditch stolen loot, don't you think?"

"I suppose so. If anyone searched the house, they wouldn't find it. But then, why didn't the thief go back and retrieve it later?"

They sat in silence for a moment, drinking their tea and watching the water change to deep velvet blue and then black as the sun's last rays faded.

"Maybe it was for safekeeping," Elaine suggested in a sleepy voice.

"*Ooh,* I like that idea," Jan said. "Someone wants to steal it, so the girl who owns it hides it where it's safe."

"Or maybe the fiancé wants it back, and she wants to keep it."

Jan nodded. "Or her mean father wants to sell it to support his gambling habit."

Elaine laughed. "Now you're talking. But all of those imply a sad ending. Why wasn't it ever retrieved?"

"She must have died a tragic death," Jan said. "No woman would forget about a ring like that."

As if providing sound effects for the mournful scene Jan had painted, the eerie cry of a loon echoed across the quiet lake.

CHAPTER NINE

Elaine had scheduled the interviews throughout the day on Friday, and the first prospect arrived at nine o'clock. She was the older woman, who said she was looking for a part-time job to fill some of her hours now that her youngest had moved out.

Elaine and Jan agreed after the interview that they both liked the woman, but she had two strikes against her. She lived in Augusta, about twenty miles away, which the cousins felt was a long drive for a part-time job. It could also be problematic in bad weather. The second thing that made Elaine hesitate was the woman's appalling grammar.

"*I don't got nothing else to do,*" she had said with a laugh.

Elaine couldn't help it. That set her teeth on edge, although it was said in a friendly, cheerful tone. She smiled and concluded the interview, telling the woman they would phone her the next day if they wanted to hire her.

After she had left, Elaine said to Jan, "Be honest. What did you think of her?"

Jan shook her head. "Not quite the tone we want to set. I mean...tearoom, Queen Anne house...I was hoping for a bit of refinement."

"Exactly. I'm glad we agree. If we host a special event, I want the customers to feel they've stepped back in time to a lady's drawing room."

The second applicant came at eleven, somewhat windblown, brushing back tendrils of wheat-colored hair that had escaped her long braid. A young man in a leather jacket waited down in the driveway beside a motorcycle.

The woman greeted the cousins with a disarming smile. "Hi. I'm Rose Young. I hope you don't mind, but my car's in the shop, and a friend brought me on his bike for the interview."

"Oh." Elaine might have expected this of the high schooler, but this was the applicant in her twenties. She eyed the young man hesitantly. He grinned and waved. "Uh, would he like to come in? He could sit in the other room while we talk. Or he could walk around the porch and down to the deck if he wants. We're right on the lake, and he might enjoy that."

Rose turned and called, "Jordy, you want to look at the lake? They have a deck out back."

He grinned and unsnapped the strap on his motorcycle helmet as he mounted the steps. He pulled it off, revealing shaggy blond hair and a boyish face.

He nodded at Elaine and Jan. "Don't mind if I do. Will the bike be okay there?"

"Oh yes," Elaine said, pointing toward where the porch wrapped around the side of the house. "Just walk on back there, and through the screened porch. There are steps down to the water."

"Thanks." He ambled off around the corner.

"Well now, Rose, come on in," Elaine said.

Jan had scooted into the east parlor, where they were conducting their interviews. She had set out a fresh tea tray on one of the tables. After Elaine and Rose were seated at another, she said, "Would you like some tea?"

"Oh, thank you, I would," Rose said. She glanced about the room and looked at Elaine with wide blue eyes. "The tearoom will be in here? Beautiful house for it."

"Yes. Thank you."

Rose leaned toward Elaine. "Jordy's not a boyfriend or anything. He lives down the road from my folks, and he mows the lawn for us. He had today free and offered to bring me over here."

Elaine nodded. Rose certainly had no trouble talking to strangers, and she didn't seem nervous. "Your résumé says you live in Lancaster."

Rose nodded. "I've been in Portland for a few years, working as a nurse. But, well, to be honest, it wasn't quite right for me. I know I want to take care of people, but I'm not sure that nursing is the best fit. So I'm kind of starting at square one." She straightened her trousers. "So I wanted to move back home for a while. I'm here at least for the summer, maybe permanently, if I get a job."

Jan brought over two teacups and saucers and placed one before Rose and one at Elaine's elbow.

"Thank you." Rose lifted hers and smelled the brew, then took a sip. "*Mmm.* Earl Grey."

Two points for Rose, Elaine thought. Not everyone would be able to identify the kind of tea she was being served. Elaine hoped that meant Rose had as much passion for tea as she and Jan did. She had already decided she liked the forthright young woman. "Where will you live?"

"With my dad for now," Rose said, which made Elaine assume that Rose's parents were no longer together, but she didn't probe. If they were to hire Rose, Elaine knew they'd gradually get to know her.

Jan came and sat down at the table with them, carrying her own cup of tea and a plate of sweets.

"Have a cookie, Rose," Jan said.

"Thanks." Rose smiled at her and looked at the cookie plate. "I love gingersnaps. Oh, and you've got filled cookies. Are you making all the food for the tearoom customers?"

"Yes, we are," Jan said with a touch of pleasure in her voice and a gleam in her eyes.

"Jan is chief baker," Elaine said. "Rose, what would you like to do for a job, if you could do anything?" Elaine asked.

"Something creative, maybe." Rose smiled. Despite the wispy braid, Rose was dressed suitably for the interview. Her olive-green blouse looked professional enough for work, and her nails were neatly manicured, without nail polish. She wore a minimum of makeup. An outdoorsy girl, Elaine thought.

"Do you like boating?" she asked.

Rose grinned. "Boating, fishing, water skiing, you name it. I grew up swimming in Chickadee Lake. That's something I really missed in Portland."

"I think I'll go offer your friend some cookies and tea," Jan said.

"That's nice of you," Rose said. "Jordy's a good kid. And he's always hungry."

Jan chuckled and rose to carry out her mission.

"We plan to host special events here," Elaine said, drawing Rose's attention back to the interview. "If we have a high tea, we'll probably dress in period costume. Would you object to wearing a Victorian dress? We'd supply it, of course."

"Sounds great." Rose looked around the room, taking in the carved woodwork, stone fireplace, and large windows. "I think you and Mrs. Blake are very brave, starting something this big and new. It's a fantastic old house."

"Thank you." Elaine asked a few more questions, and she liked the young woman more and more. Rose was intelligent and responsive. "I'll check with your references and let you know tomorrow," she told Rose when she was satisfied. They walked together through the kitchen and the screened porch, where wicker chairs and a galvanized tub of magazines and newspapers awaited the cousins during leisure hours. Jan and Jordy sat on the deck below, munching cookies and apparently enjoying a lively conversation. Elaine opened the door, and both looked up.

"All finished?" Jan asked.

"Yes, thanks," Elaine said with a wave.

"We'll be right up." Jordy tipped his glass up to drain it and stood, setting the glass on Jan's tray and grabbing his motorcycle helmet almost with one motion. Elaine led Rose back into the entry hall, where the young woman gazed unabashed at the decor and architectural details.

"I think I'd love working in a place like this," she said.

Jordy came from kitchen, smiling. "Thanks a lot, ma'am. Your cousin sure knows how to cook. You know, there's trout in that lake."

Elaine smiled. "Yes. I remember fishing with my dad in the lake when I was a girl. Thank you for bringing Rose."

The two young people went out the door smiling. Rose put on her helmet and climbed onto the seat behind Jordy. She waved to Elaine. "'Bye!"

As the drone of the motorcycle's engine faded, Jan came up behind Elaine, wiping her hands on a dish towel.

"You like her."

"I do," Elaine said, closing the door. "Do you?"

Jan nodded. "I like Jordy too, not that it matters. We're not hiring him. But he seems like a responsible kid."

"That's good."

"Yes. I know his mother's cousin, it turns out."

Elaine chuckled. "You're amazing. How long did it take you to figure out you're only three degrees of separation from Jordy?"

"About four minutes. And Jordy knows your friend Nathan. At least, he's been to the auction barn."

"How about that?" Elaine went into the east parlor and gathered the notes she had made while interviewing Rose. "I'll call the references, and if they give her a good word... She gave me her father's number too. He's just down the lake."

"Do you think we need to interview the girl who's coming after school?"

"As a courtesy," Elaine said. "I can handle it, if you want to get back to your baking."

"Thanks. I want to freeze some more cookies and work on that Russian tea blend you recommended. If we're opening a week from tomorrow, we have a lot to do."

Elaine went right to the office and made the calls. She emerged well pleased with the reports she'd received from Rose's father and one of Rose's former teachers. Rose had also given a phone number for a coworker in Portland, but had asked Elaine not to call her current boss, as she wanted to tell her in person that she was leaving her job.

While Elaine's tender heart hated to disappoint anyone, she was ready when the last applicant arrived later on her bicycle.

It was obvious almost at once that she and Jan had made the right choice. The teenaged girl was hopeful and adamant that she would work hard, but she couldn't start until the public schools let out, three weeks into June.

"I'm sorry," Elaine said. "We really need someone who can start right away. But I'll keep your application on file in case we need another server later in the summer."

The girl's face crumpled for a moment. "Okay. Thanks."

Elaine sighed as she watched her go.

From the parlor doorway, Jan said, "We can't hire everyone."

"I know. This is a business, not a social service. I just wish I could help everyone who needs it."

Jan smiled. "I know. For now, we'll be helping Rose. Now, if you don't mind, my cookies are out of the oven, and I'd like to walk over to the Bookworm and see if Bristol carries magazines. I didn't get the June issue of *Code Busters*, and I'm sure it's out."

"Mind if I tag along?" Elaine didn't share Jan's passion for logic puzzles and cryptograms, but she had also been wanting to visit the bookshop.

"That would be nice."

"I'm sure Bristol could order a book I've been looking at online about teapots," Elaine said.

"A whole book about teapots?"

"Yes, and I'd rather do business locally than have it shipped, if possible."

Jan turned toward the hall. "Just let me get my pocketbook!"

THE COUSINS HAD debated off and on all week about whether or not to attend the auction on Saturday.

"We don't really *need* anything," Jan said on Friday evening, but she had a feeling that Elaine wanted to go. Several times she had brought up Nathan's Web site on her laptop and studied the catalog listings for the upcoming auction.

"I know, but it's so much fun," Elaine said.

Jan smiled. "And one can never have too many cream-and-sugar sets."

The breeze off the lake was chilly, and Jan had built a fire in the east parlor fireplace. They had brought in two comfortable rocking chairs from the porch and placed them near the hearth to make a little seating area at that end of the room. On cool days, guests might appreciate being able to sit near the fire.

"Of course, we'll have to clean out the ashes in between," Jan had noted practically, but Elaine hadn't seen this as a reason to forgo the warmth and coziness of an open fire.

"Maybe Nathan will have some rocking chairs in the sale," Elaine said. "We could use more for the porch if we're going to keep these in here."

"Yes, or we could get a settee to put in here. Or a couple of upholstered chairs. Then the rockers can go back outside."

"Or we could get a swing for the porch." Elaine's blue eyes glittered. "There's still money in the account for fixtures."

"Nathan doesn't have a porch swing in the auction, does he?"

"If he does, it's not listed, but there is some furniture. Oh, let's go, Jan."

"All right."

"Are you sure? I don't want either of us to feel guilty for taking the time."

"I think I'm ready for a break from baking. I'm not going to make anything else for the business until next Friday, and then I'll make the last-minute things."

"All right," Elaine said readily. "Then I'm going to work on Rose's dress tonight. She said she could come by Wednesday for a fitting." They had decided to wear costumes on opening day. If the long, full skirts were too cumbersome, they could change, but the grand opening of the tearoom was a special occasion. Elaine brought the nearly finished dress down and worked on it while they chatted, and Jan put the finishing touches on her own costume. They had each chosen different colors—blue for Elaine and moss green for Jan, with rose, of course, for Rose.

"I can hardly wait for opening day," Jan admitted, "but I guess I'll have to."

Elaine smiled as she threaded her needle in preparation for sewing on the buttons. "It's only a week away."

THEY SET OUT early on Saturday, arriving at the auction hall an hour before the sale would open. Other buyers were already strolling the perimeter of the hall, where the merchandise to be sold was displayed. In some spots, items were stacked several boxes deep, and Jan wondered if they would be able to get a good look at everything in advance. Those seemed to be the less valuable items, however. Maybe Nathan would sell them by the box. She and Elaine each got a bidding number, though Jan had already decided she wasn't buying anything.

Elaine made a beeline for a locked glass case near the office door, and Jan followed. Several people were examining the small, valuable pieces in the case.

"Look," Elaine said, pointing. "See that brown teapot? That's the one Nathan showed me. He said it's from the Qing dynasty. I can't wait to see what it goes for."

Jan was more eager to see what Nathan Culver looked like. She knew he was a longtime friend of Elaine's, and that bond seemed to go deep. Always upbeat, today Elaine seemed extra vivacious. She greeted complete strangers with cheerful enthusiasm, as if they were all off on a picnic together.

When a tall, lean man came out of the office and walked toward the auctioneer's platform, Jan knew he was Nathan.

She could tell because Elaine was suddenly on high alert, and her gaze zeroed in on him like a heat-seeking radar. He was handsome, all right, though in Jan's opinion not quite as good-looking as Robert Claybrook. Nathan's brown hair had a sprinkling of gray, and his keen blue eyes darted about the hall as he spoke to one of his staff.

"Do you want to go and speak to him?" Jan asked softly.

"No, he's busy. Let's see if there are any teacups. We could use more of those."

Jan ambled along with Elaine, peering at the varied merchandise.

"Oh, look! Jan, there's something you'll love." Elaine drew her to a table on which a small black-painted cabinet rested. Its small drawers were arranged in four rows, with the words "Coats and Clark" stenciled in gold above them.

"A thread cabinet." Jan gazed at it, picturing the piece in their sewing room, with her skeins of embroidery floss in the drawers. She threw both hands up. "No. I'm not spending money today. Get me out of here."

Elaine laughed. "Okay, let's look at the fine art."

Some of the paintings and prints were lovely, but Jan agreed with her cousin that none of them struck the right note for the tearoom, although Elaine lingered over a primitive portrait with evident longing. Jan caught sight of a framed sampler among the other artworks. That was more to her taste. The tiny cross stitches made a mosaic of thread that formed a weeping willow tree and two swans.

"See something you like?"

The deep voice behind them startled both women, and as they turned toward it, Elaine's face broke into a huge smile.

"Nathan!"

"Hi. Glad you made it." He let his hand rest for a moment on Elaine's shoulder.

"This is my cousin, Janet Blake."

Nathan took Jan's hand. "Nice to meet you. Elaine's told me about your new venture. I think it's great."

"Thank you," Jan said. "She showed me your Chinese teapot. We'll be watching to see what happens when that goes on the block."

"Me too." Nathan chuckled. "Sometimes I get surprised, either in a good way or a bad way."

"I hope it's a good way today," Elaine said.

"Thanks. And did you take your teapot to Heather?"

"I did. She thought she could help us find its true personality. She had a backlog of work though, so I haven't heard from her yet."

"She won't keep you waiting too long." Nathan nodded toward the primitive. "Do you like that painting?"

"Yes, but I don't think my checkbook would," Elaine replied with a chuckle.

"It's a nice one. Could go high. Or not. Jan, what do you like?"

"Who, me?" Jan wasn't sure if he really wanted to know, or if he was making small talk. "Uh, there's a sampler here that interests me." She pointed to the stitched willow picture.

"Oh, a mourning sampler," Nathan said.

"Is that what it is?"

"Yeah, weeping willows are usually a sign that somebody died. That and urns. Tombstones, angels, crying mourners. This one is actually not as dreary as some." Nathan gazed at the needlework and nodded. "The swans are a nice touch."

"Is something like this apt to sell quite high?" Jan asked.

Nathan pursed his lips for a moment. "Maybe in the hundreds for that one. There's no date, and it's not in the best shape." He pointed to some stains near the bottom of the sampler. "But there is a name there, and it could be the deceased's name, rather than the stitcher's. A little research might give you some provenance, and that would add to the value."

Jan nodded. "Thank you. I'll watch for it when it comes up, though I came more for the entertainment."

"Nathan will give you that," Elaine said.

He laughed. "My dad was a pretty good teacher. I think I learned more from him than from auctioneer's school."

One of his staffers came over with a silver platter in his hands and stood waiting for Nathan's attention.

"Excuse me," Nathan said. "Duty calls—but I'm glad you ladies came, and I hope you enjoy the sale."

His disarming smile made Jan feel she really was in for an entertaining day. She could see what attracted Elaine to him now. He was both knowledgeable and charming. Add to that their longstanding friendship...Yes, Nathan would be a good friend to have beside you in a difficult time.

CHAPTER TEN

Elaine strolled around the auction hall with her cousin, taking special notes of dishes, linens, and artwork that might be suitable at Tea for Two. Jan took out a pocket notebook and jotted something down.

"What's that?" Elaine asked.

"Just writing down what we said we'd be willing to pay for that Sheffield pitcher. I don't want to get confused when the bidding starts."

Elaine smiled. Trust Jan to take a practical approach to things, especially when it might cost them money. "That's a good idea. Why don't you do the bidding for things we like for the business? That way, we won't be in danger of bidding against each other."

Jan frowned, and Elaine sensed her discomfort with that suggestion. Jan had probably never bid at an auction in her life, and holding up her paddle with her bidding number on it might be a scary experience. After all, Jan had watched her pennies for years out of necessity, as a widowed mother of three children.

"You have a lot more experience with this sort of thing," Jan said. "Why don't you do the bidding, and I'll keep tabs. We can't spend too much, after all."

Elaine nodded. "I will, if you'll jot down some more figures for me. You can help me watch for the things we want to come up for bids. Those biscuit tins, for instance. If he sells them separately, we might pay ten or fifteen dollars each. If they go as a lot...maybe fifty as our limit?"

"That seems like a lot of money," Jan said.

"I know. But the paint is in good shape, and I doubt they'll lose value." Elaine took out her phone and started tapping it. "Maybe I can check eBay and see what they've sold for recently."

Jan soon joined her, looking up items that had caught their interest online. A sidelong glance told Elaine that her cousin even took a cyber peek at an old thread cabinet similar to the one Nathan was offering.

"What's the price?" Elaine asked.

Jan flushed. "Too much. One went for eight hundred dollars on eBay." She wrote something in her notebook, and Elaine wondered if it was a reminder, so that when the cabinet came up for bids, she would restrain herself.

"Oh well," she said. "You might find something that will give you as much pleasure for a lot less money."

"That's what I think too," Jan said.

They found seats so that they were assured of a good view of the podium. Jan offered to stay there while Elaine made a final viewing circuit. She circled the hall again, watching for furniture and dishes they might be able to use, but saw only one box lot of interest that she hadn't already noticed. She wasn't really thirsty, but she remembered how Nathan had always brought her a bottle of pop, so ten minutes later, when she had finished surveying the items for sale, she stopped at the refreshment booth and bought two diet colas. Back at their seats, she handed one to Jan just as Nathan stepped onto the platform and turned on his microphone.

"Good morning, folks. We're glad to see you here. The sale is about to begin. I hope you've all had the opportunity to look over the merchandise." He ran through a few of the basic policies of the auction house and called for the first item to be sold, a boxed pair of dueling pistols. Since she had no interest in buying firearms, Elaine sat back and enjoyed watching Nathan and listening to his patter. He was truly a master of the art.

She paid close attention, and she bid on several items during the first hour. She prevailed on the biscuit tins, buying four for seven dollars each, much to Jan's delight, and she also wound up with a stack of vintage tea towels.

"Thank you," she said as a young man serving as one of Nathan's runners delivered them to her.

Up front, another of Nathan's staff carried the thread cabinet over and set it on the table in front of the auctioneer.

"Folks, this is a very nice, early thread cabinet with the Coats and Clark logo on it," Nathan said.

Jan sat up straighter.

"*Ooh,* it's your cabinet," Elaine whispered.

"It's not mine," Jan whispered back.

Nathan gave a little more description of the item and set the bid in at two hundred dollars. A man down the row from the cousins raised his bidding card, and Jan sank back in her chair.

"I knew it would be too much."

"At least you have good taste," Elaine said.

Jan chuckled. They watched as Nathan pitted two eager buyers against each other and ratcheted the price up gradually to seven hundred fifty dollars.

"And sold!"

Jan let out a deep sigh. "What good would something like that do me anyway, stuck in my sewing room where no one could see it?"

"Beauty is good for the soul," Elaine said.

"Well, I'll settle for lower-priced beauty, thank you."

Elaine eyed her keenly and decided that, even though she sounded a little disappointed, Jan was having a good time.

"Look, that's the box with the teacups," Elaine said. "I think you should do the bidding this time."

"Why?" Jan's eyed widened, and she shifted in her chair. "Don't you want to?"

"I think you need the experience. It's exhilarating. Just don't go above twenty dollars."

"What if I make a mistake?"

Elaine smiled. "As long as it's not a huge one, it's okay. And if it's a really big mistake, well…" She winked at Jan. "I know the auctioneer."

Jan hauled in a big breath and sat up, eyes glued to Nathan as he described the box lot.

"...and there are a couple pairs of salt and pepper shakers in here, a cheese grater, and a few other kitchen items. So, folks, what am I bid?"

"Five dollars," someone called from behind them.

"I'm bid five," Nathan said. "Who will make it seven?"

Jan lifted her card timidly, but she was too late. Two other bidders had had also jumped in, and Nathan pointed at a woman with flaming red hair.

"Seven over here, and now ten. Seven, and now ten." Nathan scanned the crowd.

Jan glanced at Elaine and stuck her card in the air.

"Ten to the lovely lady in green," Nathan said.

Jan's face went scarlet, but she smiled.

"And twelve over here," Nathan said, pointing toward the first bidder. "Fifteen?" He looked toward the redhead, but she didn't respond. "Fifteen?" He looked at Jan.

She nodded and held up her card.

"And now seventeen?" Nathan arched his eyebrows, but apparently the bidder behind them had dropped out. "Anyone for seventeen?" His gaze swept the hall. "I have fifteen, looking for seventeen."

Everyone was quiet.

Nathan brought down his gavel. "Sold to the lady for fifteen dollars."

Jan gasped and looked over at Elaine, her face flushed.

Elaine patted her arm. "You did great."

When the runner brought the box, Jan accepted it with an air of pride. She held it on her lap and carefully rummaged around in it. "Wow. You didn't tell me it had so much stuff in it." She picked up a saltshaker shaped like a bluebird. "These are cute."

Some of the items from the vault came up for bids over the next hour, and Elaine watched breathlessly as Nathan sold his plain little Chinese teapot for more than eight thousand dollars.

Jan let out a sigh when the gavel came down. "Well, I suppose that's most of what we came to see. We don't care about the other guns and paintings. Should we go?"

Elaine looked toward the platform and saw that the last item she'd had her eye on was among the things to be brought up in the next few minutes.

"Soon," she said. "There's one more thing..."

As she spoke, Nathan gestured to one of the runners to hold up a framed piece.

"Oh," Jan said, sinking back in her chair. "I forgot about that."

"Now, folks, we have this fine, early sampler. It has the willow tree motif, and some swans. It's a mourning sampler, done in silk thread on linen. We don't have a date, but my best guess is 1840. Who'll start it at a hundred?"

Jan's jaw dropped when Elaine raised her card.

"You're bidding on that?" she whispered.

Elaine smiled. "Thought I would."

"But..."

Jan kept quiet. Several other bidders joined in, and the price was soon one hundred eighty dollars. Elaine held her breath, sure someone else would raise it again. She had set a mental limit for herself at two hundred.

To her surprise, Nathan cut the bidding off rather quickly.

"All in and all done? Going once, going twice..." He paused for only a second and whacked the gavel. "Sold. One hundred eighty dollars."

Elaine exhaled and looked over at Jan.

"You...you..."

Elaine smiled. "It's not from the business budget, Jan. I'm buying it as a gift. I know someone who will love it."

Jan swallowed hard. "Do I know this person?"

"You know her very well. Don't make a fuss."

Jan sat for a moment then pulled in a deep breath. "Anything else?"

"Nope. I'm ready to go."

They gathered their purchases and stood. One of the runners came to Elaine's side.

"Here's your sampler, ma'am. Need help?"

"Thank you. We're going now. If you could carry these things, I'll pay for them, and my cousin can show you where the car is."

"Sure. Be glad to."

She placed the box lot in his arms. Elaine took Jan's card along with her own to settle both their bills at the cashier's window. As she waited in line, Nathan called a break.

"Ten minutes, folks," she heard him say over the speaker system. "Stretch your legs, then we'll resume with the rest of the gun collection."

Just as she turned away from the window after paying, he walked up to her.

"Hey, sneaking out on me?"

She chuckled. "I think Jan and I have spent all we can afford for one day. But we both had a lot of fun."

"Good. You got the sampler."

"I sure did. We'll enjoy that."

"How about my Yixing teapot?"

"Yeah," Elaine said. "I *think* that was a good price."

"I'm happy. Now, don't be a stranger." Nathan's eyebrows rose in question.

"We'll be back. For sure."

"Good." He clasped her hand for a moment and then headed back toward the platform.

On Monday, after several hours of cleaning and poring over her accounts, Elaine was ready to do some sleuthing. She and Jan took an afternoon break from the hundreds of details in their preparation for opening, and Elaine brought her laptop into the sitting room. She loved family research, and she opened a genealogy site she had used to trace her own family. She was happily browsing when Jan came in with two cups of her latest tea blend.

"What are you doing?" Jan set Elaine's mug on the end table beside her chair.

"Looking for Binnses," Elaine said. "I found a few families in Maine, but not in Lancaster, and I have no idea whether they connect to the one we bought the house from."

"Why don't you go over to see Mark Payson at the town office?" Jan asked. They had advanced their acquaintance with the Paysons at church, and had met several more members as well.

"I've been meaning to for quite a while, but I hate to take the time," Elaine said. "If we're going to wear our costumes Saturday, I need to work on Rose's dress and pinafore, and I haven't done the hem on my dress yet."

"Oh, go on," Jan said. "That ring has been bothering you since the day the electrician found it in the wall. And once we open, we'll be tied here most of the day."

"What will you be doing?" Elaine picked up her mug and eyed Jan over the edge.

"Oh, I've got plenty to do. Don't worry about me."

Elaine took a swallow. "*Mmm.* I do like this one. The cinnamon gives it a little kick, but it's not overpowering."

"I agree," Jan said. "You come up with some good ones. This is not on the menu, but maybe we can offer it as 'flavor of the day' or something."

"That's a great idea. We can have specials and put them on a chalkboard every day. If you want to try some new baked goods, we can offer those as specials too, and see how the customers like them."

"I like that, but you should go and see Mark."

Elaine sighed. "You're right. Just let me drink my tea, and I'll go. I really do want to know how that ring got in the wall."

At the small town office, Mark rose and came out from behind his desk.

"Hello, Elaine. Glad you made it. Let's see, you wanted to know who used to own your house, right?"

"That's correct."

Mark's thick eyebrows came together as he pursed his lips. "Let's look at the property maps."

He led her to a stack of thin pull-out trays that held large books. Some of them looked very old, with frayed covers. Others were more modern, with fabric-encased board covers connected by metal posts that held the maps firmly in place. Mark opened one of the newer ones.

"This is your property." He pointed to their lot. Elaine had no problem seeing the clearly marked boundaries: Main Street in front, the lake behind, and lots marked "Payson" and "Flood" on either side.

"This must be the Bookworm," she said, pointing to the one marked "Payson."

"Right. We were able to buy the property a few years ago. We're still paying for it, but Bristol loves running the store, and it's making a profit now."

"That's great," Elaine said.

"Sylvia Flood is on the other side. She lives over her shop."

Elaine recalled that Sylvia's Closet took up the first floor of a two-story house.

"Now, your house and lot were owned by Maynard Binns," Mark went on.

"Maynard?" Elaine asked.

He nodded. "He died a few months ago, and his son inherited the property. You bought it from... uh... Jonathan."

"That's right. So how long did Mr. Binns own it?"

Mark opened another book and leafed through some pages. "Maynard bought it in 1968."

Elaine's mind whirled. She and Jan both thought the ring had been in the wall longer than that. "If you don't mind a little more work, who owned it before that?"

"I thought you'd ask." He consulted the book with a smile. "Looks like a family named Gardner sold it to Mr. Binns." A little more searching brought him more information. "Here we go. Harold Gardner bought the house in 1903. His son, Paul, inherited it from him about twenty years later. Members of his family lived in it for forty-five years. They're the ones who sold it to Mr. Binns."

"Well, that makes it easier for me," Elaine said. "Only two families in the last hundred years. Do you have any more information about the Gardner family?"

"Hold on." Mark walked across the room and opened a file drawer. Elaine waited while he flipped through the folders inside.

Meanwhile, two more people had come into the office. One was standing before the counter talking to a clerk who worked with Mark. Elaine could tell from their conversation that he was renewing his car's registration. The woman who came in afterward stood behind him.

Mark looked over at her and nodded. "Hello, Marjorie. We'll be right with you."

About a minute later, he jotted something on a piece of scrap paper and came back to Elaine. "Paul Gardner's wife was named Rachel, and his mother—that is, Mrs. Harold Gardner—was Beatrice. That's about all I found." He handed her the slip of paper with the names on it.

Elaine took it and tucked it in her pocket. "Thank you so much, Mark. I won't take up any more of your time, but I really appreciate this. Now I may be able to find them on a family history site."

"Good luck." Mark smiled and went to speak to the waiting woman.

CHAPTER ELEVEN

The cousins spent most of the week in preparation for the opening. Jan and Elaine pitched in to clean the house thoroughly and make sure the dishes, glasses, and flatware sparkled. Rose came for two afternoons to help them, and by Friday evening they were tired, but everything on their many to-do lists had been done.

Jan stood on the stair landing, looking down into the hall below. "The sign's up, the tables are covered, the teas and pastries are ready. I honestly don't think there's one more thing we could do to be more prepared."

"Except relax this evening and get a good night's sleep," Elaine said.

They settled into their sitting room upstairs. Jan was beginning to feel quite comfortable there, with her blue plush-covered sofa and armchairs and the television set she had used for the last ten years. The sampler Elaine had bought for her now held a place of honor over the fireplace, and wedding photos graced the walls above the window seat. Both cousins had mounted one framed picture from each of their married children's weddings—Elaine's Jared, and Jan's Brian and Amy. A wicker shelf unit on the inside wall held smaller pictures of their two single daughters, Sasha Cook and Tara Blake, and all of their grandchildren.

Plants, side tables, and a bookcase helped fill out the furnishings, but the large room could still use a couple more chairs, Jan thought. In fact, there would be plenty of space for a card table. The kids could use it for table games when they visited, or she and Elaine could start a jigsaw puzzle on it. An electric teakettle might be a nice addition up here too, so they could make hot drinks in the evening without going down to the kitchen.

They watched the local and national news together, and when it was over, Jan turned off the TV. Above the set was a wooden shelf supported by decorative wrought iron brackets. So far they had not decided what should perch on it. Jan had stuck a potted African violet on one end, but it looked lonely.

"What do you think we should do with that shelf?" she asked Elaine, who was already turning on her laptop's browser.

"*Hmm*? Oh, the one over the TV? I don't know. I almost think we could take it down."

"I was thinking the same thing. Or..." Jan turned around, scanning the walls. "I think it would look better over there." She pointed to the wall near the hall door. "It kind of overshadows the TV where it is now."

Elaine nodded. "If you think so. We can probably move it ourselves. Unless you want to call Bill Bridges."

"Heavens, no. I like Bill, but we don't need to pay his wages for that. If you and I can't handle it, I'm sure Brian could."

Elaine was engrossed in one of her genealogy Web site now. Jan went over and took a look at the screws holding the brackets to the wall and decided to go downstairs and get a screwdriver.

She knew her restlessness was partly from the looming of the big event—opening day. She couldn't sit still long, even though she agreed with Elaine that they should relax this evening.

When she came back with a level and two screwdrivers, just to be sure she had the right one, Elaine looked up.

"The Gardners had several children living here during the 1930s. Mrs. Gardner's mother lived with them for a while too, during the Great Depression. I think one of the daughters stayed on here after the older generation passed on."

Jan considered that as she approached the shelf. "I suppose we can't rule out any of the Gardner women. Mr. Martel seemed to think the ring was made in the thirties. But I don't know about the mother-in-law. An old woman with a new ring like that? I don't think so."

Elaine nodded. "It probably belonged to Beatrice Gardner or one of her daughters."

"How many did she have?"

"Three, and there was the son, Paul, and another boy, David."

"I guess we can't be certain the ring isn't older than that."

"Right," said Elaine. "He was going by the style of the setting, I think, and he did say it could be older."

Jan frowned at the wrought iron brackets. "Remember Carlene Eastman saying she lived here?"

"Yes. She's too young for the Great Depression though. And Eastman is probably her married name."

Jan turned to look at Elaine. “So is she part of the Binns family that bought the house later?”

“Good question. I’ll see what I can find out.”

It took Jan only a few minutes to move the African violet and take down the shelf. After setting it on the floor, she stood contemplating the bare spot on the wall.

“Elaine.”

“What?” Her cousin looked up. “Oh. They didn’t move the shelf when they wallpapered? That’s weird.”

“I think they did, but they scraped it or something when they were putting it back up.”

Elaine set the laptop aside and rose. “Let me see.”

The both stared at the slash in the wall covering, revealing another layer beneath. The one-by-six-inch slash definitely uncovered another design of wallpaper. It had a small rose pattern on a cream background.

“That’s kind of pretty,” Elaine said.

“Yeah, but Carlene said when she lived here, this room had yellow striped wallpaper.”

“You’re right.”

Jan ran a hand over the spot, feeling the edge of the torn paper. “Maybe I can find pictures of this pattern online.”

“The top one or the underneath one?” Elaine asked.

“Either. Both.”

“Well, while I’m up, I may as well help you hang the shelf again. Where do you want it?”

They decided on a spot, and with Elaine’s somewhat clumsy aid, Jan at last managed to put the shelf on the wall straight. At nine o’clock, she decided to turn in whether she felt like it or not. She didn't have another project, and Elaine had scoured the Binns family tree, searching for Carlene Eastman, without success.

"Let's pray together," she said to Elaine. "You know—for the business."

"Yes, let's."

They sat close together on the couch and clasped hands.

Jan closed her eyes. "Lord, thank You for bringing us here and for letting us have this house and the tearoom."

"Please let everything we do here honor You," Elaine added.

"Don't forget to set your alarm," Jan said after their amens.

"No worries about that!" Elaine gave her a hug. "Sleep well."

Jan didn't say so, but she doubted she would sleep at all, she was so excited. At ten in the morning, they would open the doors for business at Tea for Two.

ELAINE OPENED THE back door to Rose at eight on Saturday morning. The young woman's face was flushed with excitement.

"Hi! I came early in case you need help."

Looking past her, Elaine saw a small motorboat tied up at the dock below. Rose had come nautical style today. "That was thoughtful of you. Did you eat breakfast?"

"Just toast. Too nervous."

"Well, Jan's in the kitchen, and if you want something more, there's plenty of stuff out there. Almost everything is done, but we can fill some cream pitchers and keep them ready in the fridge."

"I can do that." Rose closed the door to the screened porch carefully and followed her into the kitchen.

"Hi," Jan said with a wide smile. "Fresh apple fritters. Want one?"

"Oh, it smells so good in here!" Rose accepted one of the treats on a small plate.

"Your costume is up in the guest room, where you changed for the fitting," Elaine said. "I laid out a sales pad and two pens on the bed. You can put those in the pocket of your apron."

Jan nudged Rose toward the small round table near the back door. "Sit down. I'll get you something to drink with that. Tea, orange juice, or milk?"

The next two hours flew. At two minutes to ten, Jan and Elaine went to the front door together in their long, full skirts. Rose waited behind the checkout counter in the entrance hall.

"Ready?" Elaine looked into Jan's eyes.

"I sure am."

"Okay, here goes." Elaine flung the door open. Three cars were parked in the driveway, and more occupied the spaces painted along Main Street in front of the house. Waiting on the porch were Kit and Marcella Edmonds, Julie Yeaton, Sarah Ryder, and several women Elaine didn't know. Below on the walkway, Brian, Paula, and their two daughters, Avery and Kelly, waited.

"Welcome!" Elaine's delight at seeing so many well-wishers almost overcame her. Tears sprang into her eyes, and her heart pounded. She stepped back a little. "Please come in and sit wherever you'd like."

Rose came from behind the counter and guided the guests, smiling. "Hello. We have tables in both the front rooms." She handed small laminated menu cards to the guests.

Jan greeted the customers as they filed in. "Marcella! How wonderful to see you and your mom."

"We want tea," six-year-old Marcella said gravely.

"You shall have it," Jan replied.

Julie grasped Elaine's hand. "Hi. Everything looks lovely in here. I told all the selectmen about you at our last meeting. They were happy to hear we have a new business opening, and that a couple of former residents have returned to Lancaster."

"Thank you," Elaine said and turned to greet Sarah Ryder, the minister's wife.

Meanwhile, Paula Blake and her girls had entered, and Brian followed, his arms full of flowers.

"Oh my!" Jan clapped her hands to her cheeks. "What's all this?"

"A housewarming gift," Paula said. "Congratulations!"

"Thank you so much." Jan waved a hand toward a narrow table against the wall. "Put them there, I guess, Brian. Oh, they're beautiful. Elaine, look!"

"Just gorgeous," she said, taking in the basket of early tulips and white and purple lilacs. "Thank you, Paula. And you, Brian." She smiled at Avery and Kelly. "Nice of you girls to come too."

"You two look charming," Paula said.

“Thank you, ma’am.” Jan gathered handfuls of her skirt material and dipped a little curtsy.

“Can we sit anywhere?” asked eleven-year-old Avery.

“Of course,” Elaine said.

Jan stepped up and laid a hand on her granddaughter’s shoulder. “You might like this room best.” She pointed toward the east parlor. “It has a window seat and a fireplace.”

Kelly, who was two years younger, gazed up at Jan. “Grandma, can we come stay over at your new house sometime?”

“Kelly,” her mother said softly, but a warning nevertheless to use her manners.

“You bet you can,” Jan said. “And soon, I hope! We’ll talk about it later. Come on, I’ll show you to a nice table.”

The two front rooms stayed busy throughout the morning, and Elaine spent quite a bit of time greeting people and manning the cash register. Jan kept the food coming from the kitchen, and Rose served the customers constantly. Elaine joined her whenever she wasn’t needed at the checkout. Nearly all the people paying their bills told her how much they liked the tearoom, and that they would be back. Several also said they would recommend it to their friends.

One woman was not so cordial. She brought her sales slip to Elaine and held out a five-dollar bill.

“That’s three-fifteen. Let me get your change.” Elaine punched the amount into the register. “Did you enjoy your tea?”

“It was all right.” The sour-faced woman’s face wrinkled up. “I thought the scone was a little dry.”

"Oh, I'm sorry," Elaine said. "May I give you a few cookies to take home as our gift?"

The woman hesitated and flicked back a lock of her straight, graying hair. "All right."

Elaine quickly pulled out one of the zippered plastic bags of three ginger chews they had made up before. "Just in case," she had told Jan, but she hadn't really expected to use them.

She handed the woman her change and the bag with a smile. "I hope you like these."

"Thanks," the woman said grudgingly. She looked so dour that Elaine pegged her at sixty, but then thought perhaps she was younger. If she would only smile!

She didn't turn away immediately, so Elaine asked, "Do you live in Lancaster?"

"I'm Macy Atherton."

Elaine frowned. The name Atherton sounded vaguely familiar. Had she known anyone by that name in her youth?

"Of Green Glade Cottages," Macy added.

"Oh, of course. I see your sign all the time. Do you have summer guests yet?"

"Just a few," Macy said. "Most are coming in the first week in June."

Elaine nodded.

"We'll be full up after June tenth." The pride in Macy's announcement was unmistakable. "Mostly repeat customers."

"How nice," Elaine said. "Your guests must love it at your place." Two more women came from the west parlor, chatting as they got out their payments. "Do come again, Macy."

"Hmpf."

Macy turned away, and Elaine wondered if she would ever darken the doorway of Tea for Two again. But she did tuck her bag of cookies carefully into her purse.

Elaine smiled to greet the next customers. "Hi. Did you enjoy your tea?"

"Absolutely," said one of the women.

"This place is great," her friend chimed in. "I'm so glad you started it."

Their praise and promises to tell everyone they knew cheered Elaine and helped in a small measure to make up for Macy Atherton's dreariness.

As they left, Brian, Paula, and the girls came out of the tearoom and approached the counter.

"Elaine, this is terrific," Paula said. "If you're this busy every day, you'll do very well."

"Thanks," Elaine said. "I'm pleased with the turnout. And most of the summer people haven't arrived yet."

"My grandma said we can come back tomorrow afternoon and see the rest of the house," Kelly told her.

"That will be wonderful." Elaine could already picture the girls making a clubhouse in the third-floor tower room.

"We'll come over after dinner," Brian said.

"Are you sure you won't be too tired?" Paula asked.

"No, we'd love to have you come. I've been wishing you and the girls could see the house. And, Brian, the kitchen's all finished now. Jan is so proud of it!"

Brian nodded slowly. "Well, I'm glad. I have to admit, I'm impressed with the place. You two have done a lot of work."

"Thank you." Elaine smiled at him. Brian, it seemed, was beginning to see their vision.

Paula glanced at him. "Why don't we have Elaine and your mom over to dinner tomorrow? Give them a chance to eat someone else's cooking?"

"Sure," Brian said.

Elaine eyed him cautiously, but Brian seemed sincere in seconding the invitation.

"Why, thanks. That would be nice. I'll tell Jan. We probably wouldn't get there until nearly one o'clock though," she said, calculating how long it would take them to get to Brian and Paula's house after church let out.

"That's okay," Paula assured her. "I'll put a roast in the slow cooker tonight, and it will be done by the time we all get home from church."

They arranged it so that the family would follow her and Jan home the next day for the promised tour of the house.

By noon, the traffic through the tearoom had cleared out somewhat. Jan prepared sandwiches, and Rose and Elaine took turns serving while the others ate lunch in the kitchen. Elaine told Jan of Brian and Paula's dinner invitation, and Jan looked pleased.

"I haven't been around to visit for a couple of weeks, and I used to get over there every few days. I'm glad they asked us."

Around one thirty, more customers arrived, and Elaine went to help Rose serve. She walked briskly to a table where a couple in their midthirties was seated. Both were dressed casually but smartly. Elaine put on her best smile.

"Welcome to Tea for Two. I'm Elaine, and this is our menu."

"I love what you've done to this place," the woman said.

"Thank you."

"I'm Rue Maxwell, by the way, and this is my husband, Ned."

Elaine nodded at the husband.

"We own Northwoods B and B," Ned said, watching her face.

"That's great," Elaine said. "Thanks for coming by."

"We had to see if we thought our guests would like to come here," Rue said frankly.

Elaine chuckled. "Well, after you've eaten, you can tell me the verdict."

"You do have coffee, right?" Ned asked, scanning the menu.

"Yes, we do. Several varieties, but we hide them on the back so that faithful tea drinkers won't be insulted."

Ned laughed. "I like you."

"Oh, look, honey," Rue said. "Scones and cream puffs. I want one of everything!"

"I can bring you a sampler plate to share," Elaine said. "It's listed at the bottom."

Rue found it and nodded vigorously. "Definitely. Thanks!"

They gave their beverage orders, and Elaine hurried to the kitchen. She took extra care preparing her tray for the Maxwells. Recommendations from people like them—and even Macy—could add significantly to their summer clientele.

After she had served the couple, she hurried to the check-out, where a customer was waiting to settle up. When she had finished and wished the customer well, she turned to find Rose leaning over the counter toward her.

"You know that Mrs. Atherton you told me about earlier? The one with the cottages?"

"Yes," Elaine said cautiously.

Rose grinned. "She sent some people here."

"You're joking."

"No, I'm not. Her daughter-in-law is here with two other ladies, and she said Macy told them we had wonderful ginger cookies."

Elaine laughed and squeezed Rose's shoulder. "Thanks. You made my day."

JAN RELAXED WHILE Elaine drove toward home Sunday afternoon with Kelly and Avery in the back seat. Paula's pot roast dinner had made her a little sleepy, but Jan managed to keep up a lively chatter with Elaine and the girls. Brian and Paula were following in Paula's car.

"When can we stay overnight, Grandma?" Kelly asked.

"Soon," Jan said. "How about the week school gets out?"

"But that's a long time from now," Kelly said, scowling.

Jan turned partway around in her seat. "No, it's only about three weeks from now. You can visit in between, but you need to concentrate on your schoolwork now. The exams and other things at the end of the year are important."

"We're just getting started with the tearoom too," Elaine said, glancing in her rearview mirror at the girls. "By the time you're done with school, we'll have it down to a routine, so we can spend more time with you."

"Yeah, and you've got your karate tournament coming up," Avery said to her younger sister.

Kelly sat back, not thrilled, but accepting.

"How will you girls keep up with your sports this summer?" Elaine asked.

"I'll have gymnastics twice a week at the Boys & Girls Club," Avery said. "My regular coach teaches all summer. I just won't have the stuff I usually do at school. And Kelly got into a special karate program this year."

"That's *if* I do well at the tournament." Kelly sounded cross, and Jan wondered whether the upcoming competition had her worried.

"When is it?" she asked.

"A week from Saturday," Avery replied.

Kelly sat straighter. "Thirteen days."

"What level are you, Kelly?" Elaine asked.

"She has a blue belt," Avery said.

"She's talking to *me*." Kelly swung her fist sideways, punching her sister on the arm.

"Ow!"

Jan lowered her chin and looked over the top of her glasses at Kelly. She knew Paula and Brian were very strict about bickering between the girls. "That's no way to behave, Kelly. I don't think you want Cousin Elaine to stop the car, do you?"

"No," Kelly said in a small voice.

"Grandma will make you ride with Mom and Dad if you hit," Avery said.

Kelly scowled and shrank down in her seat.

"I think you know what else you need to say," Jan said.

Kelly heaved out a deep sigh. "Sorry."

"You don't sound sorry," Avery said.

Kelly took two breaths before she turned her head to look at Avery. "I'm sorry I hit you. Will you forgive me?"

"Sure." Avery leaned forward. "She's really very good at karate, Grandma."

"I know," Jan said. "I was there when she was awarded her blue belt."

"What color comes next?" Elaine asked.

"Green." Kelly sounded somewhat mollified. "But it will probably take me all next school year to earn that one."

"It will be worth it," Jan said.

"Elaine, did you get to see any karate senseis perform when you lived in Japan?" Kelly asked.

"No, but I did watch the army troops drill. They use some martial arts in their training. It was very interesting. Do you take your karate lessons at the Boys & Girls Club?"

"No, I go to the dojo."

They were nearly home, and Elaine drove smoothly along Lancaster's Main Street. Jan could see the tower of their house, and then the roof, then the front porch.

She caught her breath. A motorcycle was pulling out of the driveway.

"Look! Is that Jordy?"

"I don't know," Elaine said.

The bike had only one rider, impossible to identify at this distance. The red-and-white helmet made an effective mask, and the driver turned in the opposite direction from them at the end of the driveway. By the time they had reached the house, the motorcycle was out of sight.

CHAPTER TWELVE

If that was Jordy, why would he come here on Sunday?" Jan asked. "Rose isn't here today."

"Good question," Elaine said. She pulled into the garage of the lakeside house and smiled. "Come right in, girls. What do you want to see first?"

"The dock," Avery said.

At the same time, Kelly said, "The tower."

Elaine chuckled and shut off the engine. "We can't do both first, but I think we can accommodate both of you in good time."

They had already seen the tearooms, so they started the tour with the dining room, then Elaine's office, where she told the story of how the ring was found in the wall. The girls were fascinated by the tale, and by the little door Bill had neatly framed into the wall. They took turns opening it and stooping to peer in and see the old bricks of the chimney in the wall.

Avery and Paula both took a strong interest in the remodeled kitchen.

"I would love to have this place to cook in," Paula said, gazing around at the new granite countertops, the work island, gleaming appliances, and rich walnut cupboards. Jan had decorated with old kitchen utensils and tins, and a bright-blue Fiesta bowl full of lemons on the counter by the coffeemaker added a splash of color.

"Grandma, can I help you sometime, making the cookies and muffins and stuff?" Avery, at eleven, was intrigued by baking, and her eyes shone.

"You sure can," Jan said. "In fact, I made a little something for you girls."

She opened a drawer, took out two items of folded cotton material, and held them out. Avery and Kelly shook out the striped bib aprons with their names appliquéd on the front. Avery had dark blonde hair and blue eyes like Paula, and her apron was blue striped. Kelly, who favored her dad, had Brian's brown hair and eyes. Jan had stitched a red-and-white apron for her.

"Neat," Avery said. "Thank you, Grandma!"

Kelly held hers out and nodded, obviously pleased but not as delighted as her older sister.

Brian by this time had wandered out to the screened back porch and was gazing down at the lake.

"Time to move this tour group to the next station, I think," Jan said.

The back deck near the water and the dock sticking out into the lake intrigued everyone.

"You should have a boat," Brian said.

"We've actually thought about getting a rowboat," Elaine told him.

"A canoe," Kelly said eagerly.

Jan cocked her head to one side. "*Hmm,* that might be fun. We'll see." She looked at Brian for a moment. Was he accepting the permanence of her move here?

His gaze caught hers, and he smiled. "Really nice view, Mom."

"Thanks. Now, who wants to see the upstairs?"

The guest room, warm and inviting, made the girls renew their questions about staying over, and Paula agreed that they could come for a night or two as soon as school was out for the summer.

"Okay," Elaine said, leading them toward the stairs that went up to the third story, "I think we saved the best for last. We haven't had a chance to decorate up here—in fact, there's nothing up here, so we thought maybe you girls would like to make it into your own special place."

Avery and Kelly both fell in love with the small bedrooms on the top floor, and Kelly immediately suggested the unfinished attic as her personal dojo, where she could practice her karate moves. But the small tower room was the prize, and the girls proved they could get along by at once beginning to plan how they could use it.

Elaine and Jan gave them permission to have lemonade and cookies up there, provided they carried their own tray up and returned all the dishes to the kitchen afterward. Meanwhile, the cousins sat down on the screened porch with Brian and Paula and a pot of chai tea.

They talked for another half hour, at which time Brian looked over at his wife and said abruptly, "We should get going."

"Right," Paula said, rising. "The girls have school tomorrow, and you have another big day. Thanks so much for having us in."

"Thank you for coming," Elaine said.

"I'm glad you and the kids got to see the rest of the place at last," Jan added.

Brian went to round up the girls, and Paula helped Jan and Elaine carry their dishes into the kitchen.

"I hope everything goes well tomorrow and every day." Paula kissed each of older women on the cheek.

Jan smiled and waved to them from the front porch with Elaine, but she darted glances about, in case the motorcyclist had left them a note or some other evidence of his identity. She couldn't help wondering who the rider was. Had Rose borrowed Jordy's bike and come to get something she'd forgotten? Maybe Jordy had stopped in on the off chance that Rose was here.

Or maybe today's visitor wasn't Jordy at all.

THE TEAROOM OPENED Monday morning without the immediate rush they'd had on Saturday, but a steady stream of customers came in. Elaine, Rose, and Jan wore nice pants and blouses with their aprons, leaving the costumes in the guest room closet for the next special occasion. Jan stayed happily in the kitchen, making up the orders Rose and Elaine brought her, and Elaine did most of the cash register duty.

Maureen Oakley, whom she had met at church, came in with her neighbor. Maureen and her friend had just come from the Bookworm, and when Elaine went to serve them, they gave her a rundown of the new books Bristol was stocking that morning.

"And there are several new mysteries." Maureen pulled a small paper bag from her tote and extracted a paperback novel. "It's by one of my favorite Maine authors."

"I've never read any of her books," Elaine said, interested at once.

"Oh, they're terrific," Maureen assured her. "Alan and I devour them."

"I'll have to step over there and let Bristol show them to me." Out of the corner of her eye, Elaine saw more customers enter the west parlor. "Excuse me, ladies. Enjoy your tea break."

The newcomers had paused to look at the corner display that the cousins had made. The corner cupboard they had bought was the perfect size, and Roland the electrician had come back to install a couple of small spotlights inside that showed off Nana's teapots at their best. Elaine loved to gaze at the two square pots and the scenes on their sides, with birds flying over the Chinese town and tiny people crossing an arched bridge. The lower shelves held Elaine's international teapots and a few choice bone china cups and saucers.

As they turned toward a nearby table, Elaine realized that one of the women was Carlene Eastman. Her short blonde hair looked freshly coiffed, and she wore gray pants and a fashionable lime-green blouse today, in contrast to the casual look she'd presented on her first visit. Fighting a slight apprehension, Elaine picked up a couple of menu cards and took them over to the guests.

"Hello, Carlene," she said with a smile. "Welcome to Tea for Two."

"Hi. Elaine, right?"

"Yes." Elaine handed her and the other woman their menus. "This has our regular menu, and our cookie of the day is oatmeal raisin."

"That sounds good," said the second woman.

"Elaine, this is my friend, Blair."

"Hi," said Blair, whose long red hair was caught back with a large butterfly barrette.

"You've been hard at work." Carlene looked around the airy room. "Love the ambiance."

"Thank you," Elaine said. "We've tried to keep the Victorian feel."

Carlene skimmed the brief menu. "I think I'll try the Sri Lanka green tea, and I'll have the cookie of the day with it."

"I'll have the Sri Lanka as well, and... *hmm.* Everything sounds so good!" Blair threw Elaine a smile and looked back at the menu. "A cranberry muffin, I guess."

"We were just noticing your teapots." Carlene waved a hand toward the corner cabinet.

"The ones on the top shelf belonged to Jan's and my grandmother," Elaine said, jotting the women's order on her sales pad. "The others are ones I picked up over the years."

"I could tell they're special."

Blair smiled up at her. "I noticed you use different teapots on the tables."

"Yes," Elaine replied. "We decided to go with mismatched china, instead of trying to buy a set for the whole place. I think customers enjoy looking at the different styles."

"It's charming," Blair said. "I collect teapots myself."

"Oh, really? How many do you have?"

"About two dozen." Blair smiled sheepishly. "My husband says I have too many, so every time I bring home a new one, I have to give away one of the ones I already had."

"That's not such a bad thing," Elaine said. "If you keep only the ones you love best, your collection will improve as you go."

"That's what I figure."

"I like that teapot on their table," Carlene said, with a subtle nod toward where three women were pouring out their hot tea from a plump teapot painted to look like a green pumpkin.

"So do I." Elaine gave a little laugh. "What am I saying? I like them all." She eyed Blair curiously. "With your expertise, maybe you can tell me if you see any among our stock that's special. We bought most of them at yard sales."

"Not yet, I haven't," Blair said. "Some of them are very attractive, but all the ones I've seen are 1960s or later. They're probably worth about what you paid for them. I suppose you have more."

"Oh yes, there are several in the kitchen waiting for more customers to come in." Elaine thought of the teapot she had left with the restorer, but she didn't mention that one. She already knew it was special. "I'll go get your order."

She went to the kitchen and told Jan that she needed a pot of Sri Lanka green tea. She grabbed a sheet of pastry tissue and put a muffin on a plate for Blair and two oatmeal cookies for Carlene.

"You'll never guess who these cookies are for."

"Who?" Jan asked.

Elaine carried the small plates over to her tray on the counter and then reached for two cup-and-saucer sets and spoons. "Carlene Eastman and a friend of hers."

"Really? Which room are they in?"

"West. They noticed our display and asked about it. Apparently the friend collects teapots."

"Huh." Jan frowned as she set a small cream pitcher and a dish of lemon slices on the tray. "I wonder why she came back."

"Maybe they just wanted a cup of tea."

"I doubt that."

Elaine paused and looked at her. "I admit I wasn't thrilled when she came in, but I suppose she wanted to show her friend what we've done with her old home. If it *is* her old home."

Jan nodded, and Elaine wondered what was going through her cousin's analytical mind.

Rose breezed into the kitchen. "A pot of orange spice tea and a cup of hot chocolate." She hummed as she set about getting the baked goods her customers had ordered.

"Everything okay in the east parlor?" Elaine asked as she picked up her tray.

"Yep. It's busy, but I'm keeping up. How about you?"

"Only three tables taken at the moment, but I may need to go out to the checkout soon." Elaine hefted the tray and went back through the hallway to the west parlor. Carlene and her friend were deep in conversation, but looked up as she approached.

"Oh, this looks good," Carlene said.

"That's a cute pot." Blair cocked her head to one side and studied the plump white porcelain teapot with a gray-and-pink rose design on the side. She glanced up at Elaine. "I don't suppose I could sneak a look at the extras in the kitchen? If you had a good one, I'd make you an offer."

"Oh, sorry, we're too busy right now." Elaine tried to keep her voice even and her features smooth, but Blair's request irked her.

"Of course." Blair picked up the teapot to pour out for herself and Carlene.

"So where do you live now?" Elaine asked, looking at Carlene.

"Winslow."

Elaine nodded.

"I'm in Vassalboro," Blair said.

"Well, thanks for driving out here today." Another customer entered. Elaine smiled and said, "Excuse me. Enjoy your tea."

She walked toward the new arrival. "Hi. We have a few tables free. Would you like to sit near the window?"

"Thanks," the woman said. "I'm staying at Green Glade Cottages, and a friend is meeting me here after she's done at the vintage shop next door."

"Great," Elaine said, mentally chalking up another point for Macy. "I'll bring you two menus. Our cookie of the day is oatmeal raisin."

After she fetched the menu cards, she saw customers in the entrance hall heading for the checkout. She reached it just as Rose came out of the east parlor.

"Oh, you got it?" Rose asked with a glance at the cash register.

"Yeah, I'm good." Elaine and Rose spent the next hour bouncing between the cashier and serving duties. When the lull that had fallen around noon on Saturday came again, Elaine went to the kitchen, leaving Rose to deal with the three remaining tea drinkers.

"Whew, I'm not as young as I used to be." She sank onto a stool beside Jan's work island.

"When did you get this shocking news?" Jan asked.

Elaine laughed. "I'd forgotten how tiring it is to spend hours at a time on your feet."

"What would help?"

Elaine frowned, thinking about it. "Maybe nursing shoes. And a stool like this behind the checkout. At least I could sit for a minute while people are paying."

"Done," Jan said, placing a glass of milk and a chicken salad sandwich before her. "Now eat, while you have a chance."

"Thanks." Elaine closed her eyes and silently thanked God for the meal. When she opened them, Jan was watching her. "What?"

"Is that Carlene still out there?"

"No, she and her friend Blair left a few minutes ago. Why?"

"It just seems odd."

"Well, she's not getting the house back, no matter what. Her story is full of holes." Elaine took a bite of her sandwich. "This is good. Maybe I was just hungry."

"There's no excuse for hunger in this joint," Jan said, doing her best scowl.

Elaine laughed again, glad she had swallowed first. "If this business fails, you can make your living as a comedian."

THAT EVENING, Elaine couldn't get Carlene off her mind. Elaine mentioned the woman again at suppertime.

"I think I'll go back to those family history Web sites after I total up today's receipts. Maybe one of the Binnses married an Eastman."

"Too bad the census records for when they lived here aren't available yet," Jan said.

Elaine nodded. "Yeah. I might run down to Augusta one of these days. The State Archives has a bride index, but it probably doesn't include modern people either. I wonder if they have a way that I could look up a bride named Carlene to a groom named Eastman. She said she lives in Winslow. Maybe the Kennebec County courthouse can help me."

Jan smiled to herself. Elaine's mind apparently worked the way she talked, making connections and following them off in different directions. Jan, on the other hand, preferred problems that had a definite, precise answer. Still, Carlene seemed to hover at the edge of Jan's mind that evening too. She went upstairs and took her laptop into the sitting room.

While Elaine pored over the day's sales slips in her office, Jan did a little research of her own, beginning with a careful examination of the bit of wallpaper showing beneath the outer layer on the sitting room wall.

About eight o'clock, Elaine came into the room with a couple of printouts.

"I thought you'd like to see how we're doing." She handed Jan one sheet of paper and sat down on the couch with the other in her hand. "I know it's early, but I'm pleased."

Jan skimmed down the sheet, which tallied all the items they had sold and the money they had brought in.

"Wow, eighteen people had the cookie of the day."

Elaine laughed out loud. "Yes, they did. I thought you'd want to see how much we made today."

"Oh, well, money." Jan looked at the bottom line. "Very nice. If we gross this every day, will we make a profit?"

"I think so."

"You gals were pretty busy out there."

"We sure were." Elaine kicked her shoes off. "There was one point where every table was occupied but one."

"Eleven tables," Jan mused. "Maybe it's time to put a few out on the side porch. We talked about that."

"Yes, and I think it's warm enough. What did we say—five tables outside?"

"I think so. That way it wouldn't be too crowded, and servers will be able to get around even if they're wearing costumes."

"We *could* fit a couple more tables in each parlor," Elaine said. "I'd rather not though. I like the way it feels now."

"I agree," Jan said. "But do we want to invest in more tables yet?"

Elaine reached for a pen. She scribbled on the edge of her printout for a moment. "After we deposit today's receipts, we'd have enough in the account to order three tables and leave the cushion we talked about."

"Maybe we should wait until the end of the week." Jan hated to cut things close financially. She'd been doing it most of her life, and it made her stomach churn if she thought they might run out of money before the monthly bills were paid.

"Probably wise," Elaine said. "After all, it could pour rain tomorrow, and nobody would come in."

"I was talking to Bristol about that," Jan said. "She says more people actually come into the Bookworm on rainy days in the summer, because they can't be out on the lake."

"I hadn't thought of that," Elaine admitted. "Well, let's go slowly and build up a little more of a reserve before we buy more furniture."

"Agreed." Jan felt much lighter when she said that. "Would you like to hear what I've learned this evening?"

"Of course." Elaine perked up, her eyes focusing on Jan's. "What have you been up to?"

"I found that wallpaper pattern that's under this one online. It's older than Carlene Eastman."

Elaine frowned. "So...if a different paper was on the wall when Carlene lived here, it would be on top of that layer?"

"It seems logical to me. I mean, it's possible that someone used older wallpaper later on, but not likely. And even the top layer is pretty old. That was easier to find. It was sold up until about twenty years ago."

"Carlene's probably in her thirties. Her folks could have redone the room when she was a teenager."

"True," Jan said. "But where's the yellow stripe? You don't peel off one layer and leave another underneath. I think it would have to be between this outer layer and the roses."

Elaine gazed at the light-gray paper that now graced the walls. The touches of white and yellow in a trellis design brightened it, but the pattern definitely looked outdated.

"So she's mistaken about the wallpaper."

"Or maybe about the room," Jan said. "Or the house. I honestly don't believe she ever lived here."

Elaine nodded slowly. "I've searched for Carlene online, and I didn't find much. She told the truth about living in Winslow, but that's about it. She's listed with her husband, Richard Eastman, in the phone directory, and I found him online with a greenhouse and garden supply store. Do you still think she's hoping to find the ring before we do? She obviously didn't know which room to look in."

"I don't know," Jan said. "Maybe you should look for her friend. Blair, was it?"

"Yeah, but I didn't get her last name, and they paid in cash."

Jan sighed. "Can't do much with that."

"No, we can't. All I know is that Blair lives in Vassalboro, and she likes old china. I don't think that's going to help much." Elaine looked over at the slash in the wallpaper. "So what are we going to do about that? I don't think we want to get into a wallpapering frenzy right now."

Jan sank back in her chair, suddenly exhausted. "No, let's wait awhile. In the meantime, let's just hang a picture over it."

CHAPTER THIRTEEN

Elaine stopped by the Bookworm at nine on Wednesday morning. Bristol had just opened for the day, but already half a dozen people were browsing in her shop.

"Busy, aren't you?" Elaine stepped up to a display stand at the front of the store counter, where Bristol was arranging a display of books on fishing, canoeing, hiking, and other outdoor pursuits.

"Yes. Summer people are coming early this year." Bristol smiled as she slipped a volume on backpacking into place, her blue eyes twinkling. "That's the way we like it."

"Absolutely. I just popped over to see if my teapot book had come in."

"Not yet, but I expect that shipment today or tomorrow. Want me to call you when it comes?" Bristol straightened and brushed back a strand of dark blonde hair.

"If you have time. If not, I'll just keep bothering you," Elaine said with a laugh. "I brought some flyers for the tearoom. You had offered to hand them out."

"Oh, great! Put them right here," Bristol said, walking to the counter with her. "I'll put them in everyone's bags when they check out."

"Thanks." Elaine laid a stack of fifty half-sheet flyers between the cash register and a pile of bookmarks.

"What's Jan up to this morning?" Bristol asked.

"I left her up to her elbows in cookie dough and cream puff filling. Rose came early to help her."

"Sounds like Jan's enjoying herself."

"She is," Elaine assured her. There was nothing her cousin liked better than creating something other people would love.

"Tell her the new *Logic Puzzles* magazine is in, though I don't know when she'd have time to work the puzzles."

"I'll make sure she knows about it," Elaine promised as she headed for the door.

Bristol's early rush of customers spilled over into Tea for Two. From the moment the doors opened, Elaine and Rose stayed busy all morning.

Two women, one in her forties, the other two decades younger, entered and looked around the entrance hall with appreciation.

"May I help you ladies?" Elaine asked cheerfully.

"We saw your ad," the younger woman said.

"My daughter and I have been shopping for her wedding gown," the older one added. "We wondered if we could see the facility."

"Of course." Elaine stepped forward. "We have tables in two rooms. This is the East Parlor." She took them in and pointed out the architectural features, including the bay window and fireplace.

"Oh, I love it," the prospective bride said.

When they entered the West Parlor, the mother and daughter looked at each other, and the daughter nodded.

"Do you do parties?" the older woman asked.

"Yes. That is, we've just opened, but we would like this to be a place for small but elegant parties. High teas, showers..." Elaine arched her eyebrows at the women.

"How about a bridesmaids' luncheon?" the daughter asked eagerly.

Elaine did some quick thinking. "Yes, of course. We're open from ten to four each day, so if you wanted to have a luncheon party, perhaps you'd like to consider the private dining room. It's this way."

She led them past the corner display, to the doorway that connected the West Parlor to the dining room. She and Jan had yet to eat a meal in this room. It was far too big for their quiet repasts, but they planned to use it when entertaining.

"Oh, this is perfect," the bride said. She and her mother walked about looking at Jan's hutch, the chandelier, the drapes, and the decorative plaster ceiling.

"When is the wedding?" Elaine asked.

"June twenty-seventh," the mother said. "The luncheon would be a day or two before that."

"I think we could make that work," Elaine said. "May I show you to a table and bring you a pot of tea? I'd need to check with my partner to make sure our schedule is open then."

"Lovely," the mother said, and they followed her back into the parlor, where Elaine seated them and left them discussing how ideal the house would be for the bridesmaids' luncheon.

A quick consultation in the kitchen with Jan confirmed what Elaine already knew—they hadn't booked any parties yet and were wide open for them.

Jan nodded and opened the oven door to slide in a tray of danish pastries.

A half hour later, when the mother and daughter had asked all their questions and received answers to their liking, they left. Elaine, who had been trying to talk to them while serving the customers already seated, was glad the slower hour around noon had arrived. She let Rose take her break first and managed the lingerers and the cash register. When Rose returned to her station, Elaine took a lunch break.

Jan was boxing up the fresh danish and cookies she had just finished baking when Elaine went to get her sandwich.

"I think I've got plenty of pastries for the afternoon, no matter how many customers come in."

"You should take a break," Elaine said. "You got up really early."

"Five o'clock," Jan admitted. "I had to be sure those cream puffs were ready for the first customers. Did you find out any more about the Gardners?"

Elaine shook her head. "I stayed up later than I should have, but I couldn't get at the newspaper archives I wanted. The *Penzance Courier* apparently hasn't computerized its old files yet."

Jan hesitated. "Well, I could go over there. All the baking is done. I mean, if you and Rose would be okay here this afternoon. Do you think you'll need me?"

Elaine set down her glass. "That's a great idea, if you don't mind."

"It would be fun." Jan untied her apron strings. "I just started the dishwasher, so if you need more cups or spoons, look in there."

"Let me run upstairs and get you my notes on the family," Elaine said.

She and Rose managed to keep the food and beverages moving. She sent up several prayers of thanks. This was what they had wanted, had prayed for. She and Rose tried to make each customer's experience at the tearoom enjoyable, and from the expressions on their faces as they left, Elaine thought they had succeeded. Several local people came in, including Will and Pearl Trexler. Elaine snatched a few moments to introduce them to Rose.

"You're lucky to be working here," Pearl told her. "This is going to be a popular place this summer. I'm telling all my friends about it."

Later on, as Elaine headed into the kitchen to fill an order, Rose was coming out with a tray.

"Oh, I just left you a message by the phone in there," Rose said. "A lady called. I took her number down."

"Thanks." Elaine took a quick look. Heather Wells, the restorer. She arranged the items her customers had ordered and took them out to their table.

About three o'clock, things slowed down a little, and she called Heather's studio.

"Hi! Your teapot is ready," Heather said. "It looks great."

"I'll drive in to get it later if I can," Elaine said. "If not, I'll pick it up tomorrow."

"Whatever works for you."

Jan returned a few minutes before closing. She began unloading the dishwasher while Rose cleared tables and Elaine cashed out the last few customers.

After turning the sign to Closed, Elaine went to the kitchen to help clean up.

"Whew. I wonder if it will be like this every day. I hope so, but it's tiring."

"The price of success," Jan said.

"I guess so."

"Not many cookies left, and I thought we had plenty," Jan observed, loading dirty dishes to be washed.

"No, Pearl bought a dozen each of macaroons and date-filled to take home. That about cleaned us out. And we sold every muffin we had."

"I'll make extra tomorrow," Jan said. "Pull a box of cinnamon snaps out of the freezer to thaw, would you?"

Elaine went to get them and asked over her shoulder, "How did you make out at the *Courier*?"

"Pretty well, I think."

Rose brought in one last tray of dishes. Jan rearranged a few items and managed to fit them all into the top rack of the dishwasher. She pushed the button to start it and stepped back.

"There! That's done." She went to the small table and pawed through her tote bag. "Here we go."

Elaine set the box of frozen cookies on the counter and went to sit beside her.

"Okay if I head out?" Rose asked. "I've wiped all the tables and swept up."

"That's great," Elaine said. "Oh, wait. I meant to ask you—what color is Jordy's motorcycle helmet? I couldn't remember."

"It's black and white. And the one he loaned me was plain white. Why?"

"We saw someone pulling out of the driveway Sunday afternoon, but that rider had a red-and-white helmet."

"I don't think it was Jordy," Rose said. "He hasn't mentioned it to me."

"It's probably not important." Elaine waved her hand. "Go on home."

Rose grinned. "See you in the morning." She hung her apron on a hook near the back door and went out through the screened porch. Elaine could hear her staccato steps on the stairs leading down to the dock.

"If I had half her energy..."

"Me too," Jan said. "Here are the notes I made. I had to look back quite a ways."

"How far?"

"Well, I figured I'd trust Mr. Martel's instincts about the ring. I started in 1930, and I worked forward from there. I found a few mentions of Mr. Gardner and his business, and one for the older son, Paul. Harold Gardner died, and his wife and kids continued to live here during the Depression. Paul was valedictorian of the Class of 1938. Anyway, I found a few later items about the family." Jan pushed a photocopied article across the table. "This is an engagement announcement for one of the Gardner daughters. See? Miss Alice Gardner, daughter of Mr. and Mrs. Harold Gardner. She got engaged in December 1941."

Elaine had picked up the sheet of paper so she could read it, but she jerked her head up, startled. "December? Pearl Harbor was December 7 that year. Was this a war wedding?"

"I don't know. I couldn't find an actual wedding announcement. Maybe the State Archives can help us with that."

"I don't know when I can get down there during business hours." Elaine looked at the article. "Does it describe her ring?"

"No such luck," Jan said.

"Nothing's that easy, I guess." Elaine glanced at her watch. "Oh, I wanted to drive into Waterville and pick up my teapot. Heather called, and it's ready."

"You go ahead," Jan said. "I'll stay here and start on the muffins for tomorrow."

Elaine frowned. "You need to rest."

"I just took a three-hour break, remember? I'll be fine."

Elaine pushed her chair back and stood. "Well, thanks. That's a great piece of information you found. I hope the ring did belong to Miss Gardner."

"So do I," Jan said, "but we have to find proof."

Half an hour later, Elaine hurried into Heather Wells's shop. A stocky young man with wavy dark hair stood behind the counter, writing something on a notepad.

"Hi," Elaine said. "I hope I'm not too late. Heather said I could pick up my teapot."

When he looked up, his dark eyebrows met in a frown. "What's your name?"

"Elaine Cook." She took the receipt from her purse. "Is Heather in?"

"She had to run an errand before everything closed, but she should be back soon. I'm Jake—her assistant."

"Nice to meet you, Jake. Here's the receipt she gave me."

He took it and glanced at it for a moment. "Just a sec." He went through a doorway into another room and emerged a moment later carrying a teapot.

Elaine stared at it. She started to say something, but stopped. Could her teapot look so different with the messy yellow coat of paint and the sloppy pansies removed? She could hardly believe it was the same little pot. It now had a stark white glaze, and the side and lid were decorated with delicate pink blossoms. Elaine eyed it dubiously. The shape was right—or nearly right. It seemed a little rounder than her teapot. The handle too, seemed a bit "off."

"Are you sure that's my teapot?" she asked.

"Yes, ma'am. Here's the work tag." Jake held up the tag that was tied to the handle.

Elaine reached out slowly and picked up the pot. She turned it over, carefully holding the lid on. "There's a marking on the bottom."

"Right. It's Staffordshire. Heather told me it's worth about three hundred dollars. She said you bought it at a flea market, so you got a good deal."

Elaine shook her head. "My teapot didn't have a maker's mark on the bottom. It was very old."

"The mark was probably painted over," Jake said. "I saw it before Heather stripped it. It was a shame somebody painted over it like that. But Heather's great at restoration, isn't she?"

For a moment, Elaine couldn't say a word.

"Let me wrap it for you," Jake said.

There was no way Elaine was leaving the shop with that teapot. In fact, if she had to stay here all night, she wouldn't leave until she had talked to Heather Wells.

"Don't bother," she said. "That's not my teapot."

CHAPTER FOURTEEN

Jake's expression clouded. "I know it looks a little different, but that's the cosmetic change. I assure you, it's got your name on it."

Elaine was about to make a bigger issue of it when she remembered Nathan's photos.

"Look, Jake, there's obviously some mistake," she said. "I'll be back."

She went outside and took out her phone. Nathan answered almost at once.

"Hi, Nathan. It's Elaine."

"Hey! Great to hear from you."

"Thanks. Remember that teapot I brought in, and you sent me to Heather Wells with it?"

"How could I forget?"

Quickly, Elaine explained the situation. "So I wondered if you could possibly come over here and bring the photos of my teapot."

"Sure, I'll be there in ten minutes. No, five minutes."

She exhaled. "Thank you so much. I'll be waiting for you."

She got into her car and sat there, watching her rear-view mirror for either Heather or Nathan to drive in. No one entered or left the shop while she waited.

When Nathan's car pulled in, a surge of gratitude warmed her. Nathan might have been in the middle of appraising someone's heirlooms, or maybe he had been cataloguing new merchandise for his next auction. Whatever he'd been up to, he had dropped it immediately and come to her rescue. Not that she wanted to get into the habit of being rescued like a damsel in distress, but this time it felt good to know she had a friend who would hurry to help her in a bad moment.

"Hey," he said, striding quickly toward her as she got out of the car. "Is Heather back?"

"Not yet."

He looked at his watch. "It's nearly five."

"I know. Have you met this guy, Jake?"

"I don't think so," Nathan said.

"I don't like him."

"You may have good reason not to. I gave Heather a call on the way over, and she'll be here soon."

"What did you tell her?" Elaine asked.

"Just that there was a controversy over your teapot. Don't tell Jake I called her though."

"Okay."

"Ready?" he asked.

Elaine hauled in a deep breath and nodded.

Nathan opened the door to the shop, and they went inside. The white teapot was no longer in sight. Jake came from the back room and paused when he saw that Elaine had returned. His gaze flicked to Nathan.

"Can I help you?"

"I hope so," Elaine said. "This is Nathan Culver, of Culver Auctions."

Jake nodded, eyeing Nathan cautiously.

"He has some photos of the teapot I brought to Heather. We'd like to compare them to the one you showed me a few minutes ago."

"Uh...sure." He disappeared into the other room.

It seemed to Elaine that he took longer than necessary to fetch the item, but it probably wasn't more than a minute. Still, she quirked her eyebrows at Nathan. He leaned close and whispered in her ear.

"Why do I feel as though I should go outside and watch the back door?"

But Jake reappeared a moment later, carrying the white Staffordshire teapot. He set it on the counter and threw Nathan a sidelong glance that Elaine construed as nervous.

"Here you go. That's the one with your tag on it."

"That's not the one I examined a couple of weeks ago," Nathan said firmly.

"Well, I don't know about that," Jake said. "All I know is this lady said her name was Cook, and that's the item with her repair tag on it."

Nathan turned the tag so he could read it. "This tag says Chinese teapot, maybe Yixing." He picked up the white teapot. "This is Staffordshire. English."

Jake shifted his weight on his feet. "Yeah. Well, as I said to Mrs. Cook, maybe the mark was covered up by the bad paint job. When she brought it in, it looked pretty awful."

"Pretty awful," Nathan said darkly. He took out his phone and clicked a few buttons. "This is Mrs. Cook's teapot. It's not the same." He held it out so that Jake could view the screen. "This next one is of the bottom. Not glazed. At all. No marks, no shiny white stuff. That is not the same pot."

Jake gulped. "Are you sure that's the one she brought in here? Maybe she brought a different one."

Elaine felt her cheeks flush. The nerve! "The one in Mr. Culver's pictures is the one I left here."

"Well, uh, I guess you'll have to ask Heather, then," Jake said. "Maybe she has an explanation. All I know is, it's five o'clock, and I have to close."

Nathan took a small step toward him, clearly invading the young man's personal space. He stood a good four inches taller than Jake and scowled down at him.

"No, you're not closing until after Heather gets here. She's on her way now. And Mrs. Cook is going to step outside and call the police." Nathan nodded at Elaine. "Please ask them to send an officer here right away, Elaine."

Her mouth went dry. Nathan was serious. He wanted her to call the cops.

She stepped outside the shop and thought for a moment. She would need the Waterville police. It took her a moment to get the number and place the call. When the dispatcher at the police station answered, she said there was a dispute at We

Restore and gave the address. The woman promised to send an officer immediately.

As she put her phone away, Elaine felt her heart pounding. She had never called the police before, and she didn't like the way it made her feel. From inside the shop, she could hear Nathan and Jake arguing—not yelling, but still, their voices were loud enough to carry out to the parking lot. The idea that she was causing a scene at the least, and perhaps making trouble for several people, made her palms sweat and her chest tighten. Elaine was always one to smooth out social wrinkles and make sure nobody got upset. After all, she had only paid ten dollars extra for the teapot when she and Jan got the cookbooks. She hadn't even known it existed before that moment. Was it worth possibly having the young man arrested?

A dark-gray car pulled into the small lot and parked in the spot beside hers. Heather got out.

"Hi, Elaine. I had to run to the shipping store before they closed. Sorry about that. Nathan called me and said there's a bit of a mix-up."

"He's inside," Elaine said. "I hope you can straighten things out."

She followed Heather inside. As they entered, Jake was saying, "You can't prove a thing."

"Jake, what's the trouble?" Heather asked sharply.

"Oh, good, you're here," Nathan said.

"Hi, Nathan. I understand there's a problem with Mrs. Cook's order?"

"Yes." Nathan picked up the white Staffordshire teapot. "This is what your employee here tried to give her."

Heather frowned. "Jake, that's not Mrs. Cook's teapot."

Jake met her gaze for a moment and then looked at the teapot. "It has her tag on it."

"Let me see." Heather took the pot from Nathan and examined the work tag. "Okay, Jake, what's going on?"

"You're asking me?" He raised his hands, palm outward. "All I did was go out back and get the item with her name on it."

Heather's chin rose a fraction of an inch. "Oh no. That's not going to fly." She turned to Nathan and Elaine. "This teapot is one I've had in the shop quite a while. Someone brought it in for repair and never picked it up." She whirled on Jake. "You switched the repair tags, didn't you?"

"No, I . . ."

"Who else could have done it? I told you I might not get back before closing. You had an opportunity to take a very valuable piece of ceramics. Now, where's Mrs. Cook's Yixing teapot?"

The door opened as Jake began to sputter. When he saw a uniformed officer entering, he clamped his lips together.

Heather and Nathan introduced themselves and quickly explained the situation. Elaine let them tell the tale and watched Jake as he shrank back against the wall and repeatedly eyed the door to the back room.

"So, Mrs. Cook, this isn't your property?" Officer Wilson asked, looking directly at her.

"It's not. Mr. Culver's pictures show the one I brought here. I showed it to him and brought it here the same day."

"She's correct," Heather said. "That is not the teapot she left with me. I stripped hers down to the original glaze, and trust me, officer, this is not the one."

"Okay," Wilson said. "So what happened? Jake, is it? What can you tell me? Ms. Wells left the shop for a couple of hours, and you switched things around?"

"No, I didn't!" Jake looked panicky now.

"Officer, I give you permission to search the premises," Heather said. "I'd start with the back room, if I were you."

She strode past Wilson and Nathan and through the door to the back room. Jake put out a hand and opened his mouth, then seemed to think better of it. He let his hand fall to his side and followed her into the back room, with Wilson close behind.

Elaine and Nathan waited near the counter. Less than two minutes later, Heather emerged triumphant. Jake followed, his head slumped forward, and Officer Wilson came last, carrying a camouflage duffel bag.

Wilson set the duffel on Heather's worktable. The zipper was undone, and he lifted out a towel-wrapped item.

"Careful," Heather said. "That thing is worth about twelve thousand dollars."

Elaine stared at her. "Really?"

"Yes, really, if Jake hasn't damaged it during his shenanigans." She looked at Wilson. "May I?"

"Please." Wilson set the item down gently, and Heather unwrapped it. Elaine caught her breath. The shape was right, but the ugly paint job was gone. She picked up the teapot and looked at it carefully.

"Is that your property?" Wilson asked.

"Yes, it is."

Wilson turned to the young man. "All right, Jake, what's the story?"

Jake heaved out a big breath. "I don't know anything about it. Maybe Heather swapped them."

"Oh, no you don't." Heather's lip curled. "Officer, if Mrs. Cook doesn't press charges, I will."

"Okay, I think we're done here. Turn around, Jake." Officer Wilson took a pair of handcuffs from a case on his belt. "I'll take him in for further questioning, and you folks can come in later or in the morning and give your statements. Sound good?"

"Sure," Heather said.

Nathan nodded, so Elaine did too.

"You're under arrest," Wilson said, guiding Jake toward the door, continuing to recite the prisoner's rights as they made their way out.

"Oh, by the way, Jake," Heather called after them, "you're fired."

Wilson was reaching for the knob when the door swung inward.

A young man in his thirties, sporting sunglasses and a tawny mustache, stood just outside. Looking startled, he reached up and removed his glasses.

"Hi. I'm River White, from the *Penzance Courier.* I was just driving into town, and I heard on the scanner that there was a disturbance here."

"It's all over with now," Officer Wilson said.

"Oh." River eyed the handcuffed Jake with interest. "Are you making an arrest, officer?"

"Yes." Wilson didn't look too happy, but he said, "Why don't you come over to the station and I'll talk to you after I book this suspect."

"Thanks!" River stepped aside and let Wilson and Jake pass. He looked hopefully into the shop. "Hi. I guess you heard. I'm River White . . . "

"With the *Penzance Courier*," Nathan said. "Congratulations. You beat the Waterville reporters on their own turf. But there's really nothing to tell you here. I'm sure Officer Wilson will give you what you need."

"Uh . . . okay. Are you sure?"

"Yes," Nathan said.

Still River hesitated. "Are you the owner of the store?"

"I am," Heather said. "Heather Wells. And there's still nothing to tell you."

"But there was obviously an incident here."

"A very minor one," Heather said drily.

"Aren't you Mr. Culver?" River asked, looking at Nathan. "The auctioneer?"

"Yes, I am. We're having a nice estate sale next week, if you want something to publicize. Call me tomorrow at the auction hall, if you're interested."

River's features cleared. "I don't think the *Courier*'s done a story on auctions for a while. I'll ask my editor about that. It might make a nice feature."

"That'd be great," Nathan said, handing River his card. "Good-bye." Nathan shut the door.

All was silent in the shop when he closed the door.

"Wow," Elaine said after a moment. "Heather, I am so sorry."

"What for? I'm the one who should be apologizing to you. I hired Jake over a year ago, and I've known for some time he was lazy. But I didn't know he'd do something like this. He figured you and I are both stupid and he could switch those teapots out before I got back and sell yours on the side." She shook her head. "I'll have to go over my records carefully and make sure it's the first time he pulled something like this. Oh, I would have known if it was something this valuable, but he might have made off with some less pricey items without my noticing. I should have fired him after his two-week trial period."

"Firing and hiring staff is stressful, not to mention time-consuming," Nathan said gently.

"Yeah, but I still should have done it. I'm sure I can get someone better."

"Well, let's look on the bright side," Nathan said. "You recovered the teapot, and the police didn't take it as evidence."

"You don't think they'll want to hold it until Jake's been to court, do you?" Elaine asked.

"Well, Officer Wilson didn't take it today," Heather said. "I suggest you just take it home now. If they need to see it again, they'll ask you."

"Maybe my pictures will be enough, provided they get a confession out of Jake." Nathan put his phone in his pocket. "Now, let's see this little gem, Heather."

Heather smiled for the first time since her arrival. "Yeah. It's really special, Mrs. Cook. I just love it."

"It's Elaine, and I do too." Elaine stepped closer to the worktable.

"I think it's early Qing dynasty, that is, seventeenth century. It could even be a little older—late Ming," Heather said.

"Ming dynasty?" Elaine's pulse accelerated. "That's really old, isn't it?"

Nathan smiled. “It’s late medieval.”

“About 1368 to 1644,” Heather said. “I can’t date this item too closely, but I’m thinking early to mid-seventeenth century. And what I said to Officer Wilson was my best estimate—twelve thousand dollars in today’s market. I never should have said it to Jake earlier though.”

Elaine took a deep breath. “I guess I did get a bargain.” Heather laughed, and Elaine couldn’t help joining her. She turned to Nathan. “Thank you for everything. I’m glad you were here.”

“Well, don’t thank me too much until you see tomorrow’s *Courier*. We may all wish we’d sat down with River and told him what actually happened. Cops never have—or give—the full story.”

“I figured Elaine wouldn’t want the full story made public,” Heather said. “Especially not the value on that teapot.”

Elaine caught her breath. “You’re right. Do I even dare to take it home with me?”

CHAPTER FIFTEEN

I can keep the teapot in my vault for you for a while if you want, until you decide what to do with it," Nathan said.

Elaine knew she and Jan would both worry if they had something that valuable in house. "That sounds like a good option."

He nodded. "And I have an auction of fine china and glassware scheduled for late July. If you do decide to sell it, I could put it in the catalog."

"Thanks. I'll think about it. For now, if you could just hang on to it, I'd feel easier."

"Sure."

Nathan sat down to write her a receipt for the item, including a detailed description and his and Heather's estimated valuation. Elaine stepped outside to call Jan and tell her what had happened.

"So I'll be a little later than I expected," she concluded.

"I am speechless," Jan said. "Elaine, you get into the strangest situations. First the ring, and then you run into Bobby Claybrook, and now this."

Elaine laughed. "Now, hold on a minute. I wasn't the one who found the ring. Roland was. And I don't think it's so odd that I bumped into an old schoolmate. After all, we saw Julie Yeaton the day of the estate sale."

"Well, yes," Jan conceded. "Anyway, I'm glad Nathan came over, and I'm glad everything turned out okay. Come home when you can. I've got clam chowder simmering, and we'll eat supper whenever you get here."

Elaine hung up smiling, for two reasons. One, she hadn't had a good New England clam chowder in years, and she knew Jan's would be fabulous. Two, Jan was still thinking about Robert Claybrook and ranking their meeting with him right up there with the sapphire ring. That had to be significant.

She went back into the shop. Heather was preparing to wrap her teapot in a sheet of bubble wrap, and Nathan was folding up the paper he had finished writing.

"Here you go. Heather and I both signed this, in case you ever need to prove you own that teapot again." He handed her the paper. "I'll put it in my vault immediately, and I won't do anything with it until I get instructions from you."

"And I printed copies of some pictures I took after you brought it in—'before and after' pictures." Heather nodded toward a manila envelope on the counter. "I do that with most of my restoration jobs, just to protect myself. I thought it would be good for you to have them in case you ever need to identify it again, or if you want to show a potential buyer what you've got."

"Thank you both," Elaine said.

"It's not going to lose value if you let it sit for a while." Heather's brow puckered as she concentrated on taping the wrap around the teapot. "You know, I'm sure I've seen this teapot before, or one just like it, but I can't remember where. Not here in my shop. I'd remember that."

"I had that feeling too," Nathan said. "Maybe we saw one at a sale?"

"Maybe." Heather shook her head and smiled. "Oh well." She slid the teapot into a small shopping bag with handles and added the envelope of pictures.

"Oh my goodness, I haven't paid you," Elaine said.

Heather's lips twitched. "This one's on me. After what happened with Jake..."

"No, no. You earned every penny." Elaine quickly wrote out a check. "In fact, that doesn't seem like enough for your work, and I'm not counting having to deal with the police."

"Well, thanks." Heather took the check with a sheepish smile. "I'm glad you did call them. Jake could have sneaked off with the teapot if you'd left, and we'd both have been losers."

"Do you think he'll go to jail?" Elaine asked, looking at Nathan.

"I hope so," he said. "But he'll probably be out on bail by morning."

"We need to give our statements to the police."

Nathan nodded. "Do you want to go over to the police station now, or wait until tomorrow?"

"I think I'd rather do it in the morning," Elaine said. "I'm tired, but I could be at the station around eight in the morning and be home before the tearoom opens at ten. I'd hate to leave Jan and Rose alone again. It's been fairly busy."

"I'll meet you there at eight," Nathan said. "We can go in together."

"I'd like that."

He nodded. "I'll go and put this teapot in my vault right now. You go home and relax and get a good night's sleep."

"All right. Thank you again. You too, Heather."

Heather nodded. "Thanks for the interesting day. And I'll let you know if I remember where I saw your teapot before."

ELAINE PERKED UP after she had eaten a bowl of Jan's chowder and had thoroughly hashed over the day's events with her cousin. Both were glad the old teapot was in a safe place and nowhere near their house. They took their tea out to the back deck to watch the sun set.

Shafts of golden light slanting across the lake faded, and the shadows of the evergreens lining the shore darkened. The water lay dark and peaceful, with small waves lapping the dock pilings. A motorboat puttered in from the far reaches of the lake and swung in to moor at the marina.

"So the most popular items seem to be muffins and cookies," Jan said. "People do like the fancier stuff, but we sell more cookies than anything."

Jan's phone rang, and she picked it up off the wrought iron table. "Well, hi, Amy!"

Elaine smiled. Jan's daughter. This would probably take a while, as Amy was the mother of active five-year-old twin boys and would no doubt have several new antics to report. Elaine reached for her laptop and turned it on. While Jan talked to Amy, she browsed the family tree sites again and focused on Alice Gardner. If the sapphire ring was her engagement ring, why had she left it hidden in a wall?

On a hunch, Elaine typed in the name of Miss Gardner's fiancé, gleaned from the engagement announcement, Andrew Clive. The genealogy database had several men by that name listed, but a few minutes of sorting helped Elaine find the right one. Though she hadn't known his birthdate, the engagement announcement had mentioned him as the son of John and Irene Clive of Lancaster. It was fairly easy to pinpoint that family group.

When Jan ended her conversation with Amy, she laid her phone on the table.

"How's Amy and the fam?" Elaine asked.

"Just great." Jan laughed. "The boys are up to their usual mischief. They dumped out a bucket of powdered laundry soap so they could use the container to catch tadpoles in."

"Oh dear," Elaine said.

"I guess it made quite a mess, but Amy caught them before they could subject any tadpoles to soapy water. So..." Jan leaned over to look at the screen of Elaine's laptop. "What are you up to?"

"I found Alice Gardner's fiancé, Andrew Clive, and his family, and a possible reason for the ring being stashed in the wall."

"Wow, I thought you'd given up on that."

Elaine shrugged. "I *had* given up on finding Alice's wedding announcement. But then I thought about the other information in the engagement piece, and I was able to find Andrew's family. The reason I couldn't find the wedding announcement was that there never was a wedding."

"Oh," Jan said mournfully, "did they break up?"

Elaine shook her head. "Worse than that. Andrew was killed in the war."

"The poor girl."

"Yeah. And as far as I can tell, Alice never married."

"And she was left with the ring," Jan said. "But why hide it?"

"*If* that was her ring," Elaine said. "We may never know for sure. If Alice never married, of course she didn't have any children, but maybe one of her sisters did. And there are the two brothers, Paul and David. We might find a descendant from that family who would know more."

"I don't know." Jan shook her head. "What good is finding the grandchild or great-grandchild of a person whose sister received an engagement ring? I think Robert was right and we should keep it. Oh, you go ahead and keep looking if you want, but I really think that's above and beyond the call of duty."

"I guess I'm just sentimental. It may not be Alice's ring at all." Elaine did a quick e-mail check and shut off her laptop. She sighed and leaned back in her chair. The lake was glassy calm now, and she was comfortable in her light cardigan. A few yards off the dock, a fish jumped and splashed back through the surface. "Don't you love it here?"

"I do," Jan said. "I truly do."

JAN ROSE EARLY Thursday morning, as she had every day since they opened the tearoom. She liked the muffins and fancy breads to be fresh out of the oven for their 10:00 a.m. customers, and that meant rising at five.

She read a short passage from her Bible and thanked God for a new day, then tiptoed down to the kitchen. She loved these quiet hours alone. She made herself a cup of tea and grabbed her recipe file. On the screened porch, she riffled through her recipes. She had already decided on the cookie of the day.

Clouds hovered low over the village, and the lake was choppy, a bleak battleship-gray with small, random whitecaps. It seemed like a good morning for cranberry-orange muffins, and she would do up smaller batches of bran and banana nut.

"Better make extra," she said as she pulled out her tried-and-true muffin recipes. Bristol's words about rainy days might very well be true.

Meow.

Startled, she looked out through the screen. On the slope below her, near the stairs leading down from the back deck to the dock below, a furry form flowed among the dew-laden grass blades. As she watched, the large, long-haired gray cat hopped onto the edge of a step and poured himself between two spindles of the handrail.

"Aren't you something?" Jan whispered. "Where did you come from?"

The cat rubbed against one of the balusters, as though scratching an itchy spot. Jan smiled. She watched the cat while she sipped her tea. He padded down to the deck and sat on it for several minutes, grooming himself. When a blue jay winged over, not six feet above his head, he barely gave it a glance.

"Pretty sure of yourself," Jan said. Reluctantly, she got up and gathered the recipes she had chosen. Most of the pastries were already baked, but she would make the muffins, scones, and the macaroons this morning, and one batch of lemon squares.

An hour later, the last batch of the day's muffins was in the oven, and she went out front to discover that the paperboy had delivered the *Courier.* She poured herself some peppermint tea, sat down at the kitchen table, and opened the paper. Below the fold on the front page was a picture of a police officer leading a young man in handcuffs to his squad car. "Waterville man accused of trying to steal rare teapot," the headline said.

Jan stared at the print for a moment, until it sank in that the news story was about Elaine's misadventure the day before. She pushed up her glasses and began to read. When her cousin entered the kitchen a few minutes later, wearing her green velour bathrobe and moccasin slippers, Jan had just finished reading the entire account for the second time.

"Good morning," Elaine said cheerfully.

"Well, it's morning, but I'm not sure how good it is." Jan held out the newspaper and tapped the headline. "It seems you made the front page of the *Courier.*"

"Oh dear." Elaine took the paper and plunked down opposite Jan. "Attempted theft by deception…rare and valuable Chinese teapot…oh my!"

"At least he didn't use your name," Jan said.

"That's good," Elaine agreed. "The officer must not have given the reporter our names. Oh, well, he got Heather's, I see. She did tell him her name as the cop was leaving. He asked if she was the owner of the shop, and Heather said she was. But that's all he—oh, wait. He mentions Nathan by name too. He recognized him, I'm afraid."

"A famous, handsome man like that," Jan said without cracking a smile.

Elaine glanced at her, then laughed. "Silly. Nathan won't mind, I'm sure. He'll say any publicity is good publicity, and the reporter even says he's the owner of Culver Auctions, so he got a little press for his business out of it. I'm sorry it happened though."

"I'm just glad he didn't print your name," Jan said. "Although he does say the teapot belonged to the owner of the Tea for Two tearoom. I guess anyone who wanted to find you could do that easily enough."

Elaine huffed out a big breath. "You know what? I'm not going to let this ruin my day. That teapot is not on the premises, and if anyone comes and asks about it, we'll tell them it's not here and sell them a cup of tea and a scone. God's given us several large blessings recently, and I refuse to worry about this article."

"Good for you," Jan said. "Then I won't either." The stove's timer beeped, and she got up to take the last tray of muffins out. Trust Elaine to look on the bright side. This was one more example of how she and her cousin differed—and how they were good for each other.

That thought set Jan to wondering: If she'd had Elaine's personality and had taken a more upbeat approach to life after Peter died, would Brian have a more positive outlook too? But Elaine hadn't been widowed early and been forced to finish raising three children on her own. How much of their contrasting attitudes was due to circumstances, and how much to genetics and other factors, Jan had no idea. Maybe she would do a little reading up on genetics and the nature-versus-nurture controversy.

"Isn't it a lovely day?" Elaine asked.

"Huh?" Jan stood with the hot pan clutched in her oven mitts and glanced toward the window. Beyond, the clouds still hovered low over the lake, and the wind whipped the light-green leaves on the trees. The water near the dock was still a dark, midnight blue, but farther out it lightened to gunmetal-gray, and if anything, the whitecaps had multiplied. *Count your blessings,* she told herself. The house with Elaine, the tearoom, new friends. Yes, things were good here. Then she remembered the cat. "It's beautiful."

Elaine turned, smiling. Her gaze fell on the pan of browned muffins Jan held. "*Mmm*! Cranberry?"

"Cranberry-orange. Would you like one?"

"Will there be plenty?"

"I made extra this morning. Besides, these two on this end are a little small. I was running out of batter, so . . . "

"So you eked out two little ones just for us."

Jan set the pan down on a hot mat, and Elaine gave her a hug.

"No one's ever made a special muffin for me before."

Jan laughed. "You've been deprived and neglected, girl."

"Sit down," Elaine said. "I'll get the plates and butter. What are you drinking?" She glanced at the clock. "Heavens, I'm supposed to meet Nathan at the police station in an hour."

"You have plenty of time to eat and get dressed," Jan said.

"Oh, I know, but I wanted to see if I could find out more about that teapot. Where did it come from, do you suppose?"

"You may never know."

"Maybe not," Elaine said, her eyes bright, "but if I have anything to say about it, I'll find out how it came to the flea market."

CHAPTER SIXTEEN

Nathan waited for Elaine in the parking lot at the police station, leaning against his car and clicking away on his phone. When she parked across the aisle and got out of her vehicle, he smiled and put the phone away.

"Good morning. How are you doing?" he asked.

"I'm fine, and I brought you one of Jan's fresh cranberry-orange muffins." She held out one of the small white bakery bags they used for takeaway at the tearoom.

"Fantastic! I'll have that with my coffee break later." He put the bag in his car and returned to her side. "Be sure to thank Jan for me. I've got to get out to Lancaster and visit the tearoom."

Elaine chuckled. "You probably won't find it nearly as exciting as the auction house, but we'd love to see you."

"I'll see if I can't wend my way out there."

They walked to the door as they talked. Elaine paused, looking at the building's façade. "You know, the last time I was in Waterville—before I moved back, I mean—the police station was still in the basement of city hall."

"You stayed away too long." Nathan opened the door for her, and they went inside. After they told the desk sergeant their errand, Officer Wilson came out into the lobby and greeted them.

"Thanks for coming in, folks. Come right this way."

Elaine and Nathan followed him down a hallway and into a small room with a long table and several chairs. From the spartan decor and the camera mounted in one corner of the ceiling, Elaine guessed it was used to interview witnesses and suspects. Officer Wilson asked them a few questions to clarify details of their encounter the day before.

"Now, Mrs. Cook, I believe you said you purchased the teapot Jake Tunney tried to steal at a flea market?"

"Yes, Mainely Bargains," Elaine said. "It was a couple of weeks ago."

"Do you remember which dealer you bought it from? What did he look like?"

Elaine's brow furrowed as she tried to remember details of the outing with Jan. "He was probably my age or a little older. He had a short beard, and he was bald on top, with a fringe of dark hair."

"How tall?" Wilson made notes as he asked.

"Let's see. He stood up when he wrapped it for me in newspaper. Maybe five-nine or five-ten." She pictured the box of cookbooks as Jan rummaged through them. "He had his little grandson with him. I think he called him Mikey. Oh! How silly of me. He called later. I believe it was that same evening."

"Oh?"

"Yes, and he told me his name. Carl something."

Wilson smiled. "I know who you mean. That's Carl Joiner."

"Yes, that's it," Elaine said, relieved she no longer had to tax her memory.

"Why did he call you?"

"He said he had another customer who wanted the teapot."

"Did he mention its value?" Wilson asked.

"He offered me fifty dollars to take it back to him. When I said no, he upped the offer to a hundred."

"Now, that's interesting."

"Yes," Elaine said. "I decided there and then to take it to Nathan. It was a few days before I got it to him, but he thought it might be valuable. On his recommendation, I took it to Heather Wells. She's the one who gave me a figure—twelve thousand."

"And I agreed with her appraisal," Nathan said.

"I see." Wilson made a few more notes. "And how do you think Mr. Joiner knew your telephone number?"

Elaine frowned. "I suppose he got it off my check. He didn't tell me who the other customer was, and I felt that if it was a legitimate mistake, then I would take it back. But he didn't give any indication that he'd slipped up on the price. I felt he simply saw a chance to make a little more money on it."

"Carl Joiner has a police record," Wilson said.

Nathan sat up straighter. "Is this something I should know about?"

"Probably. He's been arrested before for defrauding customers and selling stolen antiques across state lines."

"How come I never heard about this?" Nathan asked.

"Well, he used to have an antique store down in Auburn, but he lost it after his last run-in with the law down there. When he started selling up here and took the flea market booth, we got a flag from the Auburn PD."

Elaine didn't like the sound of that, but it might explain some things. "Do you think that's why he didn't press me any further to sell the teapot back to him? Was he afraid I'd get him in trouble again?"

"Could be," Wilson replied. "He hasn't contacted you again?"

"No. But I haven't had the teapot in the house since that day I took it to Heather. It's in a safer place now."

"Good," the officer said, closing his notebook. "My advice is, just be careful. And if Carl Joiner contacts you again, let us know, okay?"

"I will," Elaine said.

"But this has nothing to do with that Jake fellow at Heather's shop, does it?" Nathan asked. "I don't see how Joiner could have known Elaine took the teapot there."

"Not so far as I know," Wilson said. "I'll ask Jake about it though, since we've made this connection between the teapot and Joiner. There may be something we've overlooked, but I think Jake was working on his own and trying to make a small fortune on the side."

"Has he admitted anything yet?" Nathan asked.

"His court-appointed lawyer is meeting with him this morning. If he's smart, he'll plead guilty. You basically caught him red-handed."

Elaine sighed. "I'm sure he switched those repair tags, and Heather was too. She said he probably hoped she wouldn't come back before the shop closed, and he could get it out of there and sell it before she realized anything was wrong. I'm not sure how he would explain that the Staffordshire pot was missing though."

Nathan shrugged. "He'd probably just tell Heather the owner finally came back and claimed it."

"I wouldn't put it past him." Wilson stood. "That's it, unless you remember anything else. I have your telephone numbers, so if there are any questions, we'll be in touch."

"Will we need to testify?" Nathan asked.

"Well, that's not certain yet. We'll see what the district attorney says. Jake didn't actually steal the teapot, but he did make an attempt. Because of its high value, it would be grand theft." Wilson shrugged. "We'll let you know if you're needed."

Elaine still didn't like the feeling that it was her word that would put the young man on trial, and possibly in jail, even though she knew he should pay for his actions.

"Does Jake have a prior record?" she asked.

"Some minor stuff," Officer Wilson replied. "I think if he were a career criminal, he'd have gone about this a little smarter."

"You got that right," Nathan said. "And he underestimated Heather and Elaine."

"That happens sometimes. I'm glad you realized what was going on and called us in time." Wilson nodded at Elaine. "Thanks again." He escorted them out into the lobby.

"That was interesting," Nathan said as he walked with Elaine toward her red Malibu.

"Very. And it just occurred to me—do you think my teapot was stolen? Before I bought it, I mean."

"*Hmm.* Doubt it. I mean, if Joiner had stolen it and intended to fence it elsewhere, why would he have it at the flea market in the first place? Wouldn't he have recognized it as a valuable piece?"

"Yeah, that makes sense. I don't think he realized it was special until after Jan and I left with it. Sometime between then and when he called me that evening."

"Never a dull moment with you, Elaine." Nathan smiled. "So coffee? Or tea? I'm sure we could find a place that serves tea."

She laughed. "Thanks, but I'd better get home. The ten-to-noon slot has been fairly busy all week. I'm glad, but I should be there to help."

"Another time," Nathan said.

"Definitely." Elaine felt a sprinkle land on her cheek as she unlocked her car.

Nathan smiled and held her door while she climbed into the car. "See you."

SHORTLY AFTER ELAINE'S lunch break, Robert Claybrook walked into the tearoom and looked around. She stepped away from the cash register and walked toward him, smiling.

"How nice to see you. Welcome to Tea for Two."

"Thanks." Robert took her hand for a moment. "I had a hearing canceled this afternoon, and I thought I'd make good on my promise."

"I'm glad you did. Let me show you to a table." Rose was having her lunch in the kitchen, so Elaine seated him herself, but in the east parlor, where Rose usually served.

Robert eyed the fireplace and decorative ceiling and woodwork with appreciation. "Nice old house."

"Isn't it? We love it."

"So where's the other half of the Tea for Two?" he asked, glancing around as Elaine handed him the menu card.

"Oh, Jan's in the kitchen, whipping up all the goodies our customers love. I'll tell her you're here. What can I bring you? Coffee? Or would you like to try our fresh-squeezed lemonade? It's pretty good, and it's not too sour."

"You know, it's been years since I had lemonade that didn't come from a mix. I'll try it. And, uh..." He looked at the menu. "What's good to go with it?"

"Well, everything Jan makes is terrific, but she made her triple chocolate cookies today. And her mini cream puffs are always a good bet."

"Yeah, I'll try one of each."

"Great. And I'm sure she'll want to pop out and see you when she has a minute."

Elaine hurried out to the entrance hall and glanced toward the counter. No one was waiting to cash out, so she continued on to the kitchen.

"Jan, Robert's here..."

"What? Oh my!" Jan fumbled with her apron strings. "Where is he?"

"East parlor, near the fireplace," Elaine said. "He wants lemonade, a chocolate cookie, and a cream puff. Do you want to get it?"

Rose jumped up from the small table. "I'll get the sweets, Jan. You pour the lemonade." She looked at Elaine. "Is it busy right now?"

"No, you're fine. Help Jan get Robert's tray ready, then finish your lunch."

Elaine went to check on the customers she had left in the west parlor. Two ladies had come in and taken a table while she was in the kitchen. She approached with a smile.

"Good afternoon. Oh, Macy! How nice to see you again."

Macy Atherton nodded, her face fixed in what seemed to be a perpetual frown. "Thought I'd bring one of my renters in. She wanted something to do without going too far."

"How nice," Elaine said.

Macy's companion, a pleasant-featured woman in her forties with permed blonde hair and cat-eye glasses, smiled up at Elaine. "My husband decided the lake was too rough for fishing today, so he's gone to Smithfield to look at an outboard motor. No doubt he'll be gone for hours, and I was ready to do something."

"I told her to try your ginger cookies," Macy said.

"How thoughtful," Elaine said. "I'm so glad you like them, Macy. But they're not on today's menu, I'm afraid. We have several choices today, including triple chocolate, oatmeal raisin, white chocolate chunk, macaroons, and buried cherry. Check out our other pastries too. Would you like a minute?"

"Oh no, I think you snared me with the white chocolate chunk," said the customer.

"I'll try it," Macy said, handing the card back, still not smiling. "And bring me that spice tea I had last time."

Elaine gulped. "Was that the cinnamon special?"

"I think so."

"That sounds good," her companion said. "I'll try it too."

"All right, ladies. It will only be a minute."

In the entrance hall, a woman was standing near the counter. Elaine hurried to her. "Sorry to keep you waiting."

"Oh, I'm fine. Haven't been standing here long." She held out her sales slip.

Rose came out of the kitchen and directly to Elaine's side. "How can I help?"

Elaine put the slip with Macy's order into her hand. "Could you get this order ready please? Thank you!"

After she checked out the waiting customer, she went to the east parlor doorway and looked in. Only three tables were occupied at the moment. At the far end of the room, Jan was sitting down across from Robert, and they were laughing over something together. Elaine smiled and turned to the take the tray Rose was carrying in from the kitchen.

"Thanks. I'll take this to Macy. I want to make sure she knows she can preorder ginger chews anytime, and Jan will make them for her."

JAN COULDN'T STOP herself from smiling. Bobby hadn't lost his sense of humor, that was for sure. Her face would probably ache later from laughing.

"Hey, this lemonade is great." He took a sip. "Did you make it?"

"Thanks, and yes, I squeezed those lemons myself this morning."

"I'll bet they really appreciated that."

She laughed, knowing her face was red, or at least pink. Good thing most of the tea drinkers had cleared out during the lunch hour.

"I don't think I've ever been in this house," Bob said. He hooked one arm over the back of his chair and turned sideways, gazing toward the windows that looked out on the side porch.

"We've had a lot of fun decorating," Jan said. "I guess it's kind of frilly for you, Bobby."

"Ha! No one calls me that anymore."

"Oh. Sorry. Robert."

"Bob is fine." He shrugged slightly, looking around at their tatted doilies, silk flower bouquets, and vintage knickknacks. "It goes with the house. Reminds me of my Grandma Claybrook's parlor, only it's bigger and…and lighter. It's really nice." He swung around and met her gaze. "Didn't the Gardners used to own this place, way back?"

"Yes, but that was a long time ago."

"Yeah, I barely remember them. But when I was little, I seem to recall seeing the old man sitting out on the front porch. And Mr. Howell, who lives over near me now, was a friend of his."

"Mr. Howell?" Jan asked.

"Yeah, he's lived next door to me since I bought the house out on Birch Lane. My wife and I moved out there almost twenty years ago. He's pretty old now, and I don't think he's well. He's declined a lot since his wife died."

"That's too bad," Jan said. She looked over her shoulder to make sure no one else was close by. "Elaine told you about the ring we found in the house, didn't she?"

Bob blinked. "Well, she did ask me, hypothetically, if someone found something in a house they'd bought, was it theirs to keep. I didn't know what it was."

"Oh. Maybe I'm not supposed to tell." Jan swallowed hard and hoped Elaine wouldn't be upset. "We haven't broadcast it or anything."

"You can count on my discretion," he said with a gallant smile.

"Thanks. That's what it was, a ring. And it has some value. So Elaine and I—mostly Elaine—have been trying to find out more about the people who lived here. The ring is fairly old, so we think it was here before the Binns family bought the house. We can't know for sure, but we're thinking the Gardners are good candidates. They had three daughters who lived here for quite a while, besides the mother and grandmother."

Bob nodded. "Sounds logical to me. Maybe Mr. Howell could tell you something about them. I'm not exactly sure how long he knew Mr. Gardner."

"Well, the house went to one of the sons eventually. Maybe it's just too long ago," Jan said. But still, it might not hurt to ask him what he knew of the Gardner girls. Maybe he had seen one of them wearing a gorgeous sapphire ring sixty or seventy years ago.

Bob sipped his lemonade. Rose entered the room with three more customers.

"How about this table, by the bay window?" she asked the women.

Bob set down his glass. "I should probably get going. You're keeping pretty busy here."

Jan smiled. He was right—she couldn't sit out here all day, but she was glad he had come in. She liked to think it was more to see her than to support a new business in town. "If you must. Let me send a few cookies with you. I think I overestimated the popularity of the cookie of the day."

He chuckled. "I won't say no. Where do I pay for the delicious refreshments I just ate?"

"Out where you came in. I'll meet you there with a goodie bag, on the house." Good thing Brian wasn't here to see her giving away product, Jan thought.

When she got out to the counter with the cookies, Elaine was handing Bob his change with a huge grin on her face.

"Come back again soon, Bob."

"Oh, I think you'll see quite a lot of me," he said.

Jan felt her face go even redder, if possible. She held out the bag. "Here you go. Great to see you."

"Thanks." Bob waved to Elaine and went out, pausing to hold the door open for incoming customers.

"I gave him six cookies," Jan said, looking Elaine in the eye. She hoped that sounded like neither a defiant declaration nor a guilt-induced confession.

Elaine laughed. "Good for you. I took Nathan a muffin this morning. Next thing you know, they'll be complaining we're trying to fatten them up."

"Well, Bob could use a few extra pounds," Jan said. "Not too many, of course."

Elaine was smiling as she went to greet the four people who had just entered. Jan decided it was time to scoot back into the kitchen and put on her apron. More orders, coming up!

A light rain that afternoon brought the villagers and the newly arrived summer people into the tearoom in droves. The twelve tables were full for nearly three solid hours, until they flipped the sign on the door to Closed and refilled the lingerers' teacups.

"Any more macaroons?" Rose asked from the kitchen doorway at five past four. "Mrs. Richardson, from the dairy farm, wants a dozen each of those and buried cherry, if you've got it."

Jan checked her containers. "Uh, only six macaroons left, but plenty of cherry."

"Okay," Rose said readily, "she said mix it up if we didn't have those—whatever you've got."

"Perfect. I'll give her the six macaroons and oatmeal raisin, with the dozen cherry. The white chocolate chunk were gone an hour ago."

"Those were really popular," Rose said.

Jan quickly filled a lightweight cardboard box and handed it to her. Rose went out, but a few minutes later, she and Elaine both came in with trays full of dirty dishes.

"Whew," Elaine said. "Last customers out the door, and my feet have had it!" After setting her tray on the counter, she sat down at the table and kicked her shoes off.

"Oh, too bad. I was wondering if you wanted to pay a call with me," Jan said.

"To whom?" Elaine's eyes widened in surprise.

"Bob's elderly neighbor, Mr. Howell." While helping Rose load the dishwasher and wipe off the trays, Jan gave Elaine a quick rundown on what Bob had told her about the old man's past friendship with Mr. Gardner. "So I thought I'd take him a few cookies. Or cream puffs and lemon squares, I guess. We don't have many cookies left today."

"I guess it can't hurt," Elaine said. "I was sort of planning to work on that coupon we talked about, for Bristol to hand out to her customers."

"The one that says 'The Cookie's on Us'?" Jan asked.

"Yeah. Free cookie with your beverage. And I thought I'd ask Des and Jo Murphy if they'd hand out some at their store too."

"Yeah, but put an expiration date on it, okay? Like maybe the end of June?"

"Sure," Elaine said. "But if you want me to go with you to see Bob's neighbor..."

"I'll be fine by myself. I know you're exhausted, what with your trip to the police station this morning and all. Go ahead and work on the coupon."

"Are you positive?"

"Of course." Jan got out a paper plate and put two lemon squares and four buried cherry cookies on it.

"Dishwasher's ready to go," Rose said. "Want me to start it?"

Jan looked around the kitchen, but couldn't spot any dirty dishes or utensils that Rose had missed. "Let her rip."

"Thanks for helping, Rose," Elaine said, pushing herself up out of her chair. "See you in the morning. Jan, I'm going to go change."

"Okay," Jan said. "I'm heading over to Mr. Howell's, but I'll make sure the front door is locked." She covered the plate of cookies and went to get her purse. It was hard to keep up with Elaine sometimes, but maybe today she would be the one to dig out a clue.

CHAPTER SEVENTEEN

Jan pulled into Mr. Howell's driveway and shut off the engine of her ten-year-old Camry. A pickup truck stood in the driveway that led to the gray Cape Cod house. The lawn looked as though it could use a good mowing, and the paint was peeling a little around the front windows. Nothing major, but the place could use some loving care.

She got out of the car and walked slowly up to the front steps, balancing the cookie plate. Perennials were coming up in the flower beds, but the weeds hadn't been pulled this spring.

She knocked on the storm door and waited. A lean man with sandy hair opened the inner door. He looked quite a bit younger than Jan, though his hair was thinning. This couldn't be the elderly man Bob had spoken about. He looked familiar, but she didn't have time to puzzle out who he looked like or where she might have seen him.

"Hi. I'm Jan Blake, and I'm a friend of your neighbor, Bob Claybrook. I wondered if I could see Mr. Howell."

"Oh. Well, I guess." He unlatched the storm door and pushed it open. "Time to switch that out for the screen, I guess." He stepped back and let Jan enter.

"How's he doing?" Jan asked.

"Not too well, to be honest."

"I'm sorry to hear that." Jan held out the covered paper plate. "I brought some cookies. I didn't know if he could eat them or not. If he can't, I hope you'll enjoy them yourself."

"Oh, that's nice. I'm sure Grandpa would like to try one. I'm Keith Howell, by the way, Cecil's grandson."

"Nice to meet you," Jan said.

He took the plate from her and nodded toward a doorway on the right. "He's sitting up today, in the front room."

Keith led her into the living room, where a nearly bald, wrinkle-faced old man sat in a recliner, leaning partway back, with his feet elevated and an afghan across his lap.

"Grandpa, there's a lady here to see you," Keith said, more loudly than normal.

Cecil turned his head and squinted at Jan. "What lady? Do I know you?"

"We've never met," Jan said, walking over to his side, "but I'm an old friend of Bob Claybrook, and he was telling me about you. I wondered if you'd like to visit."

"She brought you some treats, Grandpa," Keith said.

"Well, quit shouting and let's see 'em." Cecil glanced at Jan. "He thinks I'm deaf."

Keith took the plate over and uncovered it so his grandfather could look over the cookies. Cecil studied them carefully and poked a finger toward one of the squares. Jan found Cecil an interesting figure, and she noticed a very slight lilt to his voice—a ghost of a British accent, perhaps? She hadn't had much contact with people from the United Kingdom, but she did watch some British programs on PBS, and she thought that was what she heard.

"What's that?" Cecil asked, throwing her a sharp glance.

"Lemon squares," Jan said. "The chocolate cookies have cherries inside."

"What kind of cherries?"

"Maraschino."

Cecil grunted. "I'll try the square." He looked up at Keith. "How about coffee?"

"No, Grandpa, you know you're not supposed to have coffee. How about milk?"

"Okay."

"Can I get you something, Mrs. Blake?"

"No, thanks," Jan said.

"Well, have a seat. I'll go get him a glass of milk."

By this time, Cecil had settled the paper plate on his lap and had eaten half of the first lemon square.

While Keith was gone to the kitchen, Jan dove right into the topic of her choice. "My cousin and I have bought the old house that the Gardners used to own. The one on Main Street."

"Oh?" He chewed thoughtfully.

"Yes, and Bob told me that you and Mr. Gardner used to be friends."

"Paul Gardner," Cecil said.

"Oh, I see," Jan said, recalling that Elaine had said Harold Gardner was the father's name, and Paul was his oldest son. "So did you know his father?"

"No, he had passed before I moved here."

"When was that?"

Cecil frowned. "Around 1955 or '56. Somewhere in there."

Jan nodded. "So it would be after Paul inherited the house."

"That's right." Cecil took the other lemon square off the plate and bit into it.

"I wondered if you knew anything about the house. Or Paul's sisters."

He looked puzzled. "I don't think I knew the sisters."

"I see." Jan wasn't sure if she should press him with questions or not. That might seem odd to Cecil and his grandson.

Keith reappeared at that moment, with a tumbler half full of milk.

"Here you go, Grandpa."

Cecil took a sip and handed it back to him with a sour face. "Take that away. It's skim milk."

"It's one percent," Keith said. "You know the doctor said you were supposed to avoid fat."

"Well, I don't like it. Take it away."

Keith sighed.

"I should probably be going." Jan stood.

"Thank you for coming," Keith told her. "And for the cookies."

"You're welcome." Jan walked with him out to the entrance.

"Sorry about Grandpa," Keith said. "He's a stubborn old man. Very opinionated."

"He doesn't seem to have lost his spirit," Jan said.

"No, but every day when I come over, I expect I'll find he's fallen down or something like that."

"You don't live here with him?"

"No. He insists he can take care of himself, but he can't really. I have someone bring in his lunch every day, to make sure he gets one good, balanced meal, and to check on him. I come by every day on my way home from work. But I'm afraid the day is coming—rapidly—when he'll need constant care." Keith shook his head. "Stubborn old man. He won't go into assisted living."

"He'll come around," Jan said tentatively.

"I don't know. It's expensive. And he needs some special treatments, but his insurance won't cover it. I've started sorting things to sell some of them, so that when a nursing home is inevitable, moving him won't be such a chore. But if he has anything to say about it, that day will never come. Well anyway, that's my worry, not yours."

He opened the door for Jan. "Thanks again for coming. Your visit will give him something new to talk about for a few days." Keith sounded very tired and a little discouraged.

"It's very good of you, taking care of your grandfather," Jan said. "Would it be all right if I called on him again?"

"Sure. The more people who have an eye on him, the better. If you come during the day though, and no one else is here, go around back, so he won't try to get up to open the door. He leaves the back door unlocked."

"I'll remember that." She heard the television come on in the living room as she went out.

ELAINE AWOKE EARLIER than usual on Friday, and she heard a distinct *meow* from below her window. She had left the casement open a few inches all night for the fresh air, but now it seemed she had a dawn serenade.

She got up and went to one of the windows overlooking the lake, but she couldn't see any cats below. Then she heard a squeak, which she had come to recognize—the back door on the screened porch was opening.

She threw on her housecoat and slippers and hurried downstairs, through the kitchen, and out to the back porch.

Jan was crouched on the steps leading down to the deck, holding a dish. She set it down on the edge of the deck and stood, then edged backward up the steps.

"There you go," she said softly. "Come on out and get it. I won't hurt you."

"What are you doing?" Elaine asked.

Jan jumped and whipped around, grabbing the handrail. "Where did you come from?"

Elaine chuckled. "I heard yowling out here and decided to investigate."

"It's just a cat," Jan said.

"A stray?"

"I'm not sure. I've seen him out here a couple of times, and I thought he might be hungry."

"Oh, I see."

Jan eyed her sharply. "What?"

"Nothing. But we can't have a cat in the tearoom, you know."

"I know. He probably belongs to somebody along Main Street. I just..."

"It's all right." Elaine unlatched the screen door. "Come on in here. Maybe he'll come out of hiding if we're not so close." She left Jan watching eagerly through the screen and went into the kitchen to put the teakettle on. After setting out mugs and spoons, she tiptoed back on to the porch and sidled up to Jan.

A large gray ball of fur was perched on the extreme edge of the deck below, ravenously licking up the milk Jan had set out for it. Elaine suspected she had warmed it a little.

"He's gorgeous."

"Isn't he?" Jan whispered.

"You've named him, haven't you?"

Jan threw her a sidelong glance. "No! Well, maybe. I've *thought* of it."

Elaine smiled. "What do you call him in your thoughts?"

"Earl."

"Earl? Why not Prince?"

"Earl Grey."

"Oh, I see." Elaine chuckled. "Very nice."

Behind her, the teakettle whistled. The cat leaped off the side of the deck and dove underneath it. Elaine bustled inside and grabbed the kettle. She put loose chai tea into an infuser and poured water over it in a pottery teapot. A moment later, Jan came in.

"Sorry," Elaine said.

"It's all right. He'd drunk it all anyway." She smiled sheepishly. "You don't mind?"

"No, I like cats. But we should ask around and see if anyone knows who he belongs to. Bristol said she'd try to get over and pick up the coupons. I'll ask her."

"Thanks. And I won't let him inside."

An hour later, a boat motor burbled and stopped as the boat glided up to their dock.

"There's Rose," Jan called from the kitchen.

Elaine was folding napkins in the west parlor. "She's early."

"Yes, she offered to help me with the cream puffs. And we had two cookie orders phoned in last night, so I've got more dough for those started."

Elaine walked into the entrance hall and over to the kitchen door. "Did you say two cookie orders? I knew Rue Maxwell wanted three dozen for the B and B. What's the other one?"

Jan grinned. "Macy Atherton. She asked for two dozen ginger chews, so I'm making them the cookie of the day, if that's all right with you."

"It's fine. I'll make cards we can clip to the menus."

The sunny morning didn't seem to keep the customers away. Elaine was pleased that they had steady business, though it wasn't too chaotic. Rue Maxwell came by shortly after they opened to pick up her cookies.

"Wish I could stop for tea," she said, "but we've got three couples coming in today for the long weekend."

"The season is upon us." Elaine smiled as she cashed up the purchase.

"And how." Rue lifted the lid on the take-out box. "Oh, they smell so good! It's great having someplace nearby where I can get fresh baked goods and know they'll be delicious. Does Jan do muffin orders?"

"I'm sure she would," Elaine said. "Would you like me to ask her?"

"Sure. I'll try to give her a call later about it. It hit me that it would save me a lot of time in the morning, and I'd still be able to present that home-style breakfast our customers love. What time do you close?"

"At four."

"I'll call this evening." Rue tucked her receipt into her pocket and picked up the cookie box. "Thanks again."

Several customers had entered while Elaine tended to Rue's order, and Rose had greeted them and shown those who hesitated in the entry to tables. The latest arrival surprised Elaine. Carlene Eastman had made a repeat visit, this time without her friend Blair.

Rose seated her in the east parlor, and Elaine decided to ignore her. However, a few minutes later Rose came to her at the cash register.

"Hey, a lady ordered tea and then went to the restroom. She's been gone quite a while, and I don't know what to do. Her tea is getting cold. Should I go get a fresh cup?"

Elaine had a funny feeling she knew which customer Rose was talking about. She went to the parlor doorway and quickly scanned the people at the tables. Sure enough, Carlene Eastman was missing and a cup of tea and a plate holding a blueberry muffin sat on a table near the bay window.

"Let me check the restroom," Elaine said. "Can you see if the folks in my station need anything?"

"Sure." Rose headed into the west parlor, where Elaine usually served.

Elaine walked briskly through the entrance hall, to the guest powder room. The door was ajar, and the light was off. She turned and strode across to the smaller passageway that led under the curved staircase, past her office and the private bathroom to the garage door.

Her office was empty, and she let out a sigh of relief. If she had found Carlene snooping in her desk or the files, an ugly confrontation might have ensued. But where was their guest?

She went back into the hallway and saw that the door to the private bath she, Jan, and Rose used during business hours was closed. Elaine walked a few yards toward the garage door and stopped outside the restroom. She tapped on the door panel.

"Hello. Anyone in here?"

There was no answer, so she tried the doorknob. The door opened easily. Again, she found nobody in the room, but the cabinet over the sink was open.

"All right, where are you?" She made a quick stop at the east parlor door again. Nobody sat at Carlene's abandoned table. In the west parlor, Rose was topping off a man's coffee and chatting amiably with him and his wife. A woman at another table rose with her sales bill in her hand.

"Oh, let me get that for you," Rose said cheerfully.

Puzzled, Elaine poked her head into the dining room. Nobody. Carlene had asked to see the kitchen before. Maybe, just maybe…

She hurried to the doorway. Jan was filling the stainless steel teakettle.

"Has anyone come in here?"

"That Carlene person. She came to the doorway and said hi. I said hi, and she asked if she could look around the kitchen. I said no, it was against regulations. I'm not sure that's quite true, but I wasn't going to let her poke around in here."

"Well, she ordered tea, but then she did a vanishing act."

"Let's hope she got a phone call and had to leave," Jan suggested.

"Somehow I doubt it."

With sudden conviction, Elaine whirled and hurried to the stairs. Rose was taking her customer's money, and she looked up at Elaine in surprise.

"Be right back," Elaine called and continued on upstairs. At the top, she paused. No one was in the hall, and her own bedroom door was open. She took a quick look, but it was empty, as was her bathroom. Across from her door, the sewing room was closed. A glance inside told her nobody was in there. As she shut the door, she thought she heard a faint noise from farther along the hallway. She tiptoed along and peeked in at the sitting room. The big, airy chamber was unoccupied. That left Jan's room and the guest room.

Jan's door was ajar, and Elaine walked softly to it and looked in. A light was on in the private bath, but the door was open. Maybe Jan had left it on, or maybe not. Feeling a little guilty and definitely sneaky, Elaine pushed the door farther open and stepped into the bedroom. Carlene stood before the open closet door, pushing the hangers along the rod and peering behind them.

CHAPTER EIGHTEEN

May I help you?" Elaine asked sternly.

Carlene gasped and whirled toward her. "Oh, hello. I..."

"This area is private," Elaine said. "I think you know that."

Carlene's face reddened and she gave a halfhearted smile. "I was just trying to see if the things my sister and I wrote on the wall in this closet were still there."

That was more than odd, since Carlene claimed she had slept in what was now the sitting room, but Elaine didn't voice the thought.

"You will have to leave at once, or I will call the police."

"What? No! I...I was only looking for old memories. I..."

"I don't believe you," Elaine said flatly. "I don't know what you want, but it's not childhood mementos. Please go, and don't come back."

Carlene clenched her jaw and then shut the closet. She walked stiffly to the door. Elaine stepped aside and let her pass. She watched until Carlene had reached the stairs and headed down. Then she went through Jan's bedroom to shut off the bathroom light. Everything looked neat, as usual, but she couldn't help wondering if Carlene had gone through the medicine cabinet and vanity drawers. She snapped off the light and hurried down the hall and the stairs. Carlene was just scuttling out the front door.

Coming from the east parlor, Rose stared at the closing door, then looked up at Elaine.

"Wasn't that her? Where was she?"

"Upstairs."

Rose's jaw dropped. A customer came out of the west parlor and headed for the counter. Elaine lowered her voice.

"I'll tell you about it later. She won't be back."

"Okay, I'll clear the table." Rose went back into the parlor, and Elaine went to the cash register and greeted the departing guest with a smile.

A few minutes later, she filled Rose in on the situation. They didn't have a lull for the next hour, but when things finally slowed down enough for her to catch her breath, she went to the kitchen and told Jan about Carlene's audacity.

"Unbelievable!" Jan scowled. "Are you sure she didn't take anything?"

"Not a hundred percent. Maybe you should go up and check your jewelry box."

Jan sighed. "Nothing valuable in there. What do you think she wants?"

"I don't really know," Elaine said. "But I think she's looking for some specific item. The only thing that comes to mind is that ring. Well, I'd better get back out front, but if you find anything's missing, do call the police. I don't believe her childhood story for a minute."

"Me either. Maybe she heard that a valuable piece of jewelry was lost in the house and took advantage of the opportunity to look for it."

Elaine sighed. "I don't know. She's been here three times now. But I don't think she's related to the Binns family, and they owned this place from 1968 until we bought it."

"I asked Bristol the last time I was at the Bookworm," Jan said. "She didn't know who Carlene was. If she'd lived here long, Bristol ought to know, don't you think?"

"Seems like it." Elaine wondered if she should have called the police when she caught Carlene upstairs. "I told her not to come back. I'm getting tired of this skulduggery."

Jan wiped her hands on a dish towel. "Well, I'll take a look now. If you gals need anything, I'll be down in a minute."

"THE FLEA MARKET is open until eight tonight. Want to go?" Elaine asked.

Jan looked up from loading the dishwasher. It was half past four, the tearoom was closed, and the cleanup was nearly finished. "On a Friday?"

"It's because it's Memorial Day weekend, and they figure the tourists are coming in. They'll be open every day through Monday this weekend."

"Okay. Are you looking for something special?"

"Kind of." Elaine's eyes had that sparkle that meant she was up to something fun. "I think the amount of business we've had this week justifies a couple of tables out on the side porch."

"Patio tables and chairs?"

Elaine grinned. "And more teapots."

Jan shrugged and reached for her apron strings. "Why not? I only have four dozen extra muffins to bake for Rue Maxwell, scones and squares and cookies for tomorrow, and a bridesmaids' luncheon to plan."

Elaine batted a hand at her. "Oh, silly, that luncheon's weeks away. Come on. I promise not to stay long, and I'll help you with the baking when we get home."

"You talked me into it." Jan scurried upstairs to freshen up and get her purse. She had exaggerated about the baking. Saturday's cookies were already in the freezer. Besides, she could probably talk Elaine into stopping at the fabric shop too, and she could pick up the shade of green embroidery floss she needed for the cross-stitch Christmas ornaments she had already started making for the grandchildren.

Her purse lay just where it had when she'd checked it after Carlene Eastman's visit: on her dresser. The small amount of cash she'd had on hand was intact, along with her debit and credit cards and her checkbook. That had convinced her that Carlene wasn't aiming to rob them of just anything. Elaine was probably right. Carlene had something particular in mind.

The flea market wasn't as busy as it had been the morning they had first shopped there. A few of the dealers were tucking their booths in for the night, draping them with tablecloths and consolidating display items, but most seemed ready to stay open for the extended hours.

"So I was thinking of potted orchids on the tables for the bridesmaid lunch," Elaine said as they ambled toward the first row of booths. "Or do you think they're too tall for centerpieces?"

"I'm not sure. We could ask a florist." Jan scanned the tables. "Let's start at the far end this time, where we didn't get to look before."

They strolled along, perfectly happy in one of the pastimes they both enjoyed. They didn't find any extra teapots or furniture, but Jan discovered a small basket full of crochet cotton, with several crochet hooks and a tatting shuttle at the bottom. She decided to splurge. Elaine's find was a necklace made from the handle of an antique silver fork.

As they approached the last row of booths—the first they had shopped at on their earlier visit to Mainely Bargains—Jan saw a familiar face. She touched Elaine's arm and stopped walking.

"There's the man we got the cookbooks and the Chinese pot from. He's the one who called you, right?"

"Yes," Elaine said warily. "Maybe we should avoid him tonight. I don't want him starting in on me about that teapot."

"I know what you mean." Jan hated confrontation too.

They were about to turn away when a woman who had been bent over, rooting through a carton on the floor, stood and placed a couple of items on Joiner's table. Jan caught her breath.

"Isn't that..."

"Carlene Eastman," Elaine finished. "Now I *know* I want to keep away from that booth."

Something caught Jan's eye. "Wait." Elaine paused, and Jan leaned toward her. "See what's on the table right in front of her? That's not an antique."

Elaine's jaw dropped, and she grabbed Jan's wrist. "A motorcycle helmet."

"And it's red and white," Jan said. "I'm guessing it belongs to Carlene."

"The rider we saw leaving the house wasn't heavy enough to be Carl," Elaine said pensively. "Still, that's not proof."

"No, but it makes you think, doesn't it?" In Jan's mind, the matter was settled. Carlene was the one who had gone to the house Sunday afternoon while they were away.

Carlene walked around behind the table and started rearranging the merchandise.

"Hey, what's she doing?" Jan asked.

Elaine frowned. They both hovered for a moment, watching Carlene talk to Carl Joiner. Then Carl left his seat and walked away, heading toward the refreshment window. Carlene continued to bustle about behind his table.

"Come with me," Elaine whispered.

Jan followed her over to a booth that was only two down from Joiner's. The middle-aged man tending it presided over a wide array of glassware and china.

"Excuse me," Elaine said. "Do you know Carl Joiner?"

"Sure," the man said, pointing down the aisle. "His booth is right down there. Looks like his daughter's manning it at the moment, but I saw him earlier."

"Thanks." Elaine seized Jan's wrist and pulled her away, down the aisle. They circled around and went up another row, so they could approach the exit without passing Joiner or his booth.

Once they were out in the fresh evening air of the parking lot, Elaine let out a puff of air that signaled her frustration.

"His daughter! Why didn't we think of that?"

"I know," Jan moaned. "Carl and Carlene. She was looking for the teapot!"

"But why would she think it was in your closet?" Elaine shook her head. "That doesn't make sense."

"Remember how persistent she was about seeing the kitchen?" Jan asked. "The first time she came, we wouldn't let her. The contractor was working in there. But she just barreled on into the dining room."

"And when she came with her friend, she asked me again if she could go in there," Elaine mused. "Today she sneaked out of the dining room and tried to get you to let her look around."

"Well, this tears it," Jan said.

Elaine laughed. "You sound just like Nana."

"*Hmpf.*" Jan didn't like being compared to someone she'd always thought of as old, but on the other hand, she had always loved their grandmother, so she didn't mind Elaine's comment too much. "I'll bet when I turned her away from the kitchen, nobody was out in the entry and she saw a chance to sneak upstairs while no one was looking."

"Yeah. She could check our private quarters just to be sure we weren't stashing it up there." Elaine sighed. "I'm sure glad I had Nathan put it in his vault."

"So am I." Another thought occurred to Jan. "And I'll bet that's why Carl didn't bother to phone you again. Instead of arguing with you about it, he sent his little spy to find out if you had it in the house."

"Her first visit to the house was way before we opened," Elaine said. "It was just a couple of days after we bought the teapot—and after his phone call. How did we not catch on to that?"

"Well, we know her game now," Jan said. "She probably knows absolutely nothing about the ring. Do you think she knew that teapot was valuable when they got it, and her father sold it before she could tell him?"

"I don't know," Elaine said. She unlocked her Malibu, and Jan got into the passenger seat. When they were both settled, Elaine started the engine. "The newspaper article hadn't come out yet, so they couldn't have read that. But the evening after we bought it, Carl knew he had made a mistake."

Jan lifted her chin slowly, thinking. "I've got it! That man we saw when we came out of the flea market that day."

"What man?" Elaine asked.

"He was talking on the phone and going into the building as we came out. He said something like, 'Don't tell me you already sold it!' I didn't think anything of it at the time, but…Yeah, I'm sure now. I saw him again yesterday. He's Cecil Howell's grandson, Keith."

Elaine sat with her hand on the gearshift, but not moving. "You met this guy yesterday?"

"Yes, when I took the cookies. I didn't make the connection, but that was him. He must have been calling Carl Joiner on his way to the flea market, to stop him from selling the teapot. We walked right past him with it."

Elaine just stared at her.

"It makes sense," Jan said. "His grandfather needs medical treatment, and they're selling off stuff to pay for it. Cecil's going to have to go into a nursing home eventually. Keith seemed pretty discouraged about it."

"Okay," Elaine said slowly, "you may be right, but we don't know for sure. We know Carl realized that the teapot had more value than he'd thought, and he called me that evening about it, wanting it back. We also know Cecil's grandson went to the flea market and was upset that something had been sold. But Carl told me he had another customer who wanted it."

"I think that was a ruse," Jan said. "If Keith was the one who made the mistake and took it to the flea market with a lot of other, less valuable stuff, then he had that 'uh-oh' moment and tried to get it back, well, I'm just sayin'. That could be how Carl and Carlene realized so early that the teapot was worth a lot of money."

"Officer Wilson told me Carl had been arrested before for selling stolen antiques," Elaine added. "Maybe he didn't intend to give it back to Keith at all. Maybe he wanted it back to sell for himself. He told Keith he'd sold it and there was nothing he could do about it, but Carl thought maybe there *was* something."

Jan took up the thought. "We'd have recognized Carl if he came to the house. But Carlene wasn't at the flea market when we met Carl. Her son Mikey was. She'd left him with Grandpa. So maybe she owed Grandpa a favor, in return for babysitting."

"And what if Mikey put the teapot in a box of low-priced cookbooks?" Elaine asked.

Jan nodded slowly. "Anything's possible. And then Carl sent his darling daughter out to our house a couple of days later to reconnoiter."

THE DOORBELL RANG on Saturday morning, half an hour before opening time.

"That must be the postman," Elaine said. "I'll get it."

They had received a lot of parcels lately, and she was expecting envelopes and business cards she had ordered, as well as a shipment of exotic teas. But when she opened the door, it wasn't Orin Bond, their regular postman, who stood on the front porch. Instead, Heather Wells smiled at her. It took Elaine a moment to recognize the restorer without her close-up glasses and with her dark, gray-streaked hair loose about her shoulders. Heather's outfit was also much different from the jeans and casual tops she wore while at work. Today she was dressed in a blue print sundress, topped by a short white shrug.

"Well, hi! Don't you look lovely," Elaine said. "Come on in."

Heather grinned and came into the hall. She held up one foot daintily. "Monday's Memorial Day, so I thought it was time to break out the white sandals."

Elaine laughed and brushed a hand through the air. "I'm not sure anyone cares about that rule anymore, but my mother taught me the same thing. Are you here for tea? We don't officially open for a few minutes, but I'd love to sit down and have a cup with you."

"Actually, I'm here about your teapot. But don't let me keep you from your work. You must have a lot to do in the morning before opening."

"We're fine," Elaine said. "Come meet my cousin, won't you?"

Rose was restocking the supply of clean spoons and fresh napkins in the east parlor. Elaine took Heather through to the kitchen, where Jan was boxing up muffins for Rue Maxwell. She looked up from her work and gave Elaine a tentative smile.

"Jan, this is Heather Wells, the woman who restored our Chinese teapot."

"How nice to meet you." Jan stripped off her latex gloves and walked over to take Heather's hand. "I should thank you for rescuing Elaine and our treasure the other day."

"I'm glad I got there in time. I'm still furious at Jake. He's out on bail, you know."

Elaine winced. "Officer Wilson said he probably would be soon. They are going to press charges though?"

"Oh yes," Heather said. "I have an appointment with the assistant district attorney next Tuesday. And I wanted to come by and tell you in person what I've learned about the teapot."

"You found out more? That's exciting. Good news, I hope?"

"Well, it depends on how you look at it. But my appraisal stands."

"That's good."

Jan walked toward the sink. "Why don't you ladies sit down and let me bring you a cup of Elaine's new green tea blend? This sounds like serious business."

"I'd love it," Heather said, "but you open in a few minutes."

Jan glanced at the clock. "There's time."

"Let's sit out here," Elaine said, taking her to the round kitchen table. "That way, we'll be in private, and our server, Rose, can open if we're still talking at ten."

While the tea steeped, Jan brought over a plate of scones and muffins.

"Oh my," Heather said. "These look great! Are you doing a booming business?"

"In a small way, we are," Jan said.

"We've already got a B and B having Jan make their muffins for them," Elaine said, unable to hold back her smile. She was proud of Jan's skill and the energy she had put into the baking end of the business.

"Wonderful. Are you ready for the big news?"

"I think so," Elaine said, with a glance at Jan.

"Okay. Remember I said I'd seen your teapot somewhere before? Well, yesterday, I found a photograph of it."

"*Our* teapot?" Jan stared at her. "You mean one just like it?"

"No, I mean your exact teapot. The one Elaine brought to me."

"Where would you find a picture of it?" Jan's brow wrinkled.

"In a reference book."

Elaine looked at Jan. "Okay, I think you've got both of us intrigued, Heather."

"That's an understatement," Jan said.

Heather smiled. "Your teapot is very famous among people who know about such things. I admit, it's a small, select group, but the Chinese ceramics people all know about it. See, your little teapot was part of a collection of valuable artifacts that was stolen from a museum in England about sixty years ago."

CHAPTER NINETEEN

Elaine sat still, stunned at this revelation. After a moment's silence, Jan stirred. "I think we need that tea." She poured a cup for each of them and settled back in her chair. "So you're absolutely sure our teapot is a museum piece?"

"There's no doubt," Heather said. "Right down to the irregularities in the original glaze—which weren't visible before I stripped off the paint."

"Wow." Elaine lifted her teacup. "Tell us what this means. It was stolen?"

"Yes. Do you mind? Those muffins are calling my name." Heather reached toward the serving plate.

"Please do," Jan said. "I made bran, blueberry, and lemon poppy seed this morning, because that was what the B and B ordered."

"I've got to try the lemon." Heather selected one and took a bite. A dreamy expression transformed her face. *"Mmm!"*

Jan laughed. "Glad you like it."

Heather swallowed and took a sip of tea. "Fantastic. So the museum had several items stolen in one theft—about twenty pieces in all, and they were all small, portable items. Vases, bone dishes, rice bowls. Things like that, all valuable pieces, either because of their age or their artistry. The thing is, a few years later, these pieces started showing up in the United States."

"Someone was selling them?" Elaine asked.

"Right. The theft was never solved, but here and there, these things would show up in an auction. Different auctions, different cities, and placed there by different owners. The person who consigned each one claimed he had bought it in good faith and had no idea it was stolen. And the police were never able to trace it back to the individual who had sold it to him." Heather shrugged. "Of course, that was a long time ago, and we don't know what resources they had, or how hard they tried."

"How long ago are we talking?" Jan asked.

"Well, the most recent one—before yours—turned up in 1981. It was in a private sale. The previous owner had died, and the family was selling his collection. None of them could say where or when he had purchased it, but a sharp-eyed dealer spotted it and recognized it from old articles about the British theft. Before that one, I don't think any had surfaced since 1972."

Elaine blew out a slow breath. "So photos of each of the stolen items had been published?"

"Oh yes," Heather said. "It took me a while, but I found references to old trade journals that had publicized it, hoping curators and art dealers would help recover the pieces. And most of them were eventually found. I looked online, hoping I could find copies of those old magazines, but so far, I haven't been able to get my hands on any. But I did find an account of the theft in one of my books on pottery, and it showed photos of three of the more interesting pieces—including your teapot. It stated that this was believed to be the last piece that had not been recovered." She took out her phone and showed Jan and Elaine a photo she had snapped of the illustration.

"Wow, it sure looks like it," Elaine said. She passed the phone to Jan.

"Yeah, it does. When was the book published?" Jan asked.

"In 2008. I bought it when it came out and had read that part, but I didn't remember the details until yesterday. After hours of discouraging Web surfing, I got that book out, and there it was."

"We bought a treasure," Jan said.

Elaine looked at her, dismayed. "Yeah. A stolen treasure. Heather, what do we do now?"

"Maybe Nathan can advise you," Heather said. "He may have dealt with a situation like this before. After all, he handles some very valuable lots at his auctions. At some time over the years, he must have had a case where a stolen artwork showed up in his vault."

"That's probably good advice," Elaine said. "He can tell us whether we ought to call the police or not."

Heather reached for her purse. "I should go now, but there are some accounts of the museum theft online. Mostly, they don't have a lot of detail, but I can send you a link if you'd like."

"Thanks. That would be helpful."

"I think you have my card," Heather said. "My e-mail address is on that. And thank you for the delicious breakfast."

Elaine walked out to the front door with her. "Thanks so much for coming, Heather. I'm sorry our teapot gave you such headaches."

Heather laughed. "No problem. It will be exciting if it's confirmed to be the missing museum piece."

As Elaine closed the door, Rose walked out of the west parlor.

"I was just going to change the sign and put out the Open banner."

"Is it time?" Elaine glanced at her watch. "Please do that, Rose. I'd better get my apron on."

She went back to the kitchen. Jan was clearing their dirty dishes.

"Are you going to call Nathan?"

"I thought I would. Rose can seat the first few customers." Elaine peeked out into the hall. "I'll give him a call, and then I'd better get out there. We seem to have become a popular place."

NATHAN ARRIVED AT quarter past twelve and looked around at the busy tearoom with approval. Elaine stepped out from behind the counter to meet him.

"Thanks for coming."

"That's what lunch hours are for."

"Jan said she would have sandwiches ready for us, if you want to talk in my office."

"Things look awfully busy here." He glanced into the parlor on his left, where three parties were enjoying their refreshments.

"This is nothing," Elaine said with a chuckle. "You should see us at ten a.m. Noon is the slow hour, since we don't serve meals." Rose came out of the east parlor with a tray held vertically against her side.

"This is our server, Rose Young," Elaine said. "She's a gem, and we're so glad to have found her. Rose, this is Nathan Culver."

"Hello." Rose's bright smile beamed out.

"Glad to meet you," Nathan said.

"We'll be in my office," Elaine told her. "Seat any newcomers in your station, and if it gets too hectic, come and get me."

"Will do."

Elaine led Nathan to her office and then went to the kitchen door to signal Jan that they were ready. Jan brought in a plate of sandwiches, coffee for Nathan, and water for herself and Elaine. They set up the cleared desktop as their luncheon table.

"This is great," Nathan said. "I didn't realize I was getting a meal."

"Just a picnic," Jan said. "We couldn't have you sacrifice your lunch hour for us and not feed you."

"Oh, by the way, I brought you gals something. Sort of a grand-opening gift." He reached into an inner pocket and brought out a small silver item about four inches long, like decorative tweezers with molded silver flowers on each branch.

"Sugar tongs!" Elaine took them in delight. The workmanship told her they had been carefully made by a master silversmith. "Look, Jan. Aren't they wonderful?"

"They sure are."

Nathan shrugged. "They were in a box lot, and I bought them out of the auction. But I don't suppose you serve cubed sugar here."

"No, but we can put them in our locked display case with our special teapots," Elaine said.

Jan nodded. "Perfect. Thank you, Nathan."

While they ate, Elaine caught Nathan up on what Heather had told them, and also Jan's connection between the man outside the flea market and Keith Howell.

"You think this younger Howell was the person who sold the teapot to Joiner?" Nathan asked.

"We don't know for sure," Elaine said.

"But it looks like a strong possibility," Jan added. "I mean, we heard him objecting that someone had sold something as he went into the flea market, then Mr. Joiner called Elaine saying he wanted it back for another customer. Then I saw Keith Howell at his grandfather's house, and he told me they were selling old family possessions to raise money for Cecil's medical care."

"Yes, it does seem to fit together." Nathan took a bite of his ham-and-cheese sandwich and chewed with a thoughtful look in his eyes. "It might not be him at all who sold it to Joiner."

Elaine nodded. "If I knew it was theirs, and it was sold by mistake, I would want to give it back. But if it's been stolen..."

Jan nodded emphatically. "If Keith Howell stole it, we don't want to give it back to him."

"Keith is too young," Elaine said gently. "Remember, Heather said the museum was robbed sixty years ago."

"I'd heard about that," Nathan said. "One of the great unsolved antiques thefts. No one piece was fabulously valuable, but together they added up to a nice little nest egg for someone."

"It was in England," Elaine pointed out. "But Heather did say the items that have been sold have been in America."

"Someone moved them out of the United Kingdom and into the States," Nathan agreed.

"What do you think we should do?" Jan asked. "Should we call the police?"

"And if so," Elaine added, "which department? Since I bought the teapot in Waterville, I suppose we'd go to the city police."

Jan lifted her water glass. "We could ask Robert. He might be able to advise us on that."

"He's an old friend who's a lawyer," Elaine explained to Nathan.

"Good idea," Nathan said.

"What if we just go visit Cecil Howell and ask him if the teapot belonged to his family?" Elaine warmed to the idea. "If we could visit when Keith isn't there, he might open up to us."

Jan smiled. "I like that idea. We don't need to say anything about it being stolen. Just tell him we bought one, and we wondered if it came from things they'd sold at Mainely Bargains."

"It might work." Nathan looked at his watch. "I wish I could offer to go with you, but I need to get back to Waterville."

"We wouldn't dream of asking you to do that," Elaine said. "But I'll let you know how it turns out."

"Please do. And be careful, won't you? You don't want to upset the wrong people."

"You haven't had dessert." Jan jumped up.

"No time, I'm afraid. I have someone bringing in a large lot of art glass at one thirty."

"I'll get you a to-go bag." Jan hurried out.

Elaine rose and held out her hand. "Nathan, thank you again for coming out here."

"Not sure I did anything," he said with a winsome smile. "Just do call in the police if you find anything that points back to that museum theft, won't you?"

"Of course." She walked out into the entrance hall with him, where Jan met them with cookie bag in hand.

Elaine could see that a few more tea drinkers had come in. Rose's parlor was now full, and she had put Pearl Trexler and Kit and Marcella Edmonds in the west parlor. Elaine thanked Nathan again for his gift of the sugar tongs and hurried to see if Rose had taken their order.

"I did," Rose said, "but if you can get it, that would really help me. I didn't expect this many people during the lunch hour."

Elaine went to the kitchen for her apron and found that Rose had already started setting up a tray for Kit's party. A teapot with an infuser hanging inside was waiting for hot water, and a mug near it had hot chocolate mix in it. A custard cup of marshmallows sat beside the mug. Jan was studying the order slips Rose had left on her work island. "Looks like she prepared everything for this one, and we just need to fill their teapot."

Elaine smiled. "The cocoa is for Marcella. She's here with her mom and great-grandma."

Jan poured the hot water, and Elaine placed a peppermint stick beside the plate of cookies and squares so Marcella could stir her hot chocolate. When she returned to the table with their order, Marcella's eyes widened.

"Look, Grammy! Candy!"

"I hope that's all right," Elaine said to Kit. "I always felt special when I had a peppermint stick with my cocoa, instead of a spoon."

"We always did that at Christmas time, with a candy cane," Pearl said, smiling indulgently.

"It's okay," Kit said, but leveled a stern look at Marcella. "We're headed home from here, and you can brush your teeth first thing."

"I will." Marcella unwrapped the peppermint stick, grinning.

Pearl smiled at Elaine. "It's so nice to have a quiet place right here in town where we can get a good cup of tea."

"Grammy just celebrated her eightieth birthday," Kit said.

"*Shh*! You don't have to tell everyone how old I am." Pearl's eyes twinkled.

"Congratulations, Pearl," Elaine said with a quick pat on her shoulder. "That's quite a milestone."

"I only have two more weeks of school," Marcella said, "and Daddy starts his summer job Tuesday."

"His summer job?" Elaine glanced at Kit. "That's right, he delivers the mail on the lake by boat during the summer, right?"

"Yes, and he loves it. Yesterday was his last day at the sorting center until after Labor Day. And he gets Monday off, of course."

"It's a holly day," Marcella said.

Elaine smiled. "I know."

"We're going to a parade," the little girl added. "Mommy, can we come here after the parade?"

"Will you be open?" Kit asked.

"We're planning on it. I'm told Memorial Day is a big business day on Chickadee Lake."

"There'll be lots of summer people coming in," Pearl said. "I saw three RVs headed down toward the campground this morning."

"Can we go camping?" Marcella asked.

"Not this weekend, honey," Kit said. "We may have Monday off from school, but I still have a lot to do."

"You must have a lot of papers to grade and things like that, this close to the end of the school year," Elaine mused.

"I sure do. I have more homework than the kids right now."

More customers came in, and Elaine went to wait on them. The flurry of patrons lasted most of the afternoon.

"Wow, they weren't just a-kidding about the summer people," Jan said at four o'clock, when they closed the door on the last one. "We ran out of scones and the cookie of the day."

"I hate to say it, but you'd better make even more for Monday," Elaine said. "I'll help if you like."

"I don't mind a bit," Jan said. "It means we're getting off to a good start."

"I could help you too," Rose said. "I really liked helping fill the cream puffs the other day."

"Great," Jan said. "Be here by eight Monday morning, and I'll put you in charge of cream puffs. That's a muffin day for Rue Maxwell too."

"We can make them the night before," Elaine suggested. "I'll pack them up for you Monday morning, and you can do cookies and pastries."

"Teamwork." Jan nodded. "Now let's clean up this joint."

An hour later, the parlors and kitchen were spotless, and Rose had gone home. Elaine and Jan were ready for their visit to Mr. Howell, or so Elaine thought.

"Are you sure we should do this?" Jan asked.

"I thought we were agreed." Elaine eyed her cousin's face carefully. "Are you afraid it will stir up trouble?"

"Well, I don't know. If we bring up the teapot, and he knows about it, he must know it was stolen."

"Not necessarily." Elaine thought about it for a moment. "Okay, if Keith is there, we won't say a word about the teapot. We'll just inquire about Cecil's health and give them the cookies."

"Right." Jan picked up the box of a dozen assorted cookies she had packed. "Let's go."

CHAPTER TWENTY

Keith's truck isn't here." Jan pulled into Cecil's driveway.

"Good," Elaine said. "Should we knock?"

"No, Keith said to go around back so Cecil doesn't have to get up and unlock the door."

They walked to the end of the driveway and around the side of the old house. Jan noted that the lawn had been freshly mown. Perhaps Keith had stopped by that morning, since it was Saturday, to do some chores for his grandfather. They found the steps leading up to a small back porch. Jan knocked on the door, then opened it and stuck her head inside.

"Hello? Mr. Howell, it's Jan Blake. May I come in?"

"What?" came his gruff, scratchy voice. "Who did you say?"

"Jan Blake, from the tearoom."

"Did you bring cookies?"

She smiled at Elaine. "Yes, I did."

"Well, what are you waiting for?"

They walked in through the kitchen. It had an outdated air, with cabinets of scored plywood and a porcelain sink. The dark linoleum on the floor was chipped around the edges, and the refrigerator definitely had been around for decades.

Elaine followed her through to the front room. As on their first meeting, Cecil sat in his recliner with his feet elevated and a woven afghan across his lap.

"Hello," Jan said cheerfully.

Cecil stared past her and frowned. "Who's this?"

"My cousin, Elaine. She grew up in Lancaster too. She's my partner in the tearoom business."

"Hi," Elaine said. "I'm pleased to meet you."

Cecil nodded but didn't smile.

"We brought you some cookies." Jan opened the white box and held it down where he could see the contents. She had arranged three rows of four different kinds of cookies.

"What are those?" He pointed to a row of cookies with red lumps in them.

"Oatmeal cookies with cranberries," Jan said.

"Didn't you ever hear of raisins?"

She laughed. "Sure I did. I was getting fancy for the tearoom."

"Hmpf."

"I also put in some white chocolate chunk cookies, and some gingersnaps and coconut macaroons."

"I hate coconut."

"Then it's a good thing I didn't put any in the other cookies, isn't it? You can save those for Keith, or if you don't want them here, I'll take them away. Now, let me bring you a glass of milk."

"I'll get it," Elaine said. "If you don't mind, that is, Mr. Howell."

"What I really want is coffee."

Elaine shot Jan a glance.

"Now, you can't put that one over on me," Jan said. "Keith said you're not supposed to drink coffee."

Cecil sighed. "All right, all right."

While Elaine went to the kitchen, Jan took a seat near Cecil and remarked on the weather and the amount of summer visitors flocking to their cottages on the shores of Chickadee Lake.

Elaine came back with the milk, and Jan hopped up to take the glass from her.

"Did you mention the teapot?" Elaine whispered.

"Not yet. Are you sure that's a good idea?" Jan's curiosity burned fiercely, but she didn't want things to backfire on them.

Elaine made a face—one that Jan interpreted as "We're in this now, and we can't back down."

Jan took the milk to Cecil and smiled. "Here you are."

He took the glass and set it on the end table next to his chair.

"I do hope you enjoy the cookies," Elaine said.

"You want one?" he asked.

"No, thanks. Unless you want us to eat the macaroons."

"Go ahead." He held out the box, and Jan and Elaine each took a coconut macaroon and sat down.

Jan waited until Cecil had eaten a gingersnap and selected a white chocolate chunk cookie.

"You know, I got to thinking after we met the other day. I believe I saw your grandson once before that."

"Oh?" Cecil didn't seem particularly interested.

"At the flea market in Waterville," Jan said.

Cecil's chin jerked up, but he didn't say anything.

"That's right," Elaine chimed in. "It was a few weeks ago. Wasn't Keith going in when we were coming out?"

Jan nodded. "We had bought some things for the tearoom that day."

Cecil stopped chewing. He reached for his glass of milk. He took a sip and set the glass down on its coaster. "So? What kind of things?"

"Cookbooks, mostly, and a teapot."

"A teapot, huh?" He took another bite of his cookie.

"Yes," Elaine said. "We actually bought two that day at Mainely Bargains, from two different dealers."

Cecil chewed pensively, swallowed, and said, "Keith took some stuff there to sell. Old dishes and things. He thinks I've got enough old stuff that it could help pay for my treatment."

"Are your treatments expensive?" Elaine asked.

"Yeah. And they don't think I should stay here by myself. Do you know how much those assisted living places cost?"

"Yes, I do," Elaine said. "I sympathize with you there. Any place offering assistance or medical care is sky-high these days."

"Yeah." Cecil took another bite of his cookie. After swallowing, he looked at Jan. "You make these?"

"Uh-huh."

"Not bad."

Jan smiled. "Thanks. So, uh, what kind of dishes are you selling, Cecil? You don't have any teapots, do you? We still need a few for the tearoom." She glanced at Elaine, hoping her cousin was okay with her line of questioning.

"Well, I had one." Cecil shook his head. "My wife loved it, but it didn't look like much. I'd kept it all these years for sentimental value, you know? She's been dead over twenty years now, but I held on to that thing. But it's gone now."

"Was it old?" Elaine asked.

"Pretty old."

Jan cleared her throat, sent Elaine a glance, and plunged in. "I don't suppose your wife had painted over it? One of the ones we got at Mainely Bargains had been painted over, with some pansies on the side."

"Pansies, huh?"

Jan nodded. "The background paint was a light yellow. But it wasn't the kind of paint they use for glazes on ceramics. It wasn't shiny and smooth enough. I don't think it had been fired after it was painted."

They sat in silence for several seconds. Cecil took another drink of his milk and set down the glass. "That could be the one. My wife liked pansies."

Jan wasn't sure what to say. She looked at Elaine, who seemed to be struggling as well.

"So what happened to it?" Cecil asked. "Have you got it at the tearoom?"

"No," Elaine said. "After we bought it, we had the paint removed."

"I see."

"And we learned that it is actually quite valuable. Did you and your wife know that?"

Another long silence followed. At last he said, "Just sentimental value. That's all."

Jan wished the old man would show some emotion, but she suspected he had years of experience in hiding his true feelings.

"I have a picture of it, from before the paint was stripped." Elaine took out her phone and clicked a few times. She held it out so that Cecil could see one of Nathan's photos on the screen. "Is that your wife's teapot?"

He sighed. "Yeah."

"We really like it," Jan said. "Where did she get it?"

His lips twisted. "Might have been a wedding present."

"A wedding present!" Elaine sounded cheerful about it. "That's nice. When did you two get married?"

"Or maybe I bought it," Cecil said. "Yeah, I think I probably got it for her in a bunch of stuff. After we were married, you know? For the house. Teacups and things, you know? Keith shouldn't have sold that, but he didn't know it was—that I wanted to keep it. The boy didn't know any better."

"I'm guessing you got it about sixty years ago," Elaine said, keeping that upbeat, cheerful tone.

Cecil took a sip of his milk and then sat in silence.

Jan looked at Elaine for direction, but her cousin seemed at a loss too. After a few more seconds, Jan stirred. "Well, we should probably get going. I hope you enjoy the rest of the cookies." And she really did, but knowing what she and Elaine would do next made her feel like a hypocrite.

"Do you want us to lock the back door?" Elaine asked. "Will your grandson be in tonight?"

"Just leave it," Cecil said. "Here. Put that in the kitchen." He held his empty glass out to Jan.

"Sure," she said. "Is there anything else we can do for you before we go?"

He shook his head.

"Well, good-bye then," Elaine said.

Her heart heavy, Jan followed her to the kitchen, where she paused to rinse out the glass and leave it on the drain board. She sent up a silent prayer for wisdom.

As soon as they were outside and the door was shut, Elaine said, "What now? Should we call the police?"

"I suppose so." Jan frowned, trying to think of another way to proceed.

"Maybe you should call Bob," Elaine suggested.

That sounded just right. Bob would know if their flimsy evidence was worth troubling the authorities. Jan's burden seemed lighter. Even if Bob advised them to go to the police, she would have the assurance that someone who knew the law thought they were doing the right thing. Not just someone, she admitted to herself. Bob. His opinion counted.

"That sounds like a good idea," she said, shooting Elaine a sideways glance.

Elaine looked thoughtful as she opened her car door.

ELAINE TOOK THE lead as they entered the Waterville police station the next morning at eight o'clock, and Jan and Bob followed. In the lobby, Elaine turned to consult them. Jan looked pale, leaving her coral lipstick and blue-framed glasses the only color on her face. She had probably never been to the police station before. Despite Bob's encouragement, Elaine knew she hated accusing Mr. Howell of a crime.

She touched Jan's shoulder lightly. "It's okay. Really."

Bob looked at Elaine with sympathy. "Would you like me to speak to the duty officer and explain the situation? I talk to cops all the time. In fact, I know most of the Waterville officers."

"Would you?" Elaine asked. "Thank you very much." She led Jan to a row of chairs against one wall. "Sit down, honey. We may as well relax until they're ready for us."

Bob went to the safety glass window in the wall and spoke to the receptionist behind it. She directed him to a door to one side. After a moment, a uniformed officer came out and stood talking to him for several minutes. When he turned toward the cousins, Elaine stood and took Jan's hand, pulling her up.

"Come on. I think he wants to talk to us."

"Hello, ladies," the officer said with a restrained smile. "Mr. Claybrook tells me you think you may have unknowingly bought a stolen item."

"That's right," Elaine said. "We've been told it may be part of a museum collection stolen in England sixty years ago."

The officer arched his eyebrows. "We don't get a case like that very often. Won't you please come into our interview room? I'll see if one of our detectives can take your information and follow up on this for you."

They went with him along a hall past a dispatch console and offices where people were quietly working. The patrolman seated them in the small, bare conference room Elaine had visited with Nathan recently. He returned after a few minutes with a pleasant-featured man of about forty who introduced himself as Detective Adams. He nodded at Bob.

"Mr. Claybrook. Are you here as legal counsel?"

"Just as a friend," Bob said. "Of course, if these ladies need any legal help, I'd be happy to serve them, but they're just here to give you some information."

Elaine and Jan spent the next twenty minutes recounting how they had bought the teapot, Carl Joiner's attempt to buy it back, Carlene's snooping expeditions at their house, and finally Jan's recognition of Keith Howell and their meeting with his grandfather. Elaine did most of the talking, with Jan filling in a few details. She showed the detective Nathan's pictures of the teapot. Bob, meanwhile, sat quietly at the end of the table and sporadically wrote notes on a small notepad.

Elaine took a folded sheet of paper out of her purse and handed it to Adams. "I copied a link for you to an online article about the museum theft. And this is Heather Wells's address and telephone number. She said you may contact her about this."

"Thank you," Detective Adams said. "That's helpful. And you think this man, Cecil Howell, is the one who stole the museum collection?"

"We don't know," Elaine said. "We only know that our teapot may very well be the artifact still missing from that stolen collection, and we're pretty sure it came to Carl Joiner's booth at Mainely Bargains by way of the Howells."

"And Cecil Howell has the remnants of a British accent," Jan put in.

The others stared at her.

"It's a small thing," Jan said, blushing, "but the theft did take place in England."

"It's true," Elaine said. "He does sound slightly British, even though he's lived here many years. I didn't think about it until you mentioned it, but I noticed it yesterday when we visited him."

"Okay, we'll see what we can find out about all this and pay Mr. Howell a visit," Detective Adams said.

Jan opened her mouth and then closed it.

"Yes, Mrs. Blake?" the detective asked.

Jan's face was still suffused with a lovely pink. "I was just going to say, Mr. Howell is in his eighties, and he is quite ill. His grandson said he really needs more care than he's getting. He's trying to raise money for assisted living or a nursing home."

Adams nodded, his lips pressed together. "We'll take his health into consideration, ma'am. But if he is responsible for this heist, he will be arrested."

"I understand," Jan said.

"Of course, he may not be behind it," Adams went on. "He might just be someone who bought one of the stolen artifacts. But your instincts were right. We need to get to the bottom of it."

Bob spoke for the first time since the interview began. "Or he might not be connected to the theft at all."

"True," said Adams. "Innocent until proven guilty. But you want to know if he's guilty, or you wouldn't be here."

Elaine looked at Jan and nodded. "We do, detective. And we'd also like to know what we should do with the teapot while you're looking into it. Should we bring it to you?"

"You said it's in the vault at Culver Auctions?"

"That's right. I can tell Nathan to show it to you anytime, if you'd like it to stay there."

"Let's leave it at that for now," Adams said. "You know it's safe there. If we bring in an expert to authenticate the piece and determine whether it's part of this museum theft you spoke of, we'll contact you and Mr. Culver."

"That's fine with me," Elaine said. "Jan?"

"Of course," Jan said.

When they got outside, Jan let out a deep breath. "That was a little scary."

"Are you okay?" Elaine asked.

Jan nodded. "I don't think I've ever talked to a detective before."

"Anytime you need to, I'll be happy to go with you," Bob said.

"Well, let's hope it doesn't happen again soon." Jan managed a chuckle.

Elaine smiled and held out her hand to him. "Thank you so much, Bob. I know we both felt easier about this meeting, having you with us."

"Glad to do it." Bob looked at Jan. "And I mean it. Anytime."

She grasped his hand for a moment. "Thank you. That means a lot."

Bob nodded firmly. "Have a good rest of the day."

The cousins got into Elaine's Malibu. "Should we go right to church?" Elaine asked.

Jan looked at her watch. "Sunday school will be half over when we get there."

"Maybe we should stop at home for a cup of chai tea and then go over for the worship service," Elaine suggested.

"Sounds good to me." Jan buckled her seat belt, and they set out.

Elaine was just driving into the village of Lancaster when Jan's phone rang. She took it out and frowned at it as the phone continued to ring.

"It's Bob. We just left him."

"Well, answer it," Elaine said, slightly exasperated. She put on her turn signal and eased into their driveway. Bringing the car to a halt, she waited to see what was going on.

"Hi," Jan said. She listened for a moment. "No!"

"What is it?" Elaine hissed.

"Really? Hold on, let me tell Elaine." Jan lowered her phone. "Bob says there's an ambulance at Cecil Howell's house."

CHAPTER TWENTY-ONE

Jan hung on to the armrest as Elaine quickly took the corner on to Birch Lane. She had been praying silently all the way out from Main Street. "I do hope he's all right."

"If he's not, they'll take him to the hospital," Elaine said. "He'll be in good hands."

Jan glanced over at her and decided to ask the question that was bothering her. "Do you think this is our fault?"

"How could it be our fault?" Elaine asked. Jan half expected her to make a joke about poison in the cookies, but instead, she asked, "Do you think our visit yesterday upset him?"

"He didn't seem too happy when we left," Jan said. "He knew what we were getting at. What if he had a stroke or something after we left?"

Elaine sighed. "I don't know. I suppose it's possible. If he did steal those museum artifacts, and he's gotten away with it for sixty years, I guess it would be quite a shock to have two women come poking around and asking about that teapot."

"Yeah. The last piece that was taken from the museum."

"He should have sold it when he sold the other things," Elaine said. "He would have gotten clean away with it."

"That's if he is the thief," Jan said.

"Yeah." Elaine slowed down as they came to Bob's house. He stood at the end of the driveway and waved to them. Elaine pulled in and parked behind his car.

He walked over to them as they got out, his face sober.

"Hi. I thought you'd want to know."

"Thanks for calling," Jan said. "Do you know what happened?"

Bob shook his head. "Not really. We just left the police station, and I doubt they've had time to contact him."

"You thought of that too?" Jan asked.

"Well..." Bob shrugged. "It crossed my mind that if Detective Adams had phoned him and started asking questions, he might have..."

"Had a heart attack?" Elaine asked gently.

"Yeah. But I don't think they would call him. They'd come out here in person."

As he spoke, a blue sedan with a flashing light bar on top rolled past the driveway, toward Cecil's house.

"That's Dan Benson," Bob said. "He's a state trooper, and he lives in town."

"We met him at church last week," Elaine said.

"Yeah, he was probably close by when the dispatcher got the call."

"Who called it in?" Jan asked.

"I don't know, but I think maybe Cecil's grandson," Bob said. "I walked down the road before you got here, and I saw a pickup in his yard."

"Keith had a pickup the time I saw him there," Jan said.

"He probably came to check on him and found he was ill." Bob stood staring toward the flashing lights.

"I feel terrible," Jan said. "We shouldn't have pushed him. We should have gone straight to the cops with what little we knew and not tried to question him."

Elaine walked over and put her arm around Jan. "I'm sorry. You were having second thoughts before we went over there. I should have listened."

Jan let out a big sigh.

They waited another ten minutes, and then the ambulance pulled out of Cecil's driveway and drove past Bob's house with its red lights flashing. Behind it came Dan Benson's patrol car. Bob stepped out to the edge of the pavement, and Dan stopped his car, put his flashers on, and rolled down the passenger window.

Bob leaned down to speak to the trooper. "Hi, Dan. Is Mr. Howell going to be okay?"

"Well, they're taking him to MaineGeneral to check him out," Dan said. "Officially, I'm not supposed to say much, but it could be worse. His grandson's in the ambulance with him."

"Okay, thanks. I've got Keith's number. I can give him a call later and check on Cecil."

"Yeah, I'm thinking they might keep him a couple days and try to get him into a nursing home or something—but I don't know for sure. Talk to Keith. He's the one who found him in distress."

"I'll do that." Bob stepped back and waved. "Thanks."

Dan's car rolled away, and Bob turned back to the cousins.

"So you ladies were headed to church?"

"Yes," Jan said. "We might make it on time, just."

"We should go," Elaine said. "How about you, Bob?"

"I've been going in Augusta," he said, "but I can't make it on time now. Maybe I'll go to Lancaster Community with you."

Elaine smiled. "Want to ride with us?"

"I'll bring my car," Bob said. "Don't want to make you have to bring me home again."

"Okay, see you there." Jan climbed into Elaine's car, and she pointed the car toward the village. The church bell was ringing as they pulled into the parking lot. Bob found a spot near theirs, and they entered together. Half a pew was empty two-thirds of the way back from the pulpit, and the three of them slipped in, Elaine first, then Jan, then Bob on the aisle.

Jan felt suddenly self-conscious, sitting beside him. The pianist played the introduction for the first hymn, and she pulled a hymnbook from the rack. Elaine took the other one. Jan found the page and swallowed hard, then held the book out. Bob took one side and held it low enough so that she could see the music easily. How many years had it been since she'd shared a hymnbook with a man? Not since Peter had died, that was certain. The slight giddiness she felt now annoyed her.

Preposterous. Bob was just a friend.

She told herself that several times as the service progressed. During the opening prayer, she added her own silent petition—*Calm me, Lord. Help me to focus on Pastor Mike and not be silly.*

After that, she felt more herself. But it *was* nice having a tall, handsome man in a suit beside her.

When the benediction was done and people flooded the aisles, several parishioners approached Bob with enthusiastic greetings and hearty handclasps. Jan wasn't surprised that Bob knew almost everyone and was a popular local figure.

Bristol Payson sidled up to Jan, smiling. As usual, she looked confident and charming. Her cornflower sweater set accented the blue of her eyes. "Hi! I saw Bob Claybrook come in with you."

"Oh, well, his neighbor is ill, and Elaine and I had been out there to see about him." Somehow that sounded flat.

Elaine, at Jan's elbow, smiled at Bristol and leaned in. "Bob's an old friend, and a former classmate of ours."

"How nice! Mark knows him better than I do, but he seems like a great guy."

Bob, who had been talking to farmers Gavin and Ethan Richardson, looked around as if searching for the cousins. When his gaze lit on Jan, he smiled.

She felt her face warm, and looked away after returning Bob's smile. "How are things at the Bookworm?"

"Great," Bristol said. "Since tomorrow's a holiday and the kids will be out of school, I'm doing a story time with some new children's books. I'm having Dori Richardson, Annie and Gavin's daughter, come in and help me with that."

"Sounds like fun," Elaine said.

Bob came toward them, shaking hands with more people along the way. When he reached them, he said, "I thought I'd head out and see if I can get hold of Keith. He gave me his cell number last fall, in case I noticed that his grandfather needed anything."

"Do you mind calling us with an update later?" Elaine asked.

"Sure."

"Great to see you, Bob," Bristol said.

He nodded at her. "Hi, uh...Bristol, isn't it?"

"Yes. I'm Mark's wife."

"Sure, I remember. Nice to see you." He touched Jan's arm lightly. "I'll call you later."

"Thanks," she said. "'Bye."

"Is it serious with the neighbor?" Bristol asked.

"We don't know yet," Elaine said. "Jan and I had just been over to visit Mr. Howell yesterday, and it was a bit of a shock when we heard he was going to the hospital by ambulance this morning."

"That's too bad."

"Bristol, could you use a couple of dozen cookies for your story hour?" Jan asked on impulse. "I could send some over in the morning."

Bristol's eyes widened. "Well, sure. That would be great. But you must be busy too."

Jan shrugged. "We're all in this together as businesses. Besides, we love you and your store. Since I'm making two hundred cookies anyway, what's another couple dozen?"

Bristol laughed. "Well, thank you very much. But nothing with peanuts please. I know one child has an allergy. And I hope tomorrow's a record-breaking day for the tearoom."

As they walked out to the car, Elaine patted Jan's shoulder. "That was sweet of you—no pun intended."

Jan shrugged, a little embarrassed. "No big deal."

"Well, I'm going to help you with all that baking you have planned for tomorrow."

"Great. I want to do the cookies today if I can. Rose is coming early in the morning to help with the muffins, danish, and cream puffs."

"Sounds good," Elaine said. "And if we get some good news about Mr. Howell, maybe we can go visit him at the hospital after we close tomorrow."

ELAINE SLEPT FITFULLY the next night. Cecil's plight, the mystery of the teapot, and business concerns ran through her mind. In addition, she was planning to bring her mother to the house for dinner the following Sunday. She tried to concentrate on the menu and at last drifted into sleep.

She woke and raised her head from the pillow. Had she heard something, or was it part of a dream?

After a moment's silence, she eased her head down again. Probably one of the creaks the old house was prone to make. Moonlight streamed in through her window. She had left it open a few inches, with the screen in place. Maybe she had heard a loon's call, or a lonesome dog baying.

Now that she was awake and thinking up scenarios for the noise she thought had roused her, she couldn't go back to sleep. She rolled over and began to pray silently for Cecil Howell. In her thoughts, she moved on to pray for Jan's peace of mind and the success of the business.

A *thunk* that definitely came from within the house startled her to alertness. She pushed herself up on one elbow and held her breath. All was quiet, and yet…

As nearly silent as possible, Elaine sat up and swung her legs over the side of the bed. Her toes encountered her fleece-lined moccasins on the bedside rug, and she slipped her feet into them. Cautiously, she pushed herself up and reached for the robe she had left draped over the footboard.

The moonlight gave her plenty of light within the bedroom, but the hall would be dark. She took her flashlight from the nightstand. As an afterthought, she also picked up her phone and tucked it into the pocket of her robe.

One stealthy step at a time, she worked her way to the door. Her room was over the kitchen, and as she moved, she thought she heard sounds from below. She stopped and turned her head, trying to catch every nuance. Cupboard doors closing? Maybe Jan had been restless and gone down to check her baking supplies. That was probably it.

Even so, Elaine took her time turning the knob to avoid making the door rattle, and then pulled it slowly toward her. The stairs were only a few steps away. Would they creak? She hadn't paid any attention until now to the noises that emerged when she stepped on the treads. Holding the railing, she gingerly transferred her weight to the first step. It didn't make a sound, and she brought her other foot down.

It seemed to take forever to reach the bottom of the stairs, and during that time she heard definite rustles, bumps, and squeaks from the kitchen. If the overhead lights had been on, she would have relaxed and gone down confidently to ask Jan what she was up to. But the only light coming out into the entrance hall from that end of the house was a weaving, bobbing beam. Someone was exploring the kitchen by flashlight.

Elaine hovered uncertainly, clinging to the newel post. She was sure that the person in the kitchen wasn't Jan. If she'd known that earlier, she would have gone to rouse her cousin, but now that would mean climbing the stairs again. She glanced upward, at the gloomy landing above. Did she want to risk it? And if she woke Jan, what would she do?

Lord, give me wisdom!

Who could be in the kitchen? Carlene. That seemed the most logical answer. Carlene had been to the house three times, openly curious, and maybe four if she came once on a motorcycle. The last time, she had sneaked upstairs to snoop, and she had asked more than once if she could see the kitchen. Would she be brazen enough to break in and ransack their house in the middle of the night?

Another thought struck her. Jake was out on bail. He was angry at her for exposing him, and he knew the value of the teapot. No one but Nathan, Heather, Bob, and the police knew where the teapot was, other than herself and Jan. Either Carlene or Jake might reasonably expect to find it somewhere in this house.

She was stuck in a bad place. From here, she couldn't reach Jan easily, and if she used her phone to call 911, the intruder in the kitchen would probably hear her. She pulled in a ragged breath and walked quickly to the door of the west parlor. In this room, she would be as far as she could get from the kitchen and still be on the ground floor. She flattened herself against the wall near the corner display cupboard and took out her phone.

She hesitated. What if she was wrong? What if it was Jan out there?

Maybe she could call Jan to alert her. If she was the one creeping about in the kitchen, they'd have a good laugh. On the other hand, Jan's bedroom was at the front of the house. Elaine doubted the person in the kitchen would hear her cousin's ringtone. Quickly she pressed the speed dial for Jan.

After three rings, Jan's sleepy voice said, "Hello? Elaine?"

Elaine turned into the corner and cupped her hand around her mouth and the phone.

"Are you in your room?"

"Of course! It's in the middle of the night. Where are you?"

"Downstairs. There's someone in the kitchen."

"What?" Jan's voice rose in panic. "Who is it? Are you okay?"

"I'm hiding in the parlor," Elaine said. "Call 911."

"Gotcha. Don't do anything rash."

Jan clicked off, and Elaine smiled grimly. Had she ever done anything rash? Well, maybe. She supposed coming downstairs before checking to see if Jan was in her room wasn't her most thought-out act.

She held down the button that would switch her phone to the vibrate mode, which made her feel quite smart. If Jan called her back, the ringing phone wouldn't give her away.

Above her, she heard Jan's muffled voice murmuring. That meant she had placed the call, but would the burglar hear even that quiet sound?

Slowly, Elaine tiptoed from the west parlor into the dining room. She reached out to grasp the back of one of the chairs to make sure she didn't bump into something and alert the burglar that she was awake.

The muffled sounds she had been hearing seemed louder, and now she heard footsteps. The door to the hallway that ran past her office and the private bath to the garage door stood open, and through it she saw a gleam of light. It grew brighter as she watched, and her pulse pounded in her throat. The intruder had left the kitchen and was coming down the hall.

Elaine squeezed against the wall at the side of the hutch. Maybe the bulky piece of furniture would conceal her if he only took a quick glance into the room. The rays of light illumined the long dining table and the chairs grouped around it. Would he take her pewter candlesticks? She felt the edge of the hutch, wondering what to do if he came in the room. Her fingers encountered the front of the little knickknack shelf at eye level. Elaine held her breath and gingerly groped for the item she had placed there a few weeks ago—the Shona crane sculpture. Her hand closed around the loop of the stately bird's neck.

The shaft of light disappeared. Elaine leaned forward cautiously, holding the stone crane with both hands in front of her. She could see a faint gleam. Where was he now? An unmistakable sound came from the direction of the hall: a file cabinet drawer sliding open. He was in her office, probably looking for money.

Her heart raced. Could she shut him in the office? She couldn't lock him in the room from the outside. Even if she had the key, which was up in her bedroom, he would be able to turn the latch and open it from inside.

The light beam flooded the doorway to the office, almost directly across the hall. Elaine took two quick steps back and collided with the chair at the head of the table.

All was silent for a moment, then his footsteps came, deliberate and relentless, toward her. Elaine scooted around the table and backed toward her former hiding place, but she was too late.

"Where's the teapot?"

Elaine couldn't place his low, urgent voice.

"Who are you?" She hated the quaver and swallowed hard.

"It doesn't matter. Just give me the teapot."

She hesitated, clutching the statuette so tightly that its stone shoulder hurt her hand. She sucked in a breath. "It's not here."

"Where is it then?"

She still didn't recognize the voice. It could be Jake, but it wasn't Carlene, she was certain. Carl, maybe?

She said in a rush, "I told you, it's not here. I don't know who you are. Just leave now, the way you came."

"Not until you tell me where it is." He raised the flashlight, shining it full in her face.

Elaine gasped and turned her head, squeezing her eyes tightly shut.

He was closer now, and a hand seized her around the neck. He shoved her back against the wall, next to the hutch, pressing on her throat. "Tell me."

CHAPTER TWENTY-TWO

Elaine's throat hurt, and her body went rigid. Her hands curled as she sent up a silent prayer that was more of a stifled yelp. She brought the Shona carving up quickly and struck him, and at the same moment, light flooded the room. She scrunched her eyes nearly shut and yanked to the side as the man staggered away from her with one hand to his ear. He went slowly down to his knees, letting out a moan.

"What is going on here?" Jan stood in the doorway that led to the hall. The burglar turned toward her, and she gasped. "Keith? What are you doing here?"

Elaine put her free hand to her throat and rubbed her neck lightly, trying to take it in.

"Keith? You mean this is Keith Howell?"

Jan stepped into the dining room. "Yes. I forgot—you haven't seen him since that time we passed him at the flea market."

"I didn't really notice him then." Elaine swallowed carefully. "My neck hurts. He was trying to choke me."

Jan drew in a quick breath and stared at her. "Really?"

Elaine nodded, and Jan's gaze went to the crane statue she still held.

"You clobbered him with that?"

"Afraid so."

Jan moved closer to Keith, who rocked back and forth on his knees, still holding his head.

"You might have killed him."

Elaine opened her mouth to protest, but at that moment she heard a siren in the distance.

"That will be the police." Jan bent over Keith. "Are you all right?"

"Jan," Elaine rasped out, "he tried to strangle me. I wouldn't get all sympathetic now." She shoved the statue onto the table and whirled to walk out the other door, through the west parlor, and into the entrance hall. She turned on the lights, both in the hall and on the porch, and unlocked the door.

The siren grew louder, probably waking everyone in the village. It cut off suddenly, just before a patrol car with flashing blue lights turned into the driveway. Trooper Benson got out and walked up onto the porch.

"Everything all right here?"

"We caught a burglar," Elaine said. "He was choking me, and I hit him with a stone bird."

"Slow down," Trooper Benson said.

"But he's awake," Elaine protested. "He might get away."

Benson's eyes widened. "Show me."

She led him quickly through the parlor to the dining room. Keith Howell was struggling to stand, with Jan holding on to one arm to support him.

"Mr. Howell," Dan said. "What's going on?"

"I, uh…" Keith rubbed his temple. "She hit me with something."

"It was that." Elaine pointed to the stone crane on the table.

Benson glanced at the statue and clicked his tongue. "You're lucky she didn't lay you right out." He pulled out handcuffs.

"My head," Keith said.

"Sit." Benson pulled out one of the dining room chairs.

Keith sat, still holding his head.

"Put your hands out."

Keith obeyed, and Benson put the cuffs on him so that his hands were in front of him. Keith immediately put his hands back up to the side of his head where Elaine had hit him. Benson touched a radio that was fastened to the shoulder of his uniform. "This is Trooper Benson. I need an ambulance at Tea for Two, on Main Street in Lancaster."

The dispatcher responded, and he looked at Elaine and Jan. "You both live here, right?"

"Yes," Jan said. "I'm Jan Blake, and this is my cousin, Elaine Cook."

"Nice to see you again. Now, what happened?" Benson looked at Elaine.

"I woke up, and I heard noises downstairs. My room is over the kitchen. I tiptoed down. Someone was in there with a flashlight, opening cupboards and drawers. I called Jan, who was upstairs." Elaine nodded toward Jan.

Jan met Benson's gaze. "Elaine said someone was in the house, so I called 911."

"Okay, then what?"

"I heard voices, so I came downstairs," Jan said. "When I came into the dining room, I couldn't see a thing, so I turned the lights on. Keith was—well, he sort of collapsed. I was shocked to see that it was him. I think we both were. And Elaine said he tried to strangle her."

Benson looked to Elaine, his eyebrows arched. "Is that true?"

"Yes." She opened the collar of her robe. "I don't know if you can see…"

Benson nodded soberly. "I can. Are sure you're all right?"

"I think so," Elaine said, "but I was very frightened."

"And how did you come to hit Mr. Howell with a—what is that?"

Elaine and Jan told him about the break-in, as well as their purchase of the antique teapot that led to tonight's events, and how Mr. Joiner had tried to buy it back from them.

"I went to the flea market to get it back, but Joiner had already sold the teapot to someone else," Keith said. "He wouldn't tell me who had bought it. He just said it was too late."

"Then how did you know who had it?" Benson asked.

"I saw a story in the newspaper. Some guy at a restoration place tried to steal it. And then this woman"—he shoved his chin at Jan—"came poking around my grandfather's place. I figured she had put two and two together and was trying to find out more about the teapot, so she must still have it."

"Hello?" called another male voice. They all turned toward the parlor door, and another man in uniform came in. The tall young man looked about thirty, and had wavy brown hair, trimmed short. He locked eyes with Benson and nodded. "Dan. I heard the call and wondered if you needed backup."

"Thanks. This is Sheriff's Deputy Arnie Sheffield."

The deputy nodded to Elaine and Jan, and Benson quickly apprised him of the situation.

"I've called for an ambulance in case he has a concussion," he concluded. "It should be here soon."

"I'll ride with him if you want," Sheffield said.

"Thanks," Benson replied. "But read him his rights first. I want him in custody when the ER's done with him."

"Got it."

They heard another siren in the distance. Sheffield walked over to Keith. Within a couple of minutes, he had determined that the burglar understood his rights and gotten him to his feet and out the door.

"Mrs. Cook, are you sure you don't want medical attention?" Benson asked Elaine.

"I'll be fine, but thank you."

"Okay, but I'd like to take a couple of pictures while you still have the bruises, if you don't mind. They could be crucial evidence."

"All right," Elaine faltered. First Jake Tunney, and now Keith Howell. She had a feeling she was going to become very familiar with the district courthouse. Her legs began to tremble, and she felt light-headed.

"Here, honey, sit down." Jan was at her side, urging her to take a chair. Elaine folded into it, glad it wasn't the same chair Keith Howell had used.

"Let me put the teakettle on," Jan said. "Elaine's had quite a shock." She bustled out of the room and returned almost immediately. "Trooper Benson, I think you should take a look at the kitchen before I touch anything. Keith seems to have made quite a mess out there."

"Oh no." Elaine started to rise, but Jan pushed her back down in her seat.

"You stay here, Elaine. You caught the burglar. I'll handle this part, and I'll get you some calming tea and some cookies."

By the time Benson had taken stock of the damage in the kitchen and snapped a few photos of Elaine, Jan had put together a tray, and the three of them sat at the dining table.

"Nothing's broken," Jan reported to Elaine. "He spilled several things though. I guess he was rummaging through the cupboards looking for the teapot, and he knocked over the powdered sugar and the baking soda. Then he apparently got the bright idea it might be in one of the canisters. That's all I can figure, because he dumped out the flour and the rolled oats. It's a mess, but we'll clean it up in the morning."

Jan told the trooper about Carlene's visits to the house, and Elaine filled in a few details about Jake Tunney's attempt to steal the teapot.

"I'll talk to Detective Adams about this," Benson said. "He'll want to know about this burglary attempt and assault."

"He was going to question Cecil Howell," Elaine told him, "but Mr. Howell went into the hospital. I don't know if he's had a chance to speak to him yet or not."

"I'll find out." Benson ate the last bite of his chocolate chip cookie and pushed back his chair. "I've got a lot to do. Ladies, I hope you can go back to sleep."

Elaine squinted at her watch, which showed that it was nearly 2:00 a.m. If her mind and heart would stop racing, she might get a few hours' rest.

TWO WEEKS LATER, Jan and Elaine were enjoying their breakfast on the screened porch behind the kitchen. After a heavy rain during the night, the lake was a placid sheet of blue. The sun's rays skittered off it, promising a bright, pleasant day.

As she drank a glass of orange juice, Elaine sat forward and stared down at the deck below.

"There's Earl Grey."

Jan leaned toward the screen door, her teacup in her hand, and saw the long-haired cat jump onto the deck.

"He's still beautiful," Elaine said.

Jan watched Earl gracefully mount the steps. She had been putting his dish of food closer to the porch each day. The cat was still wary, but he had yet to leave the proffered breakfast untouched.

"I know he can't come in the house," she said softly, "but do you think it would be okay to make him a bed out here?"

"A bed?" Elaine stared at her. "What sort of bed?"

"Oh, a basket maybe? Just someplace he can sleep when it's stormy or cold."

Elaine considered that. "I suppose so. But Earl might be someone else's pet, you know. Just because he comes here every morning doesn't mean he won't get another breakfast somewhere else. Or dinner."

"I know." Jan sipped her tea as the cat crept closer to the dish. He glanced warily at the porch and began to eat. He wasn't overly fat, but he didn't look undernourished either.

Elaine smiled as she poured herself a cup of tea from the pumpkin-shaped teapot. "So you want to make sort of a crash pad for Earl?"

"If he wants it." Jan reached for the small rosewood box she had brought downstairs with her. "Thanks for getting the ring out of the bank box."

"No problem. When is Tara coming to see it?"

"Around closing time," Jan said.

From inside the house, the doorbell chime echoed.

"That can't be Rose," Jan said. "She usually brings the boat if it's not raining."

"I'll get it." Elaine rose and took her dishes along, setting them on the kitchen counter by the dishwasher as she passed.

To her surprise, both Detective Adams and Trooper Dan Benson stood on the front porch.

"Good morning, gentlemen," Elaine said.

Adams nodded. "Hello, Mrs. Cook."

"We've been working together on the teapot case," Dan said. "We thought you'd like an update."

"Very much." Elaine opened the door wide and stepped back. "Jan and I were sitting on the screened porch out back. Would you join us there?"

"Sure," Dan said.

He and Adams followed Elaine past the checkout, through the entrance hall and kitchen, to the back door. As she opened the door to the screened porch, Elaine said, "Detective, this is where Keith Howell broke into our house."

He eyed the door, which had a new lockset and an additional deadbolt mounted.

"I see you've taken steps to make sure it won't happen again."

"Yes. We've been talking about whether or not we need an alarm system," Elaine admitted.

Jan had risen from her chair. "Good morning, officers."

"They came to bring us up to speed on the case," Elaine said.

"That's nice of you." Jan helped draw wicker chairs forward so that they could all sit overlooking the lake.

"You have a terrific location here," Adams said.

"Thank you. We love it," Jan said. "Can I get you some tea or coffee?"

"No, but thanks. I'm on my way to Augusta," Dan said.

Adams also declined. He took a small notebook from his pocket and flipped a few pages. "Our department has questioned the Joiners. Carl admitted to me that he sent his daughter to this address to look around and see if you had the teapot here. At first he thought you might be using it or displaying it. Apparently you had already taken it to Ms. Wells, so Carlene didn't find it."

Jan nodded. "We had no idea what she was looking for, until we realized she was related to Carl."

"The second time, she brought a friend with her and had her ask most of the questions," Elaine said, recalling the day she had served Carlene and Blair. "She probably hoped I wouldn't be suspicious if I thought Blair was the one interested in teapots."

"Is Carlene being charged with anything?" Jan asked.

"No, we didn't think charges would stick. She and her father claim they did nothing wrong and were only trying to locate the teapot for Keith."

Elaine sat up straighter. "But they told Keith they didn't know where it was."

"I know. It's questionable whether they would have told him, even if they found it. But since Carlene didn't actually take anything, and since she didn't return after you told her not to, I don't think we can make a trespassing charge stick."

"We've put a cord across the stairway now," Jan said, "and a sign that says Do Not Enter."

"If you'd had that up at the time, we might have a case against her," Dan said, and both women nodded.

"Keith Howell, on the other hand, will go to trial," Adams said. "He was caught red-handed here in the house. We'll be in touch when it's time for you to testify."

"Thank you," Elaine said. "I hope he wasn't hurt too badly."

"The doctor says he's fine," Dan said.

"Good. So what happens to the teapot now?"

Adams took some folded papers from his inner pocket. "I've brought some forms for you to sign if you still want to return it to the museum."

"We do," Elaine said firmly.

"Yes," Jan added.

The detective unfolded the papers. "I spoke to their representative by phone, and they were delighted to hear the last piece of the stolen collection had been found. If you ladies will sign this, it gives us permission to get the teapot from Mr. Culver. This second one gives us permission to give it to the museum's representative after we're done with it. They're going to send someone over here to get it, rather than trusting it to a shipping company."

"Oh my," Jan said.

Adams cracked a smile for the first time. "Yeah, big stuff. You had quite a treasure there. They're giving you five thousand pounds that was in a reward fund for this purpose. It works out to something shy of eight thousand dollars, depending on the exchange rate when you get it."

"But we didn't do anything," Elaine protested.

Dan shook his head. "Sure you did. You kept their teapot safe for them—and you could have been badly injured. Or worse."

"I'm fine now." Elaine touched her throat. The bruises had faded, and the slight soreness she'd experienced for a few days was gone.

"Let the museum do this," Adams said. "That's what they raised the money for, years ago. I'm sure you'll find a good use for it."

"Yes," Jan said. "We can discuss it, Elaine. We'll do something nice with it."

Elaine spread her hands helplessly. "All right."

"Good," Adams said. "You both need to sign this paper as well, for the museum."

As the two men prepared to leave a few minutes later, Rose was skimming toward the dock in her father's motorboat.

"It's almost opening time," Jan said. "We're not ready."

"I'll show the officers out," Elaine said. "You start steeping tea and arranging the muffins and pastries."

They had settled into a routine that no longer seemed hectic. With good planning, they were able to anticipate their customers' needs and keep ahead of their orders. Despite Brian's dire predictions, Elaine anticipated turning a small profit by the end of their first year.

Customers came in by twos and threes, starting as soon as she turned the Closed sign to Open. By midafternoon, Elaine was beginning to flag. When Macy and her daughter-in-law Zale Atherton left, Elaine put their dishes on a tray and wiped the table down. Zale, as usual, had left her a tip, and Macy, also as usual, had not.

She heard the excited voices of people entering, and a moment later, Rose came into her station.

"We've got a big party," Rose said. "I seated them in the east parlor, but if you're not too busy…"

"Sure, I'll help you," Elaine said.

"They've got kids."

Elaine glanced at the antique clock on the corner shelf. The local schools were still in session, but it was almost half past three. "Be right there."

When she crossed the hall a moment later, she caught a familiar laugh. Rose and Jan were both chatting with the newcomers—all of Jan's children and grandchildren. Not only had Brian and Paula brought their girls in, but Amy and Van were there with their five-year-old twins, and Tara, who at twenty-seven was still enjoying singlehood and a career in jewelry design.

"Hi," Elaine said with a smile. "You all made my day!"

"Isn't this a hoot?" Jan asked.

Amy came to give Elaine a hug. "We wanted to surprise you."

"Well, you succeeded."

Elaine walked over and gave Tara and Paula hugs. "Tara, it's wonderful to see you." She hadn't seen Jan's youngest since Ben's funeral.

"Same here," Tara said, brushing back a handful of curly, shoulder-length dark hair.

"We decided to celebrate again," Paula said.

"Yeah," Brian added. "You two seem to be doing all right, so we came to cheer you on."

"Thanks." Jan gave him a hearty hug. "That means a lot."

Brian patted her shoulders. "Good job, Mom. I mean it. I wasn't sure at first that this was the right thing for you, but it's starting to look like a success."

"A roaring success," Tara said.

Jan smiled. "Brian, I raised you three kids and survived it. Running a tearoom is a cinch compared to that job."

"Can't argue with you there," Amy said, rising from her chair. "Riley, don't stand on that." She crossed the room, scooped her son deftly off the window seat, and plunked him down on the cushion.

"Tara, Van, Amy, I don't think you've seen the house yet," Elaine said.

"We haven't, but what we've seen so far is beautiful," Amy said.

Elaine smiled at Jan. "Why don't you give them the tour? Rose and I will take care of my last party and set up tea and pastries for everyone."

"Sounds good, Cousin Elaine," Avery said. "Can I help?"

"We'd love that," Elaine said.

Rose smiled at Avery. "Why don't you come to the kitchen with me right now? We'll see what we can find for the twins to drink."

"There's plenty of milk in the fridge," Elaine called after them.

Jan led the others up the stairs. As Elaine walked toward the kitchen, she heard Kelly ask, "Grandma, can I show Max and Riley the tower room?"

"Yes, you may," Jan said. "But no running or yelling—we still have a few customers."

Twenty minutes later, her last patrons had left, and Elaine had finished tidying the parlors. Meanwhile, Rose and Avery had made two fresh pots of tea—oolong and peppermint—and set out a pitcher of milk and one of juice. They had loaded one of the tea carts with the day's leftover pastries, ranging from a few applesauce muffins and macaroons to raspberry brownies and lemon tarts. The family regathered in the parlor.

"Wow! If I came here often, I'd have to get a bigger wardrobe," Amy said, surveying the refreshments. "Mom, you didn't put on this kind of feast when we were at home."

"I wasn't serving dozens of people every day," Jan replied.

"Is that how many people come here?" Brian asked.

"More or less," Jan said.

Max and Riley, the twins, wriggled in their chairs until their mom had brought them cookies and milk.

"I love what you've done with the tearoom, and with your private quarters," Tara said.

"Thank you," Elaine told her. "You'll have to come visit us often."

"I'd like that."

"The guest room is open," Jan said.

Tara's smile broadened. "Do they have kayaks at the marina?"

"Loads of them." Jan grinned. "I'm told the rental fee isn't bad either, and if you want to bring your friends for a waterskiing party, they can supply everything you need for that."

"I'll think about it," Tara said. "Could be fun."

"Tara, how's your business going?" Elaine asked.

"Great. I just got a contract with a gift shop chain on the coast. They want to put my basic line in each of their four stores."

"You ought to go see the owners of the gift shops here in town," Jan said. "Maybe they would carry your jewelry."

"Not a bad idea," Tara said. "How far away are they?"

"You can walk to them from here. A Little Something has trendy jewelry, and Gift Me has only items made in the state of Maine."

"You should go there, Aunt Tara," Kelly said. "I'll walk over with you if you want."

Tara laughed. "Maybe so, honey. Let's eat some of your grandma's pastries first."

"So what happened to that fancy museum teapot?" Van asked.

"Yeah, Mom, sit down and tell us the story," Brian said, pulling a chair over from the next empty table.

Rose poured Jan a cup of tea, and she settled in between Brian and Tara.

Elaine found joy in watching them. Jan looked supremely happy with her family around her. Elaine sent up a prayer of thanks for their large clan.

"Here you go, Elaine." Rose handed her a cup of tea.

"Thanks."

"Maybe someday your kids and grandchildren will be able to come visit," Rose said.

"They're planning a trip. One bad thing about starting a new business is that I probably won't be able to travel for a while to see them. But Jared and Corrie are going to try to come here soon, and I hope my daughter Sasha can visit too."

"Maybe you can travel some when the tourist season is over," Rose suggested.

Elaine nodded. "You and Jan would probably be able to handle things in the off season. I'll think about that."

She sat down near Avery and Paula. Jan was just reaching the point in the story about the museum's offer of a reward.

"Wow, Mom," Brian said. "That might pay for all the renovations you've done—or at least part of them."

Jan eyed him sharply. "I'll have you know, we've already paid for those. We're not in debt."

"Good for you," Amy said.

Yes, Elaine thought. *Good for us. Very good for us.* She foresaw a peaceful, happy future for her and Jan. The teapot mystery had brought them a little excitement, but now both of them were ready to settle down to running the tearoom.

"So do I get to see the mysterious ring today?" Tara asked.

"Yes." Jan stood and delved into a pocket. "It so happens that we got it out of the bank Friday, just for you."

"I want to see it too," Avery said, leaning close.

Jan opened the square rosewood box and gazed down at the ring. "It really is pretty." She handed it to Tara.

"I love it. And the jeweler was sure it's a natural sapphire?" Tara asked.

"He seemed to be. How old do you think that setting is?" Jan asked.

Tara frowned. "Hard to tell. There are so many good reproductions nowadays." She eased the ring from its velvet nest, but part of the lining came with it and pulled away from the box. "Oops."

"Let me help you with that." Jan bent over the ring and freed it from the lining.

Tara tilted the ring and peered inside the band. "Wish I'd brought a magnifier with me."

Jan tugged on the corner of the velvet lining, and the whole thing came out of the box. She fumbled but dropped the small rosewood box, and Kelly sprang to retrieve it from where it landed near Elaine's feet. She picked it up and looked inside.

"Hey, it looks like there's something carved in there."

"Oh?" Elaine reached for the box and squinted at the inner side, where Kelly pointed. She saw scratches in a series of long and shorter lines. Dots maybe? "Wow, it really does. But I have no idea what it could mean." She handed the box to Jan.

Jan folded the edges of the liner under carefully. "We'll have to look at it later, when we're near a magnifying glass." She set the box on the table and deftly pushed the velvet liner in.

"That looks good," Elaine said.

"Can I try on the ring?" Avery asked.

"Oh, I think it should go back in that nice little box, and we can all just look at it," Tara said.

Jan said, "Thank you, I think that's a good idea."

Tara slid the ring into its crease in the box, and Jan handed it to Avery.

"Here. You can look at it, and then pass it around. I know your mom and dad want to see it too."

Jan looked perfectly contented as the others exclaimed over the ring, but Elaine couldn't help wondering if Jan's thoughts were heading off in a new direction. Would she stay awake half the night wondering if that little box held a new riddle for them? Maybe her creative mind and Jan's scientific one would someday find out where that ring came from.

Elaine smiled as she watched her cousin and best friend. They might be in for a few surprises along the way, but this new venture with Jan was going to be amazing.

ABOUT THE AUTHOR

Susan Page Davis is the author of more than sixty novels and novellas in the historical romance, mystery, and suspense genres. She is the mother of six and grandmother of ten. A Maine native, she now lives in western Kentucky with her husband, Jim. Visit her Web site at susanpagedavis.com.

From the Tea for Two Kitchen

Buried Cherry Cookies

½ cup butter or margarine
1 cup sugar
1 egg
1 teaspoon vanilla
⅓ cup cocoa
1½ cups flour
¼ teaspoon baking powder
¼ teaspoon baking soda
¼ teaspoon salt
1 jar (10 ounces) maraschino cherries

Preheat oven to 350 degrees. Cream together softened butter or margarine, sugar, egg, and vanilla until light and fluffy. In another bowl, whisk together cocoa, flour, baking powder, baking soda, and salt. Gradually add to creamed mixture, stirring until well mixed. Shape into balls about one inch in diameter. Place them two inches apart on ungreased cookie sheet. With your thumb, press a dent in the middle of each ball. Drain the cherries and place one in the center of each cookie. Bake ten minutes or until the edges are set. Cool cookies on a rack.

Icing

6 ounces semisweet chocolate chips
7 ounces sweetened condensed milk

On low heat in a small saucepan, melt and blend the chocolate chips and condensed milk together. Frost each cookie, using about a teaspoon on each one to cover the cherry. Makes about three and one-half dozen cookies.

READ ON FOR AN EXCITING SNEAK PEEK
INTO THE NEXT VOLUME OF TEAROOM MYSTERIES!

Tea Rose

BY ERIN KEELEY MARSHALL

The next tea Rose and Elaine will serve to you is a personal favorite, the Russian Troika."

Jan Blake paused with a smile for the two dozen guests who had come to Tea for Two's first of two Saturday gatherings they were calling "Teas around the World." For an hour and a half that afternoon, the women had been introducing several teas from various cultures. And as always at Tea for Two, pastries were plentiful.

These events would help usher in the town of Lancaster's Fourth of July fest. Outside the three-story house that Jan and her cousin, Elaine Cook, had turned into a thriving business on the shore of Chickadee Lake, the earth had released its last hold on spring, and the heat of summer reigned over the sun-dappled waves beyond the windows of the shop. The air inside the cozy yet sophisticated space was scented with exotic spices and the buttery pastries that Jan turned out daily in the kitchen.

The tables scattered throughout the double parlor buzzed with chatter as Elaine and Rose, a local young woman they had hired shortly after opening the tearoom, placed a teapot on each table.

"You'll notice hints of bergamot, mandarin, and other orange varieties in this Russian black tea. The bergamot will be familiar from the China and Ceylon teas you tried a few minutes ago, but the other citruses make this one unique. When I think of Russia, I'm reminded of cold, harsh weather with snow piled high, so the warm tone of the citrus always is a pleasant surprise for my taste buds."

Several customers nodded as Jan gave them time to sample the drink and herself a chance to sneak a glance at the list in her waist sash. Rose was up next. She tucked the list back in its hiding place, then removed her blue-rimmed glasses to wipe the lenses. She breathed another quick prayer that Rose would be able to recite her part well.

Their first summer season had been eventful so far, and Jan knew the majority of the people sitting around her at least by name. Most had been strangers weeks ago but had become somewhat familiar to her, if not genuine friends, in that short time.

Many of the men, women, and even a few children in sundresses, shorts, and polo shirts had been regular visitors to Chickadee Lake for years; not quite locals, but summer regulars. Others were year-round residents, and Jan was thankful she would be able to enjoy their company long after the summer ended. She didn't much like good-byes.

Although a longtime resident of Central Maine herself, who had grown up in Lancaster, Jan was really more of a newcomer to Chickadee Lake than many of them, and she felt like pinching herself that this dream business of Elaine's and hers had become a reality that was affording both widows a way to connect with this community.

Only a few of the afternoon's patrons remained unknown to her. Jan replaced her glasses, then watched Elaine and Rose mingle and chat with the guests about which of the teas were their favorites and why.

She didn't recall ever seeing the distinguished older man sitting in the far corner of the larger east parlor, and she couldn't decide if his stern visage was off-putting or simply reserved. He seemed to keep to himself, even among his tablemates.

Jan also hadn't met the stylish couple who chatted pleasantly with Rue and Ned Maxwell at their table on the opposite side of the room. The Maxwells were in their thirties and owned the Northwoods Bed-and-Breakfast. Jan wondered if the woman with beautiful blue-black hair and her fair-skinned husband were staying at the B and B. Toned and well dressed, they looked like thirtysomethings fresh from the big city who could use some Chickadee Lake sunshine.

She made a mental note to introduce herself to all three newcomers before the event ended.

She glanced at her watch and saw that they were on schedule to wrap up the tasting session in the next fifteen minutes. It didn't seem possible after all the planning that it was nearly over already. At least they could do it all again the following Saturday.

Chickadee Lake's population had doubled when the summer season kicked off. The guest cottages, campsites, and bed-and-breakfasts were filled with vacationers on break from their off-season lives around the country. She caught bits of conversations about the chicken barbecue and corn boil the following weekend and plans for grilling and evening fishing after the tea.

She looked forward to the holiday hoopla; even all the preparation suited her because it built camaraderie in town and helped her feel a sense of belonging in her new home.

The past couple of weeks—actually the past month, Jan corrected herself—had been stressful and somewhat weighted with the recent death of Rose's mother. She welcomed a diversion for all three of them.

Elaine and Rose returned to Jan's side. "This has been a super idea." Elaine planted a kiss on Jan's cheek. "Great job, cousin."

"Well, shucks. Thank you for handling all the research and ordering the teas. It's been fun to discover new varieties and to learn some things I never knew that I never knew about our line of work."

Elaine's smile brightened her blue eyes even more. Like Jan, Elaine was in her midfifties. She still had only an occasional gray strand in her light brown hair that she kept short. Elaine turned her attention to Rose and reached over to wrap an arm around the younger woman's shoulders. "And kudos to you for the ideas for our outfits, and for finding these getups."

"Yes, Rose," Jan added. "They've been so fun. I've always wanted to wear a sari but never had an opportunity until now. I love it."

The women often dressed in Victorian costumes when hosting, but for today they had agreed on Rose's suggestion to play up the cultural theme by donning period dress from the various countries represented by the teas. Jan wore a shimmering silver Indian sari of pure silk that flattered her petite frame; Elaine, somewhat taller, wore a traditional African tribal dress in a caramel color accented by blue, red, and yellow beading; and Rose looked classically German in a patterned red dress with crisscrossed lacing on the white bodice. Her wheat-colored braid draped over her shoulder and finished the charming look.

To the guests, Rose appeared as cheerful as ever today, but Jan noticed the slight strain in her features that gave away the extra effort of maintaining a lighthearted façade.

Rose caught Jan's glance and lifted her mouth in a smile.

Too quick, definitely forced. Jan leaned over and spoke quietly, "You're next, but if you're not up for this I'll cover for you if you'd like. I know you'll do great, but you've had a rough few weeks."

Rose rubbed her hands together. "Thanks, Jan, but I'm fine. Getting ready for this has been a good break from going through Mom's things."

"Our guests will love your tea, Rose," Elaine encouraged, "and especially the dessert. I'll bring in the pastry cart and the next tea cart while you introduce them."

"Thanks, Elaine." Rose smoothed her skirt, then stepped forward to address the room. Most of the guests had finished the Troika tea, and suntanned faces turned a few at a time until Rose had everyone's attention.

"Hi there. My name is Rose Young, and as many of you know, I've been working here for a while." She swallowed. "I'm happy to share with you a tea that's native to my heritage and also a German pastry I grew up eating."

A twinkle shone from Rose's blue eyes as she looked toward Jan. "Jan's been a great teacher in the kitchen, but she also agreed to let me talk about my family's recipe for apple *kuchen*."

Elaine and Jan began delivering plates of the dessert, and on a whim Jan headed toward the distinguished stranger in the back corner. As she set a plate in front of him, he straightened quickly and slipped a piece of paper underneath the table. Jan got the impression that he didn't want her to see it.

"Here you go, sir. Enjoy," she offered in a whisper.

When he didn't respond, she followed his gaze, which was trained directly on Rose.

"I don't believe we've met," she continued. "I'm Jan Blake, co-owner here. Is this your first time at Tea for Two?"

He cleared his throat and met Jan's gaze briefly before focusing on Rose once more. His eyes were a greenish hue, his hair dark gray, and he wore a green golf shirt and gold watch. Handsome but not necessarily welcoming, Jan decided.

"Kuchen is popular in Germany, and my mother learned to bake it as a child," Rose continued. From her skirt pocket she withdrew a worn recipe card and held it up.

"How well do you know that woman?" the man asked without looking at Jan, and not really as a question but more as a statement that expected an answer.

Rose continued. "She passed it down to me, and it seems fitting to share it with you all today." Emotion caught her voice.

Jan exchanged glances with Elaine, who was heading back to the dessert cart. She knew Elaine was also hoping that Rose's mention of her mother wouldn't undo her resolve.

Something about the man's question, and Rose's current vulnerability, sent a feeling of unease through Jan, and she chose her words carefully. "Rose has lived here all her life." Making sure she smiled, she added, "And what is your name, sir? Where are you from?"

The man lifted a hand off the table slightly, a dismissive gesture that made Jan want to frown. The woman sitting next to him raised her eyebrows, as if to say, "I can't figure him out either."

Jan left him and returned to the cart for more plates. She and Elaine continued delivering kuchen, followed by more teapots, each one unique.

As people tasted the apple pastry and sipped their drinks, Rose explained about the tea. "East Frisian tea, known as *Ostfriesen* in German, is a loose tea like the others you've tasted today. It comes from the northwestern part of Germany. Before you pour it into your teacups—or tea *glasses*, as they often are called in East Frisia—place a few of the rock candies from your saucer into the glass. These candy sugars are called *kluntjes.*

"You'll see from the menus on your tables that the word doesn't sound like it's spelled. It's pronounced 'KLOONT-yuhs.' You may already have noticed a similar thing with the word *kuchen.* We Americans would pronounce it 'KOO-chin,' but in Germany the word is pronounced 'KOO-khin.' Anyway, when you pour the tea over the kluntjes, listen as they crackle."

Around the room, guests lowered their ears close to their cups. Smiles lit their faces.

"Next, place a few drops of cream around the inside edge of your glass to make the clouds, which are another signature element of this drink. The dark copper blend of black, Assam, Java, and Ceylon teas creates a malty and somewhat spicy character. Those ingredients mixed with the kluntjes and cream clouds feel like silk on the tongue." She paused for the guests to try their treats. Standing tall, she seemed composed.

She's doing well, Jan thought, but she knew Rose was grieving the loss of her mother as she spoke of her family connections to the tea and kuchen. What had been a source of love and happiness must be bittersweet now because Rose could no longer share these memories with her mom.

Elaine seemed to sense the underlying struggle too. "Rose and Jan have been holed up in the kitchen all week making the pastries on the table," she stepped up to explain, "but this one, I have to say, is extra special. Rose told me that the buttery cake base has coconut in it, and then it's topped with apple slices, an egg yolk and sour cream mixture, and finally cinnamon sugar. Then the whole thing is baked to perfection. It's heavenly, isn't it?"

As compliments erupted from all around, Rose lifted her head toward Elaine with a gentle smile. "Elaine is kind, and she is correct about the ingredients for the kuchen. Thank you for letting me share it with you." With that, she moved to stand next to Jan.

Jan placed a hand on Rose's back. "The East Frisian blend was our final sampling today. We hope you enjoyed it, along with the Indian teas, which were the Nimbu and Chai Hara. The Nimbu had the lemon-caramel flavor in a Darjeeling, and the Chai Hara was a green tea with cardamom, cinnamon, nutmeg, coriander, and ginger." She nodded to Elaine, who spoke next.

"We also gave you the African Red Bush, or *Rooibos.* It hails from South Africa and isn't a typical tea, but rather a medicinal herb that's harvested like a tea and is famous for its energy-boosting and antioxidant power."

Jan's turn again. "And then the China, Ceylon, Irish Breakfast, and Russian Troika teas. And finally, the East Frisian. Thank you for traveling the world with us from our lakeside tearoom. Who knew when you came to Central Maine that you would actually visit much more distant places?"

Chuckles followed, and a few chairs scuffed the floor as some people pushed back from the tables to leave. To Jan's dismay, both the stylish young couple and the stern older man all rose quickly and headed for the door. Several elderly women who were frequent customers had risen as well and were moving toward Jan, Elaine, and Rose. Jan knew she would miss her chance to meet the couple or find out more about the strange man. Resigned to the missed opportunity, she turned her attention back to her other customers and friends.

Rose excused herself quietly while Jan and Elaine visited up front with lingering customers and answered more questions about all things tea related. Priscilla Gates, the local librarian, and Bree Dickerson, the receptionist at the Lakeview Clinic, chatted at the counter while Elaine rang up their to-go bags of cookies.

Jan caught Rue's eye across the room and waved before heading back to the kitchen to get Rue's regular order of muffins for her guests.

"Cranberry-walnut, lemon poppyseed, and strawberry-cornbread this week," Jan said back up front as she handed the boxes to Rue. "I picked those strawberries fresh from Orchard Hill last week."

"*Mmm,* well, the boxes may be lighter by the time I get home! Ha!" Rue's blonde curls swung around the collar of her belted sundress.

"My lips are sealed." Jan smiled. "I was hoping to say hello to the couple sitting with you today, but they skedaddled quickly."

"Oh, the Tates? Yeah, they're fun. They've been with us a couple of days. I don't know where they had to get to just now, but I think they're planning to stick around town a few weeks, so maybe they'll be back."

"Three dozen still good?" When Jan saw that her question didn't register with Rue, she clarified. "The muffins. Are three dozen still enough each week?"

"You know, I almost ordered more because we're booked through July, but instead I'm sending our guests directly here."

Jan and Elaine exchanged grins.

"Thanks, Rue!" Elaine spoke up from behind the counter as the register drawer chimed again.

Rue glanced at her husband, who was accepting change from Elaine for the muffin order, while she kept talking a mile a minute. "Or I bring them in myself. Lila and Ray—they're the Tates—they happened to be the lucky guests I talked into coming with me today. I'm all about drumming up business for each other."

She winked conspiratorially. "I was hoping to snag the entire Burgess clan because there are six of them, but they're out on the water all day. You've met them, right?"

Jan acknowledged that she'd met the Burgesses, a family with four teenagers from Des Moines, Iowa. "They've been in a couple of times." She was about to ask if the man in green happened to be staying at the B and B, but Ned finished at the counter and came to stand next to his wife.

"Jan was asking about our guests, hon." Rue wiped a crumb from his beard stubble.

"Uh-huh," Ned mumbled, leaning away from his wife's fingers. "She can't take me anywhere without cleaning me up."

Rue shot Jan a long-suffering smirk, rolled her eyes, and changed the subject. "I'll try to remember to bring in some groceries for the food drive in a day or two."

The register kept ringing as customers ended conversations and came up to choose treats from the glass display to take home. An hour later, the last ones had left and quiet mellowed the shop while the cousins wiped down tables and stacked the remaining dishes on the carts in the east parlor to take to Rose in the kitchen.

As they each pushed a cart that way, Rose emerged with her keys and purse. "Oh, I'm sorry. I guess I thought I got the last of it." She started to set down her things.

"No trouble," Elaine answered. "We can finish up. Why don't you go home and relax?"

"Absolutely," Jan agreed. "And thank you again, Rose... Are you sure you're okay?"

Rose blinked. "Thanks, you two. I'll be fine."

"Is there anything we can do for you? How are you doing sorting through your mother's things?"

To Jan's surprise, Rose lifted both hands to wipe the sudden rush of tears that had welled up.

"Rose?" Elaine questioned, moving close and pulling the woman into a hug. "What's going on?"

Rose cried for a few seconds before she collected herself and attempted to brush off the cousins' concerns. "I'm okay. At least I will be. I think." She looked from one employer to the other and her jaw dropped slightly, as if she couldn't find the right words.

They waited.

Rose shook her head quickly, as though she wanted to brush off something unpleasant. "I... it's just that I... Well, here, I'll just show you." She reached into her purse and removed a folded piece of parchment stationery. She opened it and looked at it as if it carried a disease, then shoved it toward Jan. "I found this in Mom's things last night."

Jan took the paper and studied it for several seconds. "It's a death certificate."

"Yes, it is," Rose whispered. "Read the name and dates."

Jan's heartbeat quickened and a leaden feeling weighted her body. "Tatiana Rose Schultz. Born June 6, 1990. Died November 17, 1991." Other than the names, the words were in a foreign language that Jan guessed to be German.

"Yes."

Jan looked from Rose to Elaine and back to Rose. She didn't want to think what she couldn't help but think.

Rose nodded slowly, her face flushing a deep red and more tears threatening to overflow. "Yes, my birthday is June 6, 1990. And I am Rose. Rose Tatiana. That death certificate is too close to be coincidence, Jan. It's mine."

FROM THE GUIDEPOSTS ARCHIVES

This story, by Dottie Hicks of Cobbtown, Georgia, originally appeared in the November 2006 issue of *Guideposts.*

I live in a rambling old Victorian house in the village of Cobbtown, Georgia (yes, it's as quaint as it sounds), population 325. The house has a broad porch, parlors decorated with period furnishings, original pine floors, tongue-and-groove walls and ceilings and a Chickering baby grand piano my daddy gave me when I was ten years old. I like to think it's a warm and welcoming house. But I have to admit, there was a time that even in this special place, something was missing. My husband Peter had died a few years before. My son and his wife had moved to Florida, and my daughter and her husband were up north. I guess you could say I was a little lonely, even though I tried not to notice. I kept busy writing in a journal about my life with Peter; that comforted me. I was active in church. And, of course, in a house this big, there's always plenty of work to be done, although the truth is, I'm not very handy!

One day, when I was doing some errands around the house, the phone rang. "Hello?" I answered.

"Hello, Dottie?" the voice on the other end sounded a little formal, but familiar. "This is Jack Hicks." Of course! Jack Hicks. Peter and I knew Jack and his lovely wife Janice from our church in Statesboro, before we'd come to Cobbtown. In fact, I'd even asked Janice to play the organ at our daughter's wedding. "I don't know if you heard that Janice died," he said. I was so sorry. I'd had no idea. She'd gone very quickly. He took a long pause. "Dottie," he said, "I'm having a very difficult time, and I wondered how you're coping with Peter's death." I was so moved that he'd reached out to me in that way. I told him two things had gotten me through the toughest times: my writing and my faith. Jack thanked me, and hung up.

He called a few days later and asked me to have dinner with him. I froze. I was planning a trip down to Florida to see my son's family, I was looking after my parents, and I was working and directing my church choir. "I'm sorry," I said, "I just can't fit it in right now." He said he understood. Afterward, I wondered if I'd spoken in haste. Had I passed up a great opportunity for friendship? I wondered. I prayed for guidance.

Before I left for Florida, I sent Jack a note and asked him to call me when I got back. He did! We made dinner plans. Was this...a date?! At our ages—Jack, sixty-seven, and me, fifty-seven? Would we have enough to say to each other? Would it be awkward? I couldn't still my mind. But sitting in a restaurant in Savannah, all my worries vanished. We had plenty to discuss—our families, the ways we'd coped with our losses. Our hope that life would someday hold joy for us again.

"Dottie," Jack confided in me, "I was so scared of being alone after I lost Janice. I prayed that I'd meet a spirited woman to share the rest of my life with. Your name dropped into my heart."

On Valentine's Day 1998 Jack and I married. He came to live in the big Victorian house in Cobbtown. Soon I learned that God had not only sent me a sweet and gentle partner, but also an excellent handyman! There isn't much he can't do. With Jack there, the house was looking grander than ever.

My daughter, Shan, came up with an interesting idea. "Your home would be perfect for a Victorian tearoom," she insisted. She imagined British charm mixed with the best Southern hospitality. I had spent some time in England, and that's where I first had a proper afternoon tea, served in dainty porcelain cups—complete with cream and scones. I had always loved Victoriana. And to my amazement, I had amassed quite a collection of fine china and vintage linens and I even had some antique furnishings. I was intrigued with the thought.

Later, Jack and I discussed the idea. We had been blessed with this big, beautiful place. Wouldn't it be great to open it up for others to enjoy?

Now, people come from all over to visit our Victorian tearoom, which we named SereniTea. I know Jack and I brought such serenity to each other's lives when our hearts needed mending. Serenity, and love. That's what we hope to share with all of our guests when they sit down with us to tea.

We love to meet people and to offer a calm respite from a busy world. And would you believe Jack makes the most delicious scones? Everyone raves about them. Really, there's nothing he can't do!

A NOTE FROM THE EDITORS

We hope you enjoyed Tearoom Mysteries, created by the Books and Inspirational Media Division of Guideposts, a nonprofit organization that touches millions of lives every day through products and services that inspire, encourage, help you grow in your faith, and celebrate God's love.

Thank you for making a difference with your purchase of this book, which helps fund our many outreach programs to military personnel, prisons, hospitals, nursing homes, and educational institutions.

We also create many useful and uplifting online resources. Visit Guideposts.org to read true stories of hope and inspiration, access OurPrayer network, sign up for free newsletters, download free e-books, join our Facebook community, and follow our stimulating blogs.

To learn about other Guideposts publications, including the best-selling devotional *Daily Guideposts*, go to ShopGuideposts.org, call (800) 932-2145, or write to Guideposts, PO Box 5815, Harlan, Iowa 51593.

Find more inspiring fiction in these best-loved Guideposts series!

Sugarcreek Amish Mysteries

Be intrigued by the suspense and joyful "aha" moments in these delightful stories. Each book in the series brings together two women of vastly different backgrounds and traditions, who realize there's much more to the "simple life" than meets the eye.

Miracles of Marble Cove

Follow four women who are drawn together to face life's challenges, support one another in faith, and experience God's amazing grace as they encounter mysterious events in the small town of Marble Cove.

Secrets of Mary's Bookshop

Delve into a cozy mystery where Mary, the owner of Mary's Mystery Bookshop, finds herself using sleuthing skills that she didn't realize she had. There are quirky characters and lots of unexpected twists and turns.

Patchwork Mysteries

Discover that life's little mysteries often have a common thread in a series where every novel contains an intriguing mystery centered around a quilt located in a beautiful New England town.

Mysteries of Silver Peak

Escape to the historic mining town of Silver Peak, Colorado, and discover how one woman's love of antiques helps her solve mysteries buried deep in the town's checkered past.

To learn more about these books, visit ShopGuideposts.org